Torn

~The Crystal of Despair~

A Thief of Life Novel

Torn

Torn

Torn

~The Crystal of Despair~

A Thief of Life Novel

By Christi Anna

Also by Christi Anna

Book 1: Wonder-Heart of Captivation

Book 2: Jealousy-Legacy of Love

Next to come:

Book 4: Yearning-Deadly Desire

This book is dedicated to Angel Hurtt. An awesome content editor and great friend, who from the very beginning, as we chatted about my first, unfinished book over pizza, embraced my vision for this story and pushed me to be a better writer than I ever thought possible. Thank you for never blowing smoke up my butt and for keeping my characters in line, especially Miles.

Many thanks go out to my amazing editing staff, Christy Elkins, Angel Hurtt, Julia Crist and Sabine Marsico. I am truly blessed to have such wonderful and selfless friends helping bring this book to fruition. Your endless hours of proof reading and corrections have made this book one of my best so far. Thank you!

Torn

A feeling of great distress by the pull of contrary forces;

a rage or passion, an outburst...

or violent fury.

Torn

Victory Torn

In this competition, I am the prize,
Though, to win my heart, is to destroy it as well.
Yet each contender fights with unparalleled determination,
Both eager to prove their worth,
Contestants in this fencing game of love.
Between them I am the referee
I make the calls
I award the points
I declare the victor.
Like a blade across my senses,
My options slash at me from all sides.
I cringe at the decision before me,
Knowing any choice will result in pain.
My heroes each spar with grace and dignity,
Each move, cunning and smooth,
However, the match must be awarded to someone,
And so it is.
I look at my hands
In them lie the remnants of my heart,
An award for my champion.
Will he claim his prize?
Or discard it,
A worthless first place ribbon,
Which has been withered to shreds,
And will forever remain…*Torn*.

"There are many things that go through your mind while running for your life. For me there was only one…

I don't want to die."

Chapter One
Daniela

Razor-sharp rocks tore into the soles of my bare feet as I moved quickly over stony ground. Struggling to maintain balance on the treacherous land, I focused on the path ahead. I came upon a small ledge, then, without hesitation, jumped, safely landing many feet away on the other side. Terrified, but relieved by this small victory, I picked up pace and ran toward the next ledge. With the rumbling sounds of many hundred footsteps behind me, I dared not look back. The smell of salty sea air burned in my nostrils as I panted heavily, my chest aching and heart straining. My body was tiring quickly. I couldn't go on much longer, but fear kept me in motion. If I slowed, if I stopped for even a moment to catch my breath, it would only be a matter of seconds before they were on me.

As I came to another ledge, it was not hard to see this one was much wider than the minuscule fissures I'd so easily jumped before. Instinctively I hesitated, slamming on the breaks just as I reached the ridge. I cried out in pain as I slid to the ground; my feet and legs ripped open by the jaggedness of the unforgiving terrain.

However, I hadn't stopped quickly enough and my momentum carried me skidding over the edge. I flailed my arms around, attempting to grasp anything that would save me from a dark decent to the bottom of the ravine. My scream echoed off the canyon walls and I cringed as my body left the ground, falling into the vast depression.

But then, unexpectedly, something caught my arm!

Opening my eyes, I looked up with great relief into the glorious face of Miles Chadwick!

"I've got you Dani. Take my other hand," he instructed in a calm tone.

Dangling in his firm grip, I reached up and took hold. He effortlessly pulled me to safety and then steadied me on my feet. I stared in horror at the enormous crowd of emovamps. He had rescued me from the fall, but the graveness of our situation hadn't changed.

They all stood glaring at me like a choice cut of steak. I trembled, backing towards the edge of the canyon once more, awaiting their charge. Miles protectively wrapped his arms around me tightly. I let out a frightened breath and hugged his broad chest, knowing this was the end—there was no way for him to protect me from so many. His finger skimmed down my arm and I instantly felt the pulling of severe heat. I leaned back and narrowed my eyes at him. He was drawing out my energy.

A malicious grin swept his face. "Come on Dani, it isn't all that bad, is it?" he asked. I opened my mouth to answer, but to my relief, was interrupted.

"Let her go, Chadwick!" Robert yelled.

I turned around as my hero stepped forth from the crowd. Surprisingly, Miles let me go with no resistance and Robert held out his hand with a gentle smile. Immediately I ran to him, throwing myself into the warm sanctuary of his embrace and sobbing my gratitude. Petrified, I looked around at the large mob as they stood rigid, as if awaiting orders.

"Why aren't they attacking?" I whispered frantically.

Robert stroked my hair, and then, leaning back, gazed down into my face with compassion. "It has to do with seniority."

"Seniority? What do you mean by seniority?" I asked with confusion.

He gently caressed my cheek and then smiled wickedly, "You know, first-come, first-served. It means I found you first, so I get to eat first."

My eyes widened as shock took hold of me. I opened my mouth and released a horrifying scream, but it was silenced immediately by his mouth of razor sharp teeth!

"Daniela—Daniela wake up honey—Daniela wake up!" he yelled.

Opening my eyes, I stared in horror at Robert's face and immediately began a terrifying backstroke that sent me hurdling off the bed with a noisy *crash!*

I smashed into the lamp and hit the floor with a hard *thud!* "Stay away—you just stay the hell away from me!" I screamed.

Robert raised his hands in a surrendering motion, approaching with caution. "Daniela, it's me—Robert. I'm not going to hurt you, sweetie, just calm down." My eyes darted to the open bedroom door and I shifted nervously as his distance lessened. "It was just a nightmare, but it's over now. You're safe. Come on," he said, reaching for me. I looked at his outstretched hand, back to the door, and then bolted for my escape.

"No—Daniela, please don't run!" He lunged forward, grabbed me from behind and wrapped his arms around my shoulders. I screamed and kicked against his strong hold, trying desperately to break free. "Sweetie don't fight me, I'm not trying to hurt you!" He held me in a tight lock against his chest, attempting to calm me, but petrified and determined to get away, I lowered my mouth onto his forearm and sank my teeth into his tough flesh! He let out an agonizing cry, releasing me momentarily.

I scrambled towards the stairs, but Robert was on me once more. Before I could reach the end of the hall, he tackled me to the floor with all of his weight. I let out another squawk of opposition, but this time felt the warm sensation of pleasurable heat as it entered my skin and my body relaxed from this soothing touch. I rested my head against the cold wood of the hallway floor and began crying into the rich mahogany. Finally, Robert softened his grip and rolled me over, looking down at my tear swollen face with kindness and understanding.

It had all been a nightmare. I'd been having them every night since Tobias attacked me more than a week earlier. He'd hid on my balcony during a thunderstorm, then smashed through the doors and attacked me. He'd had plans to rape and feed on me, all because of the potent energy I emitted. However, if my odd power wasn't enough to entice him, Tobias had been even *more* excited about the prospect of taking my virginity, and that detail had made for some of the worst nightmares this week.

Thankfully though, Ryan had interrupted before Tobias could go through with it. Since Ryan was merely human, it was only a temporary distraction, one that nearly claimed Ryan's life. However, it provided just enough time for Robert to get there and save the day. Now, as if ghastly dreams of Tobias and his slimy hands all over me wasn't enough, I was also having flashbacks during the day as well, making it difficult to distinguish between reality and trauma induced hallucinations.

I looked at my hero sitting on the floor with me, his bare, muscular chest exposed, wearing only a pair of flannel pajama bottoms and hair tasseled about. He'd no doubt been asleep when he sensed my nightmare and came rushing into my house to wake me, just as he'd done so many other times this week.

Suddenly overcome by a rush of relief, I threw myself at him, wrapping my arms around his neck in an emotional storm of guilt and reprieve. "Robert I'm so sorry, I didn't know what I was doing!" I wailed.

He held tight, rocking me and stroking my hair. "It's alright—I know sweetie."

As he ran his hands over my shoulders, I gasped in horror at the bloody teeth marks on his arm! "Oh Robert—oh God! I bit you!" I cried, hysterically grabbing his arm and holding it still for closer inspection. "I'm a freaking psycho!"

"No you're not, it was an accident, don't worry about it," he assured.

"But how is that possible? You're supposed to be indestructible, I don't understand how I even broke the skin, let alone do that!" I said, pointing to the gnarly wound.

Robert sweetly tucked a lock of wild hair behind my ear and smiled thoughtfully. "Emotional energy is what makes us resilient, but I've been giving you the majority of mine for the last week and a half now. It's weakening me, while at the same time making you extremely strong," he explained.

"That's awful! Why didn't you tell me this?"

"Because I didn't want you to worry and I know you need it more than I do right now," he said earnestly.

"Well, I don't want you to do it anymore then. It's fine every once in a while, but not all the time. I don't want you to become run down because of me. If anything happened to you because you were too weak, I would never forgive myself."

Robert leaned his head against mine lovingly. "You don't have anything to be afraid of. I'm weakened, but believe me; I'm only fragile in comparison to you because you're so strong right now."

"I don't care; I still want you to stop," I insisted. "Promise you won't project to me anymore for a while."

He didn't answer, but instead stood up and lifted me to my feet. "Come on, I'll make you some breakfast," he said, strolling off toward the kitchen, avoiding my demand.

"Robert, I mean it," I warned, following him down the stairs, but he didn't comment. "I'm serious, no more projecting." Still, he gave no response. Finally, we reached the kitchen and Robert immediately took out a first aid kit and bandaged the hideous bite mark on his forearm, then went about gathering ingredients and cooking utensils as if it was no big deal. He made no attempt to hide the fact that he was not going to agree to halting the exchanges.

At last I grabbed his bicep and firmly demanded, "Robert Elliot Hollin, I am not kidding. No more projecting to me or…or…or I'll—"

Suddenly, he swung around and pulled me swiftly into his arms, lifting me off the ground with a laugh! "Or you'll what?" he challenged with an ear to ear grin.

I narrowed my eyes, thinking of an answer. With a victorious grin I folded my arms with determination and replied, "I won't make you any more cookies."

"That's playing dirty. You know how much I love your cookies," he pouted. I remained quiet, gazing off distantly with fortitude. "But they make up nearly half my food intake now," he argued.

"Not one—more—single—cookie."

Robert let me down slowly, a look of defeat. "Okay, you have me. I promise, no more projecting, at least for a day or two."

"Not good enough. One week," I demanded.

Robert shook his head. "Two days," he said stubbornly.

"Six."

"Three days," he offered.

I shook my head. "Nuh-uh—at least five."

He took my hips, pulling me against him. "I love it when you argue with me," he said, his voice soft and full of desire. "You pucker out your little lips and look so serious—so beautiful."

I breathed in his intoxicating scent and nearly backed down, but held fast to my bargaining chip. "Five days," I repeated sternly, awaiting his submission.

He slowly ran his lips up my neck, his warm breath skimming over my skin, causing me to tremble with excitement. In a low husky voice, he asked, "How about we meet in the middle, say—four days?"

I leaned back and narrowed my eyes, feeling certain this was the best I was going to do. "Alright, four days—but only if I need it," I insisted. Robert nodded his agreement and slowly leaned in for a kiss. Immediately, I placed a hand against his mouth, halting the attempt. "Ah, ah, ah…that's four days starting *now*."

With a sigh of defeat, he nodded again and let me go. Satisfied with my morning victory, I took a seat at the bar and watched my favorite sexy chef prepare breakfast while hunger pangs gnawed at my stomach. Good gravy, he had skills—cooking skills too. Although most of my need to eat was intense munchies caused from the exchanges; how could any girl watch a shirtless Robert cook, and not work up a massive appetite?

As I leaned dreamily on the counter, watching my favorite cooking show with the unbelievably gorgeous host, Dr. Robert Hollin, again I noticed a faint glow around him. I had been seeing it with greater frequency as of late and had come to the conclusion it was visible when I was heavily charged with energy, and directly after an exchange. It only lasted a few minutes or so and was in varying colors, though I wasn't sure why. I felt certain it had something to do with emotions, just wasn't sure if they were his or mine.

This morning's color was the same as it had been all week; a bright emerald green. I still hadn't brought it up to Robert, silly as that sounds. I wasn't entirely convinced it was something good though. I tried to probe him for more information about gifts, but hadn't heard him say anything about one that involved seeing color. In a way I suppose I kept it a secret out of fear. It was just one more thing that made me a weird anomaly, like the energy I emitted. I already felt like a freak as it was.

"You know, I wouldn't have to project to you so much if you let Michael place the block," Robert suddenly said, halting my food for thought.

"I already told you, I'd rather not."

"I know, but it would really help you. Michael's very experienced and I know he would be careful that you didn't lose any important memories," he assured. "I understand you're worried, but I promise, the benefit outweighs the risk. You can't keep on like this for long, it's not good for you."

"I know—it's not good for you either," I said remorsefully.

Robert came around the island and took my hand, kissing it gently. "I can handle it; it's you I worry about."

My heart ached from his deep concern. After all, here he was worrying about *my* well being, when he was the one with a huge set of teeth marks in his arm. "I'll think about it; okay?"

"Fair enough," he replied, returning to his cooking with a smile of momentary victory.

I watched dreamily as he carried out his culinary duties with grace and perfection. Finishing up, he slid my plate across the counter, flipping the hand-towel over his shoulder. I smiled at this small action because it reminded me of the morning Miles cooked my crazy, smiley face breakfast. Well aware Robert could pick up on my emotion I quickly switched all thoughts to mundane visuals of baseball in order to mask my feelings.

"Would you like some coffee?" Robert asked.

I smiled warmly at his thoughtfulness. "That'd be wonderful."

Diving into my plate, I savored each extraordinary bite, trying hard to keep my mind on non-Miles related things, but much as I tried, thoughts drifted back to him. The day after Robert and I returned from England, I had paid a visit to Miles and accepted a job offer to paint a mural in his office at Chadwick law. Robert was furious about it. However, I'd made it quite clear that I believed it to be a legitimate offer and not an attempt on Miles's part to sleep with me. My stomach fluttered with the thought.

In light of the near death experience with Tobias the week before, Robert felt it best that I take some time to settle down before I took on the stress of a job. Submissively, I had moved our meeting to today. Though the postponement was reasonable, it was more likely an attempt to delay the job in hopes that I would change my mind. I had not.

Additionally, I was extremely apprehensive about the project, having had no *actual* experience, other than painting on my own walls (which I would like to point out I hadn't even completed). I moved before I finished the first mural, and the one I'd begun at my new house was almost entirely destroyed by the battle with Tobias. Robert was having the walls repaired and had promised to try and salvage as much of the original mural as possible, but I insisted he paint over all of it. I preferred to start with a clean slate and at this point wasn't sure when I would get back to it if the painting job with Miles worked out. My stomach flipped again.

Hence, my other reason for being nervous. I was hoping when the time came to begin the painting job, Miles would leave me in his office to work alone, but my instinct told me it was not in his character to do so. Inevitably I was plagued with thoughts of spending a lot of time with the man who quite literally made my toes curl. Suddenly, a sharp pain of jealousy shot through my chest and I immediately looked at Robert.

"What time is he supposed to pick you up?" he grumbled, handing me the coffee with an aggravated expression.

"Um…eight," I answered guiltily, glancing at the clock. "Flippin' crap! It's almost eight now!" I yelped, jumping from my seat and rushing for the stairs.

Robert was instantly in front of me, arms around my shoulders. "Did I tell you how good you look in my clothes?" he asked playfully.

I rolled my eyes at his timing. "I need to go get ready," I said, struggling lightly against his strong hold.

"You need to finish your breakfast."

"I can't, he's going to be here any minute."

"He can wait, you need to eat. Now sit down, relax and have some breakfast with me," he insisted sweetly, walking me back to my seat.

I couldn't refuse and did love eating with him. We sipped at our coffee, all the while smiling flirtatiously and taking turns feeding little bites of food to each other. These were some of my favorite moments with Robert. Quiet, loving—uncomplicated, they were the way I wanted it to be always. However, just as always, it was a moment of peace destined to be shattered.

Chapter Two
Daniela

Robert let out an aggravated sigh and glared at the door with disgust.

"He's here, isn't he?" I asked. With a nod, he started toward the door. Quickly, I moved to run upstairs. "Sit down and finish your breakfast or you're going to be starving in an hour," Robert insisted, motioning me back to the bar. I knew he was right and obediently sat back down and hastily nibbled at my food.

He opened the door to the brilliant white smile of Miles Chadwick, who without invitation, strolled in as if he owned the place. I can't be sure, but I swear Robert rolled his eyes.

Miles came directly over and sat down at the bar next to me with a devilish grin. "Good morning, la mia belle," he said, planting a kiss on my cheek. I tried to suppress my giggle, but it escaped as I gripped the barstool with my toes.

"Good morning to you too," I replied.

Robert walked around to the other side of the island, picked up his coffee and sipped it, glaring at Miles with irritation. Miles glowered back at the shirtless Robert with equal disdain.

"You could at least put on some clothes," Miles remarked dryly.

Robert gave a wicked smile as he took another sip of coffee. His chest muscles flexed and twitched, sending my mind reeling with excitement. I couldn't help smiling a little. I knew he did it on purpose, aware of the effect he had on me and knowing full well Miles could sense all of it. Robert continued to smile as he finished his cup. Lifting his arm to take another drink, the bandage on his forearm caught Miles's attention.

"So what happened, did you get into a fight with a vampire or something?" Miles joked.

Robert shot him a disgusted look, but didn't reply.

"Actually it was me," I confessed remorsefully.

Miles's eyes widened with astonishment and he smiled ear to ear. "*You* did that? WOW!" he exclaimed. "You know, if he won't leave you alone, I can show you a couple of good self-defense moves," he popped off.

I rolled my eyes at his offer, "It wasn't like that. I attacked him."

Miles laughed, but couldn't let it go. "Well, doc, they do say forty percent of domestic violence is women abusing men."

Robert remained quiet, trying to ignore Miles's battering. Attempting to lighten the mood, I pushed Miles playfully. "I had another nightmare and Robert came in to wake me up. I was just confused," I assured.

Miles watched Robert, who was already looking more than irritated at his pompous remarks. I sent up a silent prayer that Miles would let it go before it turned into a fight, but as usual Miles had an inability to pass up a chance to egg Robert on. It came as no surprise when he opened his mouth and spouted another asinine comment.

"I wouldn't be too hard on yourself, Dani, I'm sure you're not the only woman who's ever bitten him."

With that, Robert puffed up and slammed his coffee mug down, sending pieces of it shattering in all directions!

"Whoa! Got a bit of a temper there, maybe I really should show her some self-defense moves," Miles exclaimed.

Robert tightened his fists and roared, "I would never do anything to hurt her!"

The air in the room became icy cold and I cringed. I wanted to crawl under the counter and barricade myself in the cabinet with the pots and pans. However, I knew when I accepted Miles's job offer things were not going to be easy. I was going to have to deal with that decision and try my best to keep the peace.

"Y'all stop it!" I shouted, throwing my hands up between them. "You're both acting like children! Now, I just got my house put back together, so either settle down and get along or I'll throw you both out and you can go kick the crap out of each other in the parking lot while I finish my breakfast!"

Miles and Robert stared at me in disbelief and then Miles let out a light laugh. "Well alright, angel, you don't have to tell me twice," he said, taking my hand and giving it a kiss. "I can play nice."

Robert glared at Miles with contempt, but said nothing. Instead, he began cleaning up the shards of porcelain that now covered my kitchen.

Nonchalantly, I pulled my hand back from Miles's warm grip and hesitantly smiled. "I better go get ready," I said, heading for the stairs. "I'll be quick."

"Take your time, sweets, I'm not going anywhere," Miles called after me.

I showered and dressed quickly, choosing a simple outfit of denim overalls and a white cotton tank-top. I simply wished to be comfortable, *and* in something durable I was confident wouldn't rip. The first time I'd met Miles, I'd clumsily knocked over a vase on his desk with dozens of marbles. I'd been down on my hands and knees trying to reach one of them that had rolled under a desk when I felt the back of my skirt give way from the strain on the seam. If that wasn't bad enough, to my horror I turned around to find Miles watching all of it with enjoyment.

Embarrassment seemed to be a repeat pattern with me. Though the entire meeting was a humiliating experience, it was one I cherished deeply. It was things just like this which had me extremely nervous about allowing officer Kavenius to place a block in my mind. I couldn't stand the thought of him altering them, whether by accident or intentional.

I pulled my long blond hair up into a loose ponytail and dabbled on a little makeup (a must with the ominous circles that encased my eyes). The lack of sleep, or more so, lack of rest, had really taken its toll, but I was still in denial and felt capable of handling the flashbacks and nightmares. *Surely they would pass on their own,* I thought.

Of course, night terrors weren't the only thing keeping me on edge; I was also struggling with thoughts of Becca. My best friend had been the unknowing victim of Tobias (pompous, scum, emovamp). He'd been using her for months, draining her energy and sanity it seemed. The last time I'd spoken with her, I tried to warn her that he was no good, but jealousy ensued and she felt I was only interested in stealing him away.

I rubbed my cheek, still feeling the hurt from the slap she'd given me that day. Tears welled in my eyes from the painful memory. She was staying with her mom, I knew that much, but she still refused to speak to me. My heart ached at her rejection. Robert tried to convince me I shouldn't take it personally, but I couldn't help it. For whatever reason, I felt responsible for her getting mixed up with him.

Although she was suffering terribly, I did feel a small amount of relief now that she was away from him. Tobias made the mistake of attacking me, the one human who happened to have a boyfriend capable of draining him in record time. Unfortunately for Tobias, it was a lesson that didn't come with a second chance to change his ways. The last I saw of him, he was nothing more than an explosion of blue particles.

I gathered my nerve and then walked back downstairs to Robert and Miles. Both were glaring at each other fiercely, like toddlers fighting over a toy, but as soon as they felt my presence, they immediately turned their attention to me. Miles's stood up as I approached, his eyes sparking with glee.

"Well that definitely looks better than those awful pajamas you had on," he remarked sarcastically. "If you ask me you should donate those poor things to charity, or better yet, just toss them."

"They may be ugly, but there's a reason they are her favorite," Robert defended arrogantly, coming around behind me. Turning me to face him, he gently pulled me into his arms, hugging tight and burying his face in the crook of my neck. While inhaling my perfume he shot Miles a cocky grin from over my shoulder and exclaimed, "God you smell good." Childish as it was, Miles had really asked for it with all the times he'd goaded Robert in the same way. "I'm really sorry for breaking your coffee cup," he apologized.

"It's technically *your* coffee cup," I smiled.

"Still, I shouldn't have lost my tempter."

"Well, I forgive you then."

Robert leaned his forehead against mine and smiled sweetly. "How about I make it up to you with dinner tonight? I'll take you out someplace nice." I sighed with disapproval. "*Or* if you like, we can stay in and I'll make you anything you want. We can go for a nice walk around the pond or maybe get a movie and snuggle on the couch. We haven't done that all week. Whatever you want, I'm yours to command," he proclaimed.

Miles let out a deliberately loud groan of irritation. "Or, you can just invest in indestructible, N.A.S.A. quality coffee cups."

The game of tug-of-war between Miles and Robert had begun with a loud *bang*! I was already feeling pulled in two different directions.

I rolled my eyes at his sarcastic remark and then turned my attention back to Robert's offer of contrition. "Dinner and a movie at home sounds wonderful."

"What would you like? Just name it and it's yours."

"How about you surprise me," I replied.

"That I can do," he said in a sultry tone, and then quickly covered my mouth with his. The kiss was forceful and passionate. From it surged his heated energy, like liquid fire it flooded my bloodstream and sent my mind turning from the pleasurable emotion that I was being gifted with. Robert knew we had made a deal, but couldn't resist the opportunity to remind Miles that I was his.

He pulled back slowly, giving me a look of uncertainty. My scowl was all the proof he needed of my disapproval.

"We agreed on four days," I scolded.

"Sorry," he grinned sheepishly. "Four days starting now."

I stepped around him and looked to Miles. With hurt in his tone, he asked, "Are you ready to go?"

I smiled apologetically. "Yeah, just let me grab my coat."

I'd hardly moved a foot when Robert was already beside me, coat in hand. "Have a great day, honey, and I'll see you tonight," he said, slipping it on and giving me a gentle kiss on the cheek.

As Miles assisted me into the car, I glanced up at Robert standing in the doorway, his features wrought with the uncertainty of this choice I was making to take the job. It was a choice which could cost me everything.

Chapter Three
Daniela

Miles and I lay out in the warm sun on a beautiful patchwork quilt. He had packed a scrumptious picnic lunch, but for now we relaxed and talked as I drew out different ideas for his office. I had hoped for a somewhat traditional business meeting, but when it came to Miles, he was anything *but* traditional. Though it was something I liked about him, more often it proved to be problematic when it came to getting anything serious done.

"Stop that," I scolded, shooing Miles's hand away.

He gave a light laugh then reached up and tickled under my chin. I giggled instinctively, but again, pushed his hand away with annoyance, glaring down at his face with disapproval. He was sprawled out on the blanket with his head laid back in my lap.

"You're not making this easy," I said, indicating I had nowhere to sit my sketchpad. Miles smiled mischievously, but didn't move. "You know you could contribute some design ideas, after all this is your office," I stated.

"How about a mural of two people—*lovers*, lying out on a blanket, passionately kissing?" he asked, slowly running a finger down my arm. Abruptly, I sat the sketchpad down on his face, continuing to draw and using him as a table. Miles rolled out of my lap with a laugh. "Come on Dani—relax with me for a little while. We can go over designs later," he insisted, tugging at my ponytail.

"I'm not here to relax, I'm here to work; remember?" I sighed, never looking up as I sketched.

Miles crawled around behind me and then gently slid the band from my ponytail, releasing the long locks of blonde hair to hang around my shoulders.

"I love it when you wear your hair down," he said in a low voice close to my ear.

28

Immediately, my hand stopped and breathing quickened. Miles began to play with my hair, running his hands through it slowly. I leaned my head back, allowing the warm rays of sunshine to wash over my face.

"See how good it feels to simply enjoy yourself? There's always time for work later. Right now just take in this moment," Miles said softly, brushing his fingers through the long strands seductively. Then, pulling them gently to one side, he placed a light kiss on my neck.

Suddenly, my head bolted upright and I nearly jumped off the blanket. "That's it!" I yelled, "I knew this was a big mistake. Robert was right, apparently it's not my painting skills your interested in. Jeez, I can't believe I actually thought you liked my work. I'm such an idiot!" I ranted as I scrambled to gather my things.

Miles caught my arm, halting my escape. "Come on, don't leave," he begged.

I turned and glared at him, jaw clenched tight with irritation. "Careful, I bite; remember?"

Miles smiled with excitement at my warning. "Dani, sweets, with venom such as your beauty, I welcome your bite." He leaned in and added, "But might I suggest you start with my lip."

"I'm afraid I would die from comparison," I retorted cruelly.

He raised an eyebrow. "Ouch. Touché."

"Well, you deserved it."

He nodded. "Perhaps, but for your information, I adore your work and am quite honestly insulted that you would think my motives were anything but honorable. I won't deny that *your* being the artist is an added bonus to getting a great mural, but that's not why I hired you," he assured. I rolled my eyes, but deep down fell for it, and softened my stance. "I'm sorry, really I am. I was just playing around, and I promise to behave from now on," he said, crossing himself. "Come on, sit back down and show me what you have so far."

29

I remained still for a moment, but was unable to resist his reasoning and gave in. "Okay, I'll stay, but no more playing around," I scolded sternly.

With a soft smile, he nodded. "I promise."

I sat back down and flipped my sketchpad open to the drawing I had previously been working on. "Okay—what do you think of this one?" I asked.

Miles scooted up next to me and examined the design. "I like it. It looks very, what's the word? Tranquil," he remarked. "Are those anemones?" he asked, pointing to a section of flowers in the picture.

"Yeah, I especially like them for some reason, although I don't know why. I guess maybe because I see red ones in my dreams a lot."

"*Hmmm*…that's interesting. So in a way, if you paint that in my office, it will be like having your dreams on my wall. I like that," he said quietly, brushing my hair back over my shoulder.

I shivered, my blood heating quickly from such a simple gesture. This keeping my distance was going to be a lot harder than I had anticipated.

"Miles—"

"So, what else do you dream about?" he interrupted.

I let out a frustrated sigh, blowing a stray hair from my face. "I don't know; nothing pleasant really."

"Nightmares of Alistair?"

"Alistair, Tobias…" I said, and then hesitated, remembering the horrible nightmare of him and Robert just that morning. "I'm sure they'll get better as time goes on." He rubbed my back, but remained quiet. "Miles, what do you know about blocking?" I asked.

He looked at me with a surprised smile. "I know quite a bit about it actually. I have a friend who can do it; why?"

"It's Robert, he also has a friend who offered to do it, you know, to help stop all of these nightmares and flashbacks I'm having."

"So are you going to do it?"

I bit at my lip nervously. "I don't know. I want to, but…"

"But what?"

"I'm afraid I'll lose my memories," I confessed.

Miles looked at me thoughtfully. "You wouldn't lose all of them, just the bad ones from the last few months."

"Yeah, but there's a lot of really great ones mixed in there too. What if he accidently blocked one, say…when you and I met?" I asked hesitantly.

Miles smiled warmly at me for a long time, then took my hand and kissed it softly, sending a warm shimmer into my skin. "Don't worry, la mia belle, I would never let you forget *me*."

"But what if I did? I mean, I hate to think that Robert would ask his friend to remove you on purpose, but I also know how much he hates our friendship," I explained.

"Yes, he does hate that you adore me," he remarked arrogantly. "But I've known him a long time and can honestly say, as much as he hates me, he would never stoop to such an underhanded move—and it wouldn't matter anyway."

"Why?"

"Because, the block doesn't erase your memory, only makes it fuzzy, like you know something happened, but it's unclear and you're not entirely sure it happened to you," he explained.

"That's what scares me. I don't want it to seem like some story I heard. As humiliating as our first meeting was, I want to remember it just as it happened, with perfect clarity."

"You would Dani, I promise," he assured, but I still wasn't convinced. "Look, if you didn't remember meeting me, I would simply re-introduce myself and then tell you the exciting story of when we first met and how you instantly fell in love with me."

I let out a loud laugh at his presumptuous comment. But Miles wasn't laughing. Instead, he gazed at me with all seriousness. I quieted my laughter as he held my eyes for a long time. I could feel the heat of his longing for me more clearly at that moment than ever before, and I wondered if Miles knew just how close to the truth his comment fell.

"Dani, I know you're scared, but this could really help you. Even though you want to deal with this on your own, you have to realize as tough as you think you are there are times when it's not enough. This is one of those times."

"Honestly, I'm doing fine. I've had a few nightmares and flashbacks, but it's nothing I can't handle."

Miles brushed my hair over my shoulder and softly ran the back of his hand down my cheek. "You try so hard to hide your pain, but you can't hide it from me. I *feel* your fear and I'm telling you what you already know—you can't handle *this* on your own."

"I just want to be brave."

Just then, a tear spilled down my face and he caught it with his thumb, gently wiping it away. "It takes a very brave person to admit when they need help. You should do this—trust me."

I looked into Miles's sober features and felt certain he wouldn't mislead me. I was terrified of losing my memories, but was becoming more afraid of the nightmares. Though I still wasn't entirely convinced to go through with it, I was definitely giving it more consideration; especially now that I was certain Miles would see to it he was remembered no matter what.

"Just promise me you'll think about it," he said.

I bit at my lip and nodded. "Okay, I'll think about it, but you have to promise me one thing in return."

Miles eyed me with great curiosity. "Anything, my love."

"If something does go wrong—if I should forget you; when you tell me the story of how we met, will you please leave out the part about my skirt ripping?"

Miles let out a long sigh of discontentment. "But that was one of my favorite parts," he said with a devilish grin.

I rolled my eyes, but couldn't keep from smiling a little. "Please, just promise," I repeated.

"You said you wanted to remember it with perfect clarity," he reminded me.

"Uhhh! Please, everything else yes, but *that*, just that one little thing; I can live without *that* detail."

Miles took my hands, then kissed them for a long time and softly whispered, "Alright, la mia belle, I promise."

Chapter Four
Daniela

Once our '*business meeting*' was over, Miles took me home. I can't say it wasn't tempting to spend the entire day with him, and he did try to convince me to, but I was determined to keep it as professional as possible (if that *was* possible). I already doubted it.

I had just flopped down on the couch, when I heard a faint knocking sound. I turned my head and listened carefully, thinking it had been someone at my door, but not entirely certain. Several seconds went by, and again, I heard the distinct knocking sound, and this time knew it had come from the door.

I walked up to it hesitantly, remembering a time not long ago, when I would carelessly open the door to anyone, never believing I could honestly be in any danger. It was recklessness I could no longer afford. So, quietly I waited. Again there came a soft *knock*.

"Who is it?" I asked sternly.

"It's me."

Immediately, I grabbed the knob and tried to open the door with a quick *jerk*, but in my excited haste, had forgotten to unlock it. Clumsily I fumbled around, trying to undo the deadbolt. At last I managed to get it unlocked and flung the door open!

There on my porch, stood the shell of my best friend. She stared back at me through hollow eyes and with great uncertainty, doubtful I would welcome her visit.

"Becca," I gasped.

Before she could utter a single word, I threw my arms around her shoulders and hugged with all my might! Tears poured out with intense relief as I sobbed quietly, thankful to have her back

34

and alive. I knew things hadn't been set right between us yet, but felt confident that her willingness to simply show up was a huge step in the direction of mending our friendship.

"Tobias left me!" she suddenly wailed. "He just up an' left me! Not a note, not a damn goodbye—nothin'!"

I held her tight, sad for the pain and rejection she was feeling, but relieved at her assumption for his absence. "Do you want to talk?" I asked.

"Yeah."

"You want me to make us some cookies?"

Becca leaned back with tear filled eyes and squeaked, "Yeah."

I wrapped my arm around her shoulder and guided her inside to the kitchen bar. After sitting her down, I went about gathering the ingredients for our comforting treat, while she emptied the tissue box on the counter.

Everything inside me wanted to break down and tell her the truth of what Tobias was. Even though technically I wasn't held to any code of secrecy, in a way I still had to maintain my silence as a means of ensuring Robert's and Miles's anonymity, as well as my own trustworthiness. I wanted to be honest, and hoped that someday I could finally tell her the truth. For now though, I had to keep it to myself. Plus, with our friendship just now on the mend, this wasn't the time to come clean anyhow. My hope was a point would come when Robert and I would be able to sit down and explain it to her just as we had Ryan.

"So when did he leave?" I asked with obliviousness.

"A little over a week ago," she sniffed.

"I'm sorry Becca, I really am."

"No Dani, I'm the one that's sorry. I treated ya like crap when all ya was tryin' to do was warn me he was no good. I'm the dingle berry that fell for all his bullshit. The worst part is, he made me turn on my best friend," she said solemnly.

There was no way I was going to let my best friend take the blame for what Tobias had done to her. Yes, she had turned on me, and yes, she accused me of terrible things, even slapped me. However, it was only because she was addicted to the extreme high she got when he fed on her. How could I hold her any more responsible for her actions than I would a heroin addict? The answer was I couldn't.

"You know what I say? Instead of sitting around sulking over who said what, or who turned on who, let's just put all of it behind us and start fresh. No apologies, no nothing, just a clean slate; what do you say?" I asked with hopefulness.

Becca looked at me with a dazzled expression, but then her mouth slowly formed a grateful smile. "You would do that…for me?" she choked. "But why?"

I walked around to her and tucked a lock of hair behind her ear. "Because, you're my best friend," I said softly. "You never let a guy come between you and your best friend, it's against the BFF code or something like that; right?" I chuckled lightly. Becca let out a relieved laugh and then pulled me in for a hug. I squeezed her back with heartfelt thankfulness, feeling at last that I had my friend back. "Now, how about those cookies?" Becca gave me an excited nod through tear filled eyes. Handing her another box of tissue, I went back to my sugary creation. We needed comfort food and fast!

As I stirred together the ingredients, Becca sat silently watching. My heart broke at the pitiful sight. Her hair was dull and un-kept, no makeup, and clothes a wrinkled nightmare. By my own personal standards, it wasn't far from my appearance on any given day, but by Becca's standards, it was the look from hell. She was, as she would say, 'a *walking fashion disaster*'. I worried terribly for her sanity and wellbeing. Had the tie to Tobias been severed early enough? It seemed now, only time would tell.

It didn't take long before I was pulling the first batch from the oven, and the house filled with the heavenly scent of my homemade chocolate chip cookies.

"This is always the hardest part," Becca suddenly said.

"What is?"

"The waitin'. It's not so bad when yer mixin' everything. Even when they're bakin' I can handle it, but when they first come out, it's like my mind sees 'em and says they're done, and it just cain't wait till they cool off," she laughed.

"Well," I reached into a drawer and retrieved two spoons, "there's always plenty of cookie dough while we wait." I smiled, handing her one of the spoons. Jubilantly we dove into the bowl, scooping out a huge mound of raw gooey goodness.

"So, are you still staying with your mom?" I asked.

"Yeah, I actually lost my job a month ago, but Mr. Jerk-shit wouldn't let me live with him, so I had to move in with her." Abruptly, she broke down sobbing again. "I just love him so much, an' I don't even know what I did wrong," she wailed.

Quickly, I came to her side and wrapped my arms around her. "Don't you beat yourself up over him anymore. You didn't do anything wrong," I assured. "And you deserve so much more."

Gently, I took Becca's empty spoon from her hand, reloaded it and handed it back with sympathy. She wiped the tears from her raw cheeks and smiled her gratitude in return. As Becca smacked away at the creamy dough, I suddenly blurted, "You should stay here—with me." Becca stared at me for a moment, not entirely sure how to respond. "I don't mean like permanently, but at least for a while—maybe a few weeks or so, just until you get on your feet again. What do you think?"

"I don't know, isn't Dr. Dreamy payin' for all this, I mean, wont he be upset?" she asked with concern.

The question was a valid one. Even though there was a possibility Robert would get mad, with the previous compassion he had shown her, I felt it was unlikely. Plus, my best friend's wellbeing was on the line, so I was willing to take that chance and trust that he would agree with the arrangement.

"He won't, besides, he may be paying for this now, but I'm keeping track of every penny he spends and trust me, I will be paying back every cent," I assured. "What do you say? Will you room with me?"

Becca eyed me speculatively for a long time, and then slowly her mouth turned up into a sweet smile. "M'kay, If yer sure I ain't gonna be interuptin' nothin'."

"You won't, I promise!" I exclaimed, throwing my arms around her neck and hugging with all my might. "Hey, maybe Robert has a position open at his office or something."

"It's okay, I already found another job."

"Where at?"

"Another scrapbook store. It's just a little further south, in Norman, but I'm making a dollar more an hour, so I'm happy with it."

Grabbing a few cookies for the road, Becca wasted little time in leaving to pack, promising to return sometime that evening. She was still far from back to her normal self, but I was now hopeful that with time she would someday be the old Becca I remembered.

I stood in the doorway, watching her as she walked to her car, when to my delight, Robert pulled in next to her. They exchanged greetings, and though I couldn't hear them, I could tell Robert was just as happy to see her as I was. After a few seconds, they parted ways and he made his way up the sidewalk to me.

"So I take it you two made up," Robert remarked as he approached.

"Yeah, well, *that* and I kind of sort of…did something else," I said hesitantly.

As soon as Robert reached me, he pulled me into his arms for a long hug. I breathed in his tranquil scent and smiled contently to myself.

"And just what would that be?" he asked with a carefree sigh.

"I was just trying to help her, and I know I should have asked you first, but I guess I figured you wouldn't mind, after all, she is my best friend, and—"

"Daniela, whatever it is, just tell me," he insisted playfully.

I let out a respite breath and confessed. "I asked Becca to move in with me—not permanently, just for a few weeks or so, until she gets back on her feet," I explained nervously.

I watched Robert's expression, uncertain of his feelings over my proposal. I was just about to panic when Robert's mouth turned up into a beautiful smile. "I'm very proud of you."

I started at him in disbelief. It was not the response I had anticipated. In fact, it was a response I would never have thought of. "What, proud I'm taking advantage of you?" I asked with confusion.

"No, proud you stepped up to help out your friend."

"But I thought you would be upset."

"Why would that upset me? This is your house and you can do whatever you want. You don't have to ask my permission."

"No, technically this is *your* house," I argued. "I shouldn't have offered without consulting you first."

Robert smiled with amusement and then gave me a loving squeeze, burying his face in my hair. "When are you going to understand that everything I have is yours?" he breathed. The warmth of his breath on my collarbone sent my thoughts racing.

A shiver ran down my back and I struggled to remember the point I had been trying to make. Suddenly his words became clear in my head and I pushed him back to look at him eye to eye. "What do you mean everything you have is mine?" I asked tautly.

"Just that. Everything I have is yours," he answered, tugging at a strand of my hair playfully.

I'm sure most girls would find his comment a dream come true, but remember, I was Daniela Moretti, destroyer of all good things and incapable of accepting anything I didn't earn. As sweet as it sounded, the thought of it filled me with terrible guilt.

"I beg to argue. I'm *just* your girlfriend. I'm certainly not entitled to everything you own and would never expect that," I said heatedly.

Robert took my face into his hands, bringing his nose tip to tip with mine. Calm flooded my bloodstream and I quieted down instantly. "Daniela, my love, there is nothing I own I would not happily give to you. Without you I have nothing anyway."

"But—"

"You're the only thing that's important to me now, and everything else is just...meaningless," he said softly.

"But—"

"I love you," he whispered.

Oh, he was good. How was I supposed to argue with that? I couldn't, so with heavy shoulders I dropped it—for now. "I love you too," I mumbled.

"It'll be good for you to have a housemate, especially for the next month," he said.

"Why is that?"

"I'm going to be very busy in the coming weeks preparing for '*Gran Conte*', the Great Count."

"Like a census?"

"Similar, but more like tax season for emovamps. Every ten years we have to register. There's a lot of paperwork and documentation that has to be in order. What makes it harder is my entire family has to register together. The deadline is in a little less than four weeks and its going to take us every bit of that time to get it done," he explained.

"If it takes that long, why didn't you start on it earlier?'

Robert tucked my hair behind my ear and gave me a thoughtful smile. "Because, *we* were in England."

"Oh yeah," I said sheepishly, a little embarrassed by my failure to think of that. "So do you have to take off work for it?"

"No, my family and I will meet every night starting tomorrow. We'll work through until at least midnight, maybe later. Consequently, tonight will be one of the few nights we'll get to spend together for awhile."

"Well I could come with you. You know, hang out, watch TV or something, maybe even help if you wanted," I offered.

Robert gazed at me longingly and I could see in his eyes he liked my suggestion, but then he lowered his shoulders with a look of disappointment. "You can't. I'm afraid you're too much of a distraction. Not just for me, but for everyone. Your energy drives us all crazy, but for me it's even more than that. All I think about is you, even when you're not around. If you're anywhere near, I won't get any work done."

"That's why you said it would be good for me to have a housemate, because otherwise I'm going to be alone every evening; right?"

Robert nodded. I can't say I wasn't a little hurt or that I didn't feel like even more of an outcast, but at the same time, I understood Robert's point. I was all too aware that my energy was a big distraction. Additionally, I tried to imagine what it would be like trying to fill out a W2 form with him around and could see what he meant about not getting any work done. I could barely tie my shoes with him around, let alone concentrate long enough to do important paper work.

"Good, so now that we have that out of the way, how would you like to get out of the house for a little while today? I thought we could go to the garden center and pick out some flowers for *your* house," he suggested.

His offer would seem a simple and harmless one. However, in light of all that had happened to me in the past few months, it was a question that struck fear deep within my heart. I had been willing to go with Miles to the park for our business meeting, because he promised to take me someplace with few people around, but the thought of venturing out into public terrified me. I was guaranteed to be seen by others, which in my mind was the equivalent to throwing me in a tank of sharks and ringing the dinner bell.

For more than five years I had lived a quiet life, meaningless and boring, but quiet nonetheless. All of that changed the minute I began going out. Consequently, it was barely two weeks before the first attempt on my life was made. Though I in no way regretted meeting Robert or Miles for that matter, I did feel it had opened me up to a world I dealt with better under the shelter of obliviousness. If I was still unaware that I was a huge target, I wouldn't be so afraid all the time. I had to ask myself; would I rather live in fear or simply never see my death coming? It was a question with no right or wrong answer.

"Those are some pretty heavy feelings you have in there," Robert said, pulling me from my dark thoughts. I smiled musingly, but chose not to answer. "You'll have fun, and it'll be good for you," he assured.

"I don't know, can't you just pick something for me, buy me a packet of seeds or something like that?" I whined.

"You can't hide away from the world forever. If you're not going to get out and enjoy life, there is really no point in living. Come on, you'll be with me the entire time," he said sweetly.

I watched him, admiring his beautiful features, then smiled shyly, blushed and looked away. Though we were officially an item now, I was still not accustomed to the idea that someone so wonderful could be mine. Aside from a charming personality, he was gorgeous beyond compare. I still had difficulty looking at his face without turning into an eyelash-batting spaz who giggled just at the thought of him.

"Okay," I agreed, "but if you sense anyone who even remotely sends out the slightest questionable vibe, promise me you'll take me home immediately?"

He looked at me with sincere compassion, well aware of my overwhelming fear and him powerless to make it go away. He drew me in for a long hug and I relished in the safety of his arms, wishing I could stay there always.

"I promise Daniela, I will never let anyone hurt you ever again."

Chapter Five
Daniela

We held hands, strolling through endless aisles of flowers and plants. The snow had melted away, spring was here at last and everything was growing and thriving. The nursery center was buzzing with masses of people getting a jump on their gardens. I gazed around at the multitude of flowers, unable to decide on a favorite.

"Do you see any you like?" Robert asked.

"Any? I like them all!" I exclaimed.

"Well as happy as I would be to buy every last flower in here for you, I'm afraid we would have nowhere to put them all, so maybe you could narrow it down a little," he laughed.

I blushed at his statement, having all confidence he really would buy me every flower there if I only asked. His willingness to give me whatever I wanted was a level of devotion I was starting to understand about him. Though I had never been a fan of being spoiled, it made me happy to know he felt me worthy of such commitment. This brought me back to a question that had been floating in my mind all week—that of commitment.

As we continued to walk, I glanced up at him from the corner of my eye, debating whether to once again broach the subject of turning me. The last time I tried, it ended with him storming out, and me sure I had ruined the best thing in my life. However, when Tobias attacked me, Robert came to my aid, and by the time it was over, we were both so relieved to have survived, we immediately apologized to each other. That haste to reconcile is exactly what had me curious. Robert didn't say *what* he was sorry about, simply that he was. I had to wonder if he was remorseful for the fight or that he had been so unreasonable about turning me. Had he reconsidered his stand on the subject? As much as logic told me to

43

let it go, I was developing a strong will inside that was determined to gain his submission.

"What is it?" he suddenly asked. I gave him a clueless expression. "There's something on your mind; what is it?" he repeated.

I chewed nervously at my lip, thinking carefully about my words, not sure of what to say. *Okay Dani, this is it. Either bring it up or let it go,* I told myself. I was really rooting for me to let it go. Inevitably though, my will had other plans and to my disappointment I opened my mouth and asked, "What were you sorry about?"

My question came out with my usual candor. I suddenly wanted to fill my mouth with potting soil and plant a rose bush in it. Robert only stared at me for a moment, then lowered his shoulders and looked to the ground. I took that as a bad sign, and was suddenly sure this had been a terrible idea.

"You mean the night of our fight," he said with remorse. "You want to know if I was sorry for the fight or if I reconsidered turning you?"

I dragged in a hesitant breath, not fully sure I was ready for his answer. Exhaling at last, I replied, "Yes."

I stared at the ground, unable to look up for fear of breaking down. With a gentle hand beneath my chin, he slowly lifted my face. His eyes were full of so much sadness that my heart wept at the sight of their sorrow.

"I was sorry for the fight," he said. Instantly a hard lump formed in my throat, but before a single tear fell, he continued. "*And* for being so unreasonable."

I struggled to decipher his answer and began stuttering incoherently. "So, you...you mean...you are—what exactly are you saying?"

"I'm saying, I will consider it."

"Really?" I yelped, unaware I had begun to cry.

Robert pulled me into his arms and held tight. "Really." Then he leaned back and looked down at me with seriousness. "But I want you to understand, I'm not willing to change you unless I find hard evidence it's been successfully carried out before with another transplant patient. I love you too much to ever risk your life. I hope you can respect that."

"I can, I promise!" I said with quiet excitement.

Robert gently wiped the tears from my cheek and then sweetly kissed my nose. "Now, let's pick out some flowers."

I didn't argue with him, simply nodded happily and went about browsing the beautiful floral selection. There were so many to choose from, and for some reason, as I looked at them now, they all appeared even more glorious than they had just moments before.

I strolled along the path, eyes skimming over each shade and bud with delight, until at last they came to rest on a thick patch of red. Looking over them, I ran my hands lightly across their velvety petals, caressing the ruby softness with familiarity. I hadn't actually ever touched one in real life, but lately I had dreamed of the small crimson buds many times and felt connected to them somehow.

"You like these," Robert said quietly from over my shoulder.

"I do, very much," I concurred excitedly, but not feeling the need to explain why.

"You know there is a legend about the red anemone; would you like to hear it?" he asked.

I turned and gazed lovingly at him, finding his knowledge about such things charming. "I'd like that very much."

"Well it's sort of a sad tale, but I think you'll like it. The story begins with Adonis, who was one of Aphrodite's lovers. She had many, but he was her favorite. There are many versions as to how he actually died, but most often it is said that he was gored by a wild boar during a hunt, probably sent by one of her *other* jealous lovers." Robert raised an eyebrow to me, and I swallowed hard. He smiled and then continued. "Aphrodite heard his cries and went to him, but it was too late. His wounds were fatal and he died in her arms," he explained sadly. "It's said in her deep sorrow, that she sprinkled his blood with nectar and as each drop fell from his body, it turned into a red anemone," he finished, plucking a flower from the patch and handing it to me gracefully.

I gazed at him with star-struck awe. He was so incredibly romantic, a characteristic that had me ready to melt into the pavement.

I took the flower from his hand and just as I did he leaned in and gave me a kiss. It wasn't a long one, but it wasn't just a peck either. More importantly, there was absolutely *no* exchange with it. He leaned back with a pleased grin and I wondered if he meant to do it or if it was just spontaneous. Either way he seemed relieved it didn't end up with me lying unconscious in the middle of the petunias, and I was certainly not about to complain.

"I'll go get a cart so we can load these up," he said. "Look around for a few more minutes and make sure there aren't any others you'd like to have."

"Hurry back," I said anxiously, not feeling comfortable with being left alone for long. He gave me a wink and then disappeared quickly into the sea of foliage.

I continued to peruse the selection, but didn't find anything I liked as much as the red anemones. As I rounded one of the aisles, I was instantly face to face with a man! Unable to scream, I grabbed my chest in stunned silence.

"Oh I'm sorry miss, I didn't mean ta frighten ya," The man apologized, his wide smile exposing the only three teeth he had.

His clothes were worn with filth, and the skin that hugged his bony hands was wrinkled and tan. He wore an old, ragged hat, but I could see strands of white hair poking out wildly from underneath, no doubt he was long overdue for a hair cut—and a bath by the smell of things.

"That's alright, it was my fault really. I wasn't watching where I was going," I apologized.

"Well, it's hard to, when there's so many purdy things to look at," he said eyeing me shyly.

I blushed at his obvious compliment and smiled my gratitude. I knew I should have been freaking out that a stranger was talking to me, but for some odd reason, I felt completely at ease. He looked homeless by all accounts and my heart was instantly filled with pity.

"Are you here buying flowers?" I asked.

"No, I just come to look. Muh wife, God rest 'er soul, used to just love comin' here every spring," he explained.

"Oh, I'm so sorry. You must miss her a lot."

"I do, but comin' here makes me feel better. Like she's just a few aisles away, pickin' out the best flowers she kin find so she kin out do the neighbors," he said with a chuckle.

He suddenly became quiet, thinking back to the days of shopping with his wife and his eyes filled with the painful memory of his lost love. Before I knew what I was doing, I threw my arms around him and hugged. I think he was just as startled by this impulsive gesture as I was.

"I'm sorry, I don't know what came over me, it just seemed like you really needed a hug," I apologized.

"No need ta be sorry miss, I didn't mind a bit. I's just surprised is all. I don't often get people wantin' ta hug me."

Looking at his disheveled appearance, I understood why.

"I'm Daniela," I said, extending my hand for his.

Without hesitation, he shook it firmly. "Nice to meet ya, Miss Daniela. Names Ridley—Ridley James. His hand was thin and weak, making me wonder when the last time was he'd had food.

"Ridley, have you eaten today?" My question came out as if I were inquiring about the weather.

He looked at me with surprise and I have to say, I could hardly blame him. "Why no ma'am," he replied.

"When *was* the last time you had something to eat?"

He looked up as if searching the days in his mind. "I reckon it's been a few."

"Well then, I'd like to buy you some lunch," I said, reaching into my purse. I didn't have a lot of cash on me, but Robert had been known for slipping money into my purse when I wasn't looking. It was his way of making sure I always had cash just in case of an emergency. Well if I ever felt there was one, it was now.

I dug around, and to no surprise, found a fifty tucked neatly in the side pocket of my wallet, just as I suspected. I quickly pushed it into Ridley's hand and then closed his fingers around it.

"No, no, no, miss, I couldn't take yer money," he argued. But I wasn't about to hear of it.

"You know," I said, pushing the money into his palm again and holding it there. "A wonderful man told me not too long ago, '*You shouldn't be so hesitant to accept help; no one in this life gets through it without needing some occasionally.*' Please, it would be my honor to help you today."

Ridley's eyes glistened at my words and finally after a few seconds, he nodded. "God bless ya, Daniela. I hope whoever that man is, he knows how blessed he is to have ya."

I gave him another hug, and then he turned and disappeared beyond a mass of ferns. I stood quietly watching after him with deep sadness, wishing there was more I could do for him.

"That was a very nice thing you did," Robert said.

Startled, I abruptly turned around. I didn't know how long he had been standing there, but my guess was long enough to see me giving *his* money away.

"I'm sorry about the money; I'll pay you back, I just—"

"I'm not concerned about the money, sweetie, it went to a good cause," he said pulling me to him. I leaned my head against his chest, breathing in his soothing scent. "You are such a remarkable woman, always so concerned about others."

"That's really not all that remarkable. There are lots of people in the world that do way more than me," I scoffed.

"Perhaps, but there are more who do *nothing*," he countered. "Simply your willingness to acknowledge someone else's need above your own sets you apart from much of the world, especially these days. There are few people who even bother giving someone like that gentleman help of any kind. Most turn him away, assuming he is being dishonest about his need. For all you know he could be down at the liquor store right now."

"It wouldn't matter to me," I said uncaringly.

Robert leaned back and looked at me curiously. "Why is that?"

"Because it doesn't change the reason why I gave it to him. I helped him because it was the right thing to do. So what if he goes and buys beer or drugs? It doesn't change the fact that *my* heart was in the right place, that's what *I* have to live with. I know, I know, it's a pretty cornball way of thinking."

Robert gazed at me with admiration. "Daniela Moretti, I could never tire of your cornball way of thinking," he said, leaning his forehead against mine. "Not in a thousand years."

Chapter Six
Daniela

I quickly added a few ingredients to my bowl, keeping my back to Robert so he couldn't see what I was making. He leaned over me, attempting to sneak a peak, but I hunched over, further shielding my creation from view.

"Is it cookies?" he asked curiously.

"Nope."

As he went back to stirring his own pot on the stove, I stretched my neck to glimpse what he was cooking as well, but his massive frame made it impossible to see.

"Is it spaghetti?" I asked with equal curiosity.

"Nope," he replied playfully.

Robert and I had agreed to surprise each other with dinner. He was making the meal, and I was making dessert. It was a fun game, but one that was driving us nuts! I've never been good at waiting, and whatever he was cooking smelled amazing.

I had chosen to prepare a coconut cream pie, one of my favorites. Aside from the wonderfully creamy filling, I had figured out how to make thick, fluffy whipped cream, just like my favorite pie place, Pioneer Pies, and would pile on a huge mound at least four inches high! I had never made a pie for Robert, so I was excited to see what he thought of my 'Mile High Coconut Cream Pie.' It was a simple recipe really.

Now that the pie portion was complete and chilling in the fridge, I was working on the whipped cream. I flipped the hand mixer on high and after several minutes the cream began to form soft peaks. Robert glanced over his shoulder several times nosily and I smiled with delight. I loved his playfulness. He was like a little kid, never too busy for a good game with me.

As I finished up, I attempted to remove the beaters from the mixer for cleaning, but accidently flipped it back on, sending whipping cream splattering in every direction and all over me! I let out a shriek of laughter at my clumsiness and quickly turned it off. Looking around at the huge mess, I grabbed for a towel to clean it up, but Robert caught my arm and held it, gazing excitedly at my face.

"Wait," he said, pulling me up close and leaning in. "I can't stand to see good whipped cream go to waste," he said in a low, husky tone. The warm sweetness of his breath brushed across my lips and I began trembling at his closeness. He gently tilted my head back, exposing my neck and then ran his tongue along my jaw, licking and kissing away small patches of the sweet cream, continuing all the way up to my mouth and finishing with a quick nibble of my bottom lip. He stepped back, looking at me with deep want. I stared back with desire so intent, it burned from my eyes.

Suddenly, we leapt at each other, but our faces stopped just short of touching, both knowing the minute we kissed, it would be over. We held each other's gaze for several intense seconds and then I quickly began kissing and biting at Robert's neck. He pulled me tighter to him and began returning my affection with his own along my jaw line and ear. I ran my hands through his hair and took in a shaky breath as he reached under the back of my blouse and softly grazed the skin along my spine with his fingers. My mind was going crazy with excitement as I reached under the back of his shirt and ran my nails lightly across his lower back. He shivered at my caress and bit at my collarbone passionately.

Abruptly he stopped, jerking his head back. "We should stop," he insisted.

"We're doing fine, just don't kiss me," I instructed, pulling him back.

We resumed cautiously, but within seconds, Robert pulled back again. "Daniela, we *really* need to stop," he said firmly.

"Just a little longer *pleeeeeease*…remember, *you* started this," I pointed out. I undid the buttons of his shirt and laid a long kiss in the center of his chest. Leaning his head back, he momentarily gave in to my request as I finished with the last button and slid the shirt from his broad shoulders.

Abruptly, Robert grabbed my arms and jerked me back, staring at me with eyes of longing. I knew that look and was sure he was about to kiss me. Not that I didn't want that incredibly bad, but it meant an exchange and that was against the deal we had made that morning. Just as he began to pull me to him, I threw my hand up against his mouth, halting his attempt.

"Ah ah ah…remember, no exchanges for the next four days!" I quickly reminded breathlessly.

Robert's expression became one of frustration, but then, submissively he let go of me and lowered his head. Slowly, I cuddled back up to him, wrapping my arms around his waist and leaned my head against his warm chest. "I said no kissing, but that doesn't mean we have to stop," I said in a sultry tone.

"No—but we *need* to stop," he replied gravely. "Before this goes too far and I end up hurting you."

I looked up into his eyes and gently stroked his cheek. "Let's just take it slow," I whispered, running my hands up his smooth chest, and gently placing several soft kisses over his heart. Robert squeezed my shoulders tight, his breath quickening. I began unbuttoning my own shirt as I nibbled at his neck, when Robert suddenly grabbed my hands, stopping me in my tracks.

He glared at me with disapproval and then, taking my shirt in his hands, buttoned it back. "No, honey. We can't do this."

"But we're doing fine," I assured.

"It's not just about that," he said with frustration. "I respect you too much for this. As much as I want to continue, and believe me, I *do* want to continue; you're a lady and I can't disrespect you in this way."

"But I don't mind," I argued, reaching for him again.

Robert stopped me once more, holding my arms away. "But I do," he said earnestly.

I understood what he was saying, but sadly at the moment, I was worked up beyond the point of reason, so inevitably I opened my mouth to plead with him again. However, as luck would have it, we were interrupted by a knock at the door.

I looked at Robert with momentary panic and he smiled sweetly back. "It's just Becca," he said with a great deal of personal relief and I suspected he was glad for the interruption. Robert quickly began putting his shirt back on as I opened the door to my best friend, who immediately barreled in with two huge suitcases. Sitting them down, she abruptly stopped and looked at Robert, who was just finishing with the last button on his shirt.

"Uuuhh…I ain't interuptin' nothin' am I?" she asked with one raised eyebrow.

"No," Robert answered with reddened cheeks. "We were just about to have dinner. Would you like to join us?"

I gave her a sheepish smile and felt my own cheeks heat with my embarrassment. "Yeah, there's plenty for all of us, Robert made fettuccini Alfredo!" I said excitedly.

"Hey, you peeked!" he said playfully, lightly popping me with a hand towel.

I jumped and let out a squeal of laughter. "I did not! I would simply know that smell anywhere," I defended.

"Well, Daniela made coconut cream pie," Robert said.

I smiled widely. "You could smell the coconut; couldn't you?"

"No—I peeked," he confessed.

I swatted at him playfully and then turned my attention back to Becca. Immediately my heart sank at the sight of her tear filled eyes and the room became quiet and still. "Oh Becca, I'm sorry," I said pulling her in for a hug.

"It's okay, you didn't do nothin' wrong. It's just been a hard day. I'm not really that hungry right now. If it's okay with y'all, I think I'll just go on up to my room an' start unpackin'."

"Here, I'll carry those up for you," Robert said, taking the suitcases from her hand. Becca trailed behind as he and I led her to the guest room.

"I think I'm just gonna take a shower an' go to bed," she said, her voice full of despair.

My heart ached for the evident pain she was in and I wished there was something I could do to cheer her up. Nodding my head, I gave her another hug and then slipped out and rejoined Robert who was already downstairs again.

We ate dinner, though we didn't talk much throughout the meal. There was an odd tension in the air; mostly that Becca was upstairs, no doubt crying into her pillow. I wasn't even an emovamp and *I* could feel it, so I knew it had to be torturous for Robert who seemed gloomy the rest of the evening.

"I brought a treat for us tonight," he said as we finished up with the dishes. "I know you don't drink much, but I wanted to do something special for you, so I picked out a really nice wine from my cellar at home," he said, retrieving a bottle from the fridge.

I took it from his hands and studied it carefully. "Hmmm…Château Le Pin Pomerol 1999—this was the best you could do?" I asked teasingly.

Robert took the bottle from me and smiled widely at my outlandish question. "I'll have you know this is a very fine wine. As a matter of fact, I only have this one bottle," he said popping the cork with ease.

He retrieved two lovely glasses from the cabinet and filled each with a small amount of the rich, burgundy liquid and then gracefully handed one to me.

The time I spent with Robert was always fun, but was equally educational. I was learning a great deal of things about finer living and about taking time to appreciate things for more than what they appeared on the surface, especially with my heightened senses. I held up the glass to the light and inspected its color, then holding it just under my nose, breathed in slowly. Gently I swirled my glass, inhaling its fragrant bouquet again. Roberts's eyes sparkled as he watched me inspect the wine just as taught. Finally, I raised it to my lips, took a minuscule sip and held it in my mouth, allowing it to roll over my tongue and soak into my taste buds.

I pursed my lips as I pulled in a tiny bit of air and then breathed out through my nose, enjoying the different flavors of mocha, black cherry and currant. Delighted with what I had tasted so far, I took another sip. Now this time I was to draw it into my mouth with a small amount of air. I was supposed to do it *quietly,* however, I was so amused by Robert's expressions as he eagerly watched me, I began smiling mid sip and took in too much air. The silence in the room was broken by my huge *SLURP!* Robert's eyes widened with startled surprise, and he let loose a roar of laughter. I nearly spit the wine, but swallowed quickly, joining him in a good laugh at my expense.

But slowly our laughter died down and Robert gazed distantly towards the stairs with sadness.

"You can feel her can't you?" I asked.

"She's in a lot of pain, not just emotional. Her body is going through withdrawals right now, and it physically hurts," he explained. I gazed solemnly at the staircase with him, not actually able to sense her sorrow and pain, but I felt it nonetheless. "I have an idea," Robert said suddenly. "How about you take this and go spend some time with your best friend," he suggested, handing me the bottle of wine.

"Oh, I couldn't—"

"I insist. She needs you Daniela and the wine will help too. Go ahead—you're the best thing for her right now," he said, urging me toward the stairs.

I looked at him with great hesitation, but knew he was right and furthermore, found it incredibly endearing that he would give up his last evening we would have together for a while, as well as a great bottle of wine, just to help my best friend. I took a few steps and then quickly turned back and planted a long kiss on his cheek.

"Thank you," I whispered.

"Any time my love. Now go on—I'll lock up down here," he assured.

With that, I wasted no time and swiftly ran up the stairs to Becca's room. I stopped at her door and stood quietly, trying to think of just what to say. Quietly I knocked.

"Come in," her ragged voice called.

I opened the door slowly and stepped in. Becca was lying on the bed, unmoving, her face buried in a pillow.

"It's me—I brought something for you," I said softly.

Becca turned over and stared at me blankly, her eyes empty of the liveliness that used to reside there.

"You ain't gotta hang out with me, I know ya'd rather be down there with yer man," she said.

"I see him all the time. You and I haven't seen each other in months. We need a good '*girl's night.*' Just the two of us, no men and a great bottle, of what I can promise you, is very expensive wine," I said with a mischievous grin.

Becca studied me carefully and then slowly the corners of her mouth turned up into a smile. "Well that's good, cause tonight the dime store crap just ain't gonna cut it," she sniffled.

I sat down on the bed and handed her the bottle. Yes, this was expensive wine and one that probably deserved better than to be guzzled clumsily straight from the container, but tonight there were more important things than appropriateness or wine tasting skills. Tonight we both needed to let loose and relax, needed to cry, laugh and reconnect with each other. And so, beginning with a large swig, we did just that.

Chapter Seven
Daniela

Sunday morning came bright and early, especially with the slight hangover I was feeling from the night before. The empty wine bottle sat on my nightstand mocking my headache. Staring at the clock next to it, I groaned. I'd slept in until nearly ten o'clock, while Becca had already awakened and was gone to work for the day. I pulled the covers up over my head and thought back to the dream I'd been having just moments before. It was of *him*, the man with the black eyes. I shivered at the thought. He scared me terribly, yet as strange as it sounds, I preferred the nights I spent dreaming of the man with soulless eyes. I felt safe in my dreams with him, because no one else was ever there. Not Alistair, not Tobias, no one hunting or trying to kill me. It was as if he was more terrifying than all of them and I was somehow under his protection.

I was just dozing off to sleep again, when suddenly I bolted upright!

"CRAP! I start the painting job today!"

I was painting at Chadwick law, which was a very busy place during the week. Consequently, Miles had felt it best for me to work on the weekends while the building was unoccupied. Though reasonable, I wondered if he wasn't using it as a convenient means of spending more time with me while avoiding any distractions. Sadly, I ignored the little red flag waving in my head.

I quickly showered and went about my daily routine of primping. Opting for a ponytail and then topped it off with a baseball cap, something to keep my hair out of my face while I worked. I dressed in a pair of old carpenters pants with a simple white tank top; it would serve as my standard dress most days and was an unappealing outfit (intentionally so).

I had some coffee and a wonderful breakfast thanks to Robert. He had prepared a sausage casserole for me the day before, so all I had to do was heat it up when I was ready. His thoughtfulness never ceased to amaze me.

As I sipped at my cup and glanced through the paper, my thoughts drifted to Ryan. It had been more than two weeks since Robert and I had told him the truth of what Robert and Miles were. He hadn't called or come by, and though I desperately wanted to talk to him, I was afraid and really didn't know what to say anyhow. Mostly, I just missed him and needed to know he was okay.

I picked up the phone and began dialing his number, but midway through, I hung up. It was something I'd done several times the last few days. Each time I started to dial, I would lose my nerve and give up.

I knew Miles would be there at any time to pick me up, and so, I sat at the bar, looking around with boredom and a severe case of anxiety. Lord only knows the many thoughts I'd had of this day and the numerous scenarios of what could happen once I was alone with the unbelievably tempting Miles.

To pass the time, I cleaned up the kitchen, which was basically spotless. I fluffed the toss pillows on the couch and then went upstairs to make my bed. As I came back down the hall and rounded the banister, something came over me that was not in the realm of my typical behavior. Even though it had been more than twenty-four hours since my last exchange with Robert, I was still feeling extremely energetic...and daring.

Beyond my own ability to understand my actions, I climbed up on the banister and stood straight up, overlooking the living room, some fifteen feet below. My balance was incredible as I scaled the bar with no difficulty. Then an idea hit me as a gazed down at the floor—a scary idea, an exciting idea...a very, very stupid idea. I stood straight, took in a deep breath, closed my eyes and stepped off.

It was as if I fell in slow motion. My body turned and balanced itself as I glided the long distance to the floor. I wasn't afraid and I landed gracefully on my feet just below the point I had stepped off.

"Holy crap—that was…AWESOME!" I exclaimed.

Now, logic would dictate I should have enjoyed my momentary triumph and not pushed my luck by another attempt. However, like a kid who'd just ridden her first rollercoaster, I was hooked on the thrill. Within seconds of landing, I was back upstairs, ready to do it again!

If I had simply chosen to step off the edge the second time, I have no doubt, all would have gone fine. However, I reasoned if stepping off was fun, jumping would be even better. With that, I squatted down slightly and then pushed myself into the air.

Now a '*normal*' human would have probably managed a leap of around six feet, I'm guessing. However, I was no normal human at this time. I was a human pumped up on supernatural energy. So, you can imagine how surprised I was, when I went a wee bit further than six feet. Okay, a lot further.

In fact, I completely over shot my target and went sailing nearly twenty feet to the other side of the room, hit the coffee table, then the couch, flipped it *and* myself over, and crashed into the opposing wall!

I lay unmoving with my legs twisted halfway over my head, in a mangled mass of furniture and curtains. Almost instantly I began laughing hysterically at my chaotic predicament. I was just about to attempt to unwind myself and get up, when suddenly my front door burst open with a loud *crack!*

"Daniela! Are you okay?" Miles asked hysterically.

My face turned four shades of red as I tried to twist around and get upright again, but my foot was caught in the drapes. "I'm fine, I'm fine…" I muttered, trying to shake loose the pesky fabric.

After hearing the enormous collision coming from inside my house, he thought I was being attacked again and broke my door in to save me. Of course it would be *him*; who else would I expect to find me in such disarray?

"What happened? I heard a huge crash and…" Miles was at a loss for the unexplainable scene. Before I had a chance to say anything, he was beside me, untangling my foot and scooping me up. Gently he placed me on my feet. "Are you hurt?" he asked with concern, dusting me off and inspecting me for injuries.

My face heated with embarrassment and I shooed his hands away. "Stop that—I'm fine, I just…" I had no clue how to explain the frazzled state in which he'd found me. I turned to clean up the mess of broken glass and debris, when suddenly Miles caught my arm.

"No you're not, you're bleeding," he said, examining my bicep. "Do you have a first-aid kit?"

"Um, yeah, it's in the cabinet," I said pointing to the kitchen.

Miles pulled me to the bar and sat me down on one of the stools. Retrieving the small medical box and taking a seat next to me, he went about patching my injury. It was a surprisingly deep gash just on the backside of my arm.

"This is pretty serious you know. You're lucky your body's strong with energy. The amount of force it took to injure you right now could have done severe damage. If you were anyone else, I'd be taking you to the hospital for major stitches, or worse," he remarked.

I rolled my eyes, brushing off his concern as a means to hide my embarrassment. "Yes, but I'm not just anyone am I?" I smirked arrogantly as he cleaned the wound. "Ouch!"

Miles looked at me lovingly. "No—you are *not* just anyone," he said in a gentle tone. His gaze was intense. I stared longingly into the beauty of his eyes. They were green with lovely flecks of blue that filled my mind with visions of what I thought heaven must look like at night. They were an emerald sky with glittering topaz stars.

He smiled warmly, then tied off the bandage and gently pressed his lips to my shoulder just above the gauze. A warm, electric current simmered through my skin and deep into my body. I felt my blood heat and took in a deep breath of pleasure as all pain was pushed out.

Miles leaned back a little and smiled brightly, "There, how's that?" he asked.

"Good…it's good…it feels good," I stuttered breathlessly.

Miles examined me for a moment and then looked around. Returning his gaze to me, he raised one eyebrow and asked with intense curiosity. "So—exactly what *were* you doing?"

"Nothing," I lied. Quickly looking for a distraction I jumped up and began straightening everything. "Here, help me with this," I muttered, motioning to my upturned couch.

Miles effortlessly flipped it right side up and helped me move it back into place, then turning to me again, he smiled mischievously.

"What?" I snapped.

He said not a word, and instead began walking around the room, holding his hand out over various objects. Slowly he made his way up the stairs and stopped at the top railing. Running his hand along the smooth wood, he looked at me with a knowing grin. "You jumped off the banister," he accused with surprise.

Again my face heated with humiliation and I glared up at him with contempt.

"No—maybe—okay yes! There, I said it, I jumped off the banister. And I'll have you know I was doing just fine until I over shot my landing…a little."

"A little?" he laughed loudly. I pursed my lips together with disapproval, to which he immediately stopped his obnoxious chuckle.

He stared at me with the delight of a child and I glared back, indicating he needed to drop it. To my relief he did, at least for the time being, but I knew without a doubt, it would not be the last we spoke of it.

Suddenly he leapt over the balcony, landing only inches away! Good heavens; did he have any idea how much he excited me? "You're sure you're alright?" he asked softly.

"Huh?" I replied dreamily. "I mean no—I mean yeah! Yes, I'm fine…I'm good. Thanks for patching me up," I replied, patting the bandage like a goober.

"Well, we have a lot of work to get done today. I can't have my star artiste disabled on her first day, now can I?" he asked playfully.

I raised one eyebrow. "*We* have a lot of work to do? Don't you mean *I* have a lot of work to do?"

"Of course I meant you—I'll just be supervising," he said with an ornery smirk.

I rolled my eyes. "You know, you don't have to stay with me. You could just drop me off and I'll call you when I'm done for the day," I suggested with hope.

"Are you kidding?" he asked, taking my hand again and pulling it to his mouth for a kiss. "I've been looking forward to this day for months. I wouldn't dare miss the opportunity to watch you paint. Somehow I think it will be quite a show."

"Of that I'm sure," I grumbled. No doubt I was sure to do something by the end of the day to further humiliate myself. Chaos seemed to follow me wherever I went, especially when I was *anywhere* near Miles. "Honestly, I'm sure you have better things to do."

His eyes sparkled at my words. Gently he tucked a stray hair under my cap and softly cooed, "I can think of nothing I'd rather do, than to spend every day with you, la mia belle."

Ah crap.

Chapter Eight
Daniela

Miles and I stretched out a long tarp and began taping it down in place. His office had beautiful wood floors and I certainly didn't want to mar them up with paint. With my lack of grace, the tarp had been a wise decision no doubt.

"I'll go fill this up with water and get you some paper towels," he said, picking up a container. "Do you want a soda or something while I'm down there?"

"Coffee," I replied. He wrinkled up his nose with disapproval, then bowed slightly and disappeared around the corner. "Extra cream and sugar!" I shouted.

I sat down on my knees and began laying out supplies. Opening the beautifully carved box, I retrieved the lovely silver handled paintbrushes Miles had given me, and smiled. I ran my finger across the striking ornate design and the letters L.M.B. engraved on the handles. Though I didn't feel worthy of such a sweet nick name, admittedly I loved it when Miles called me *'la mia belle.'* The tone as it rolled off his tongue had everything in my body squeezing together tightly, especially my knees.

"I Thought I heard somebody up here," a voice called from the doorway.

I looked up at Miles's brother, the very handsome Edward Chadwick, leaning against the doorframe casually. Of course, like every emovamp I'd met, he was totally gorgeous. To make matters worse, he looked a lot like his younger brother.

He was only a little older than Miles. Approximately forty years, making him around two hundred seventy-two. The idea of that still felt strange, because forty years *was* only a little older in the world of emovamps. Around their eighteenth birthday their aging slowed down. From what Robert had explained, they barely aged at all for the next two hundred years and then only an average of one year for every ten. Needless to say, as I looked at Edward, who was as buff as a twenty-seven year old, it was hard to believe he was older than the steam engine.

"Edward, I didn't know you would be here today."

"I was just finishing the paperwork for…er...taxes," he said awkwardly.

"Taxes huh? Are you sure it's not for Gran Conte?" I asked with a knowing smirk.

"You know about it?"

"Yeah, Robert told me," I said smiling, proud of my growing knowledge of their kind.

"He's teaching you a lot about us. That's good," he said pleasantly. His tone was friendly. I didn't feel he harbored quite the resentment for Robert that Miles did.

I sat back on my knees, biting at my lip. Feeling a bit brave, I asked, "Why do Miles and Robert hate each other?"

Edward gave a startled look, not anticipating my question. He thought about it for a moment, letting out a long breathy sigh of contemplation. "What have they told you?" he countered.

"Absolutely nothing. All I know is that they have been this way for a long time, but I don't know why." He let out another sigh, thinking over his willingness to say. As I began to stand up, immediately Edward was there, offering his hand. Taking it, he easily helped me to my feet. I asked again, "Why do they hate each other?" Edward shifted uncomfortably, still hesitant to breach the secret. "Please, I have to know."

"Daniela, I agree that you should know the truth, but please try to understand, it's not my place to tell you."

"You don't seem to hate Robert—was it something Miles did?" I asked anxiously.

Edward shifted his stance nervously again. "Daniela, I don't hate Robert, he's a good guy, in fact we were friends many years ago, and no, it's nothing Miles did, but…"

"So it's something Robert did?" I asked fearfully.

Edward smiled with deepest compassion, knowing how much I yearned for answers. Reaching out, he took my hand. "There is so much about our world that you don't yet know, some of it is very good and some…some is dark and terrible. I wish I could give you all the answers you seek, but I can't. As much as you deserve to hear the truth, it's a question they will have to answer. However, I warn you Daniela, the answer you find may not be to your liking."

Something in the jade depths of his eyes scared me. I lowered my head in submission and simply nodded.

Edward lifted my hand to his lips for a gentle kiss. "You're such a beautiful young woman, smart and talented. Personally I don't think either one of them deserve you. Miles is lucky I'm married or he would have me to contend with as well," he said sweetly, sending a shiver down my back, causing a small giggle.

"I leave you alone for five minutes and already my brother is hitting on you," Miles said teasingly from behind Edward. I smiled apprehensively, glancing at the floor with reddened cheeks. Miles eyed us both with suspicion. Nervously I fidgeted with my shirt. "Did I miss something?" he asked.

"No…no, I was just telling her about Gran Conte," Edward replied casually.

Miles could sense the deception in Edwards reply, but for whatever reason, chose to let it go.

"*Ahhh*, Gran Conte. Dani I tell you, it's worse than tax season. Honestly, the IRS is nothing compared to the Oracle's council," Miles joked with irritation.

"Well, I only stopped in to say hello, so I'll leave you both to it. I can't wait to see the mural when it's finished." Edward strolled to the doorway. "Don't let him work you too hard," he called from down the hall.

"I won't," I called back. Miles gazed at me, a look of questioning, almost as if awaiting my coming clean about the conversation with his brother. However, something in Edward's tone had me reconsidering my desire for the truth of Miles's and Robert's feud. For the time being, I dropped it.

"So are you going to just stand there and watch me all day, or are you going to help?" I asked with annoyance.

Miles grinned at my badgering. "I don't paint anymore. So yes, I intend to simply watch you *all* day. Besides, it's my favorite show," he said in a husky tone. I rolled my eyes at his remark.

The first day of painting went well. I was really enjoying time away from home. By keeping myself isolated so much lately, I'd forgotten how good it felt to get out. Though still too paranoid to venture away from the house on my own, being with Miles provided more than just pleasant company, it was also a great source of safety and comfort.

After a couple of hours painting, from the corner of my eye, I spied Miles picking up one of my paintbrushes. He ran his fingers over the handle, stroking the soft bristles between the tips delicately with a longing I completely understood. I attempted to watch without drawing attention to myself, but his interest in the brush excited me beyond words.

Aware of my gaze, he glanced over and smiled sheepishly. "Thought maybe I would help fill in some of your outline over here," he offered, pointing out a section. "If you want?"

"Yeah—yes, that would be great," I encouraged.

Miles dipped the brush into a lovely hue of light blue and with the grace of a seasoned artist, began to paint. His eyes were filled with the memories of a long remembered passion, that for reasons unknown to me, he had given up many years ago. I was overjoyed with his renewed interest, and found his artistic skill highly attractive. My preference to work alone was overshadowed by greed for him to stay. Truthfully, I wished him to paint with me every day.

Conversation throughout the afternoon was light and playful, and I relaxed little by little, feeling more confident that Miles would behave himself. Of course it was confidence short lived. I glanced over a few feet down and glared at the wall with disdain.

Miles smiled mischievously, putting the finishing touches on a small painting. It was of a man and woman who were very apparently in the throes of passion.

"There—what do you think?" he asked confidently.

Not wishing to be prude, I played along with his game and stepped over for closer inspection. "Hmmm…" I sighed.

"That's it? Just '*Hmmm*'?"

"Give me a minute will you," I scolded. Miles bite at his lip, awaiting my opinion with interest.

Clearly the picture was of him and me, no doubt painted as an obvious joke. Nevertheless, it was exquisite in its detail. He had a beautiful way of blending colors together and shading subjects that lent warmth and beauty. Honestly, I loved it.

"Nice use of color, *interesting* subject and the shading is very good," I remarked. Miles beamed brightly at my compliments. "However, you need to work on your proportions," I continued. His expression quickly changed to one of confusion. "Right here," I said, pointing to the man in the painting. "His head should be much, *much* bigger," I said, trying hard to not smile.

Miles stared at me, a look of amusement. Taking my hand, he raised it to his mouth, kissing it for a long time. "You have a good eye for detail. I agree his head should be much bigger, but then—so should her mouth."

"Awh! Whatever," I scoffed, pushing him away lightly. With a grin of orneriness he quickly leaned in and laid a kiss on my cheek.

Yeah, this was going to be a lot harder than I thought. There was no denying my feelings for Miles went far beyond friendship. As much as I knew that this time together could lead to more, I ignored every stop sign in my head and allowed it.

Why?

I have no logical answer to that.

Chapter Nine
Daniela

The day's end came quickly and though Miles tried talking me into dinner afterwards, I respectfully declined, insisting I had promised to cook for Becca that night.

I had just arrived home when Becca returned from work. Immediately, I began dinner while she sat at the bar, telling me all about her day. Robert was right; having a housemate was good for me. Aside from easing my paranoia, it also served an even greater purpose. The fog that had enveloped the relationship between Becca and me was dissipating, our bond once again strengthening.

I wanted to tell her all about my first day of work, how much fun I'd had with the incredibly gorgeous Miles, but knew it would only serve to make her feel bad. So, I remained quiet, simply listening to the musical, countrified rambling of my best friend. We watched a little TV, nibbled on leftover pie and eventually turned in for the night.

After a quick shower, I dried my hair and then snuggled down into the deep softness of my bed. The French doors at the end of my room were darkened by the night. I shivered at the memory of Tobias crashing through them just two weeks earlier. Now adorned with very heavy bars, they provide only a small amount of comfort. Honestly I didn't believe there was a bar in the world capable of stopping an emovamp.

Then again, Robert remarked about them only being temporary and planned to install stronger ones when they arrived. Looking at the huge steel cage paralleling the doors, I had to wonder just how much stronger they could get.

I'd been a good girl, taken one of the sedatives Robert gave me, but like always, panic set in as my eyes became heavy with fatigue and though I fought hard to keep them open, they batted closed several times.

Suddenly, with one blink, my surroundings changed. I recognized where I was immediately. The rusty chain link and cold concrete floor were forever engrained in my memory. It was the abandoned kennel. After Alistair abducted me, I was brought here to die. I looked up at my arm, broken and cuffed to the fence as always. The hollow sounds of the empty corridor echoed in my head with eerie familiarity. Was this real? I couldn't tell anymore. I'd had so many flashbacks and nightmares, I could no longer discern between fact and fiction. I wanted to believe the times I spent with Robert were reality, but as I looked around my dilapidated prison, everything felt very real. The icy gate, hard ground—even the putrid taste of blood in my mouth was all *too* real.

"Dani…Dani…Dani…Dani…" The whisper echoed down the long length of the corridor.

I became rigid at once, taking in a sharp breath and holding it tight.

"Dani…Dani…Dani…Dani…" The voice was familiar, but it was not Alistair. Still I remained silent, breathing shallow and listening carefully.

"Dani…Dani…Dani…Dani…"

"Who's there?" I whispered.

Suddenly, something moved in the shadows! I widened my eyes, straining to see clearly through the blackness.

"H-h-hello? Wh-wh-who's there?" I asked again. My body trembled, heart pounded. Unable to blink, my eyes filled with tears.

"Come with me…me…me…" the voice whispered.

Snap! The fence link broke, releasing my arm. I stood up and the gate swung open. Sucking in a deep breath of frosty air, I followed the dark shadow as instructed. The corridor appeared to never end as I stumbled along the dimly lit path, trying hard to keep the shadowy figure in sight. At last the black silhouette disappeared beyond a door. The fog of my breath danced around the door's frame in an icy ballet as I breathed hard with nervousness. Light from beyond breached the cracks around the edges and I squinted, trying to see what lie in the next room, but could not make out any details. Finally, I drew in a large breath and pushed slowly against the door. Quietly it opened and I peered in with astonishment.

It was like an opening to another world. Where I stood was cold, grey, desolate, but just at the threshold, began a bedroom which was warm, bright, splendidly decorated and elegant. A huge bed draped in fabric and ivy with a multitude of pillows adorned the center of the vast chamber. I glanced around, but the shadow figure which led me to this haven was nowhere to be seen. Walking in cautiously, I glanced around for anyone, but was alone. Finally, I reached the bed, and my tired body gave over to the beckoning of warm blankets as I collapsed into the pillow-soft linens.

"Why can't every nightmare be like this one?" I asked aloud.

"Dani…Dani…Dani…Dani…" the voice whispered again.

I bolted upright, eyes darting quickly around the room.

"Hello?" I asked quietly. No answer. "Please, is someone there?"

Unexpectedly, a hand slid around my waist and hot breath stung my shoulder. Swiftly I turned! My eyes widened in horror as I stared at his wicked smile and shrieked, "YOU!"

"Don't worry Dani, I'll be gentle," Tobias hissed, throwing me back against the bed. I let out another cry, but instantly he was on me, hands grasped firmly around my wrists, pressing them deep into the mattress.

"Please…please don't do this," I begged. "Just let me go!"

"Afraid I can't do that. You're just so delicious, I can't help myself," he snarled, kissing me with agonizing, brute force along my neck.

70

All of a sudden he stopped and pulled back to look at my face. I watched his features contort with horrible pain as he stared at me. Then his eyes became dim and closed, his body instantly collapsing on mine. The weight of his massive frame was suffocating and I struggled, pushing against him. Abruptly, he was yanked off, his lifeless body tossed through the air, landing several feet away! I screamed in horror at the sight of his mangled corpse sprawled across the floor. Everything happened so fast. I was stunned, but then strangely relieved. I looked up at the man who had saved me.

The man, with black eyes.

His face was concealed, as usual, behind a mask of gold and rust, adorned with ebony feathers which matched his soulless eyes. In his hand, a silver dagger, covered in Tobias's blood. I was terrified, but not of him. I should have been. Everything about this man struck fear in my heart, yet, I longed for him in a way that made no sense.

Tossing the dagger aside, he crawled to me. As he positioned himself over my body I lay back and trembled with anticipation. "Datevi, a me…" he whispered, his words full of unyielding domination.

I can't explain what happened next, only to say I was suddenly overcome with a fervent desire. Grabbing him around the neck, I pulled his mouth to mine. His kiss was passionate and forceful, but then so was I. He drew back momentarily as if surprised by my forwardness. I immediately pulled him back, forcing our lips together again. He gave in, his lips parting at my command, our tongues twisting, hands exploring. He released a small moan into my mouth and I smiled with victory.

Then quickly he pushed back. "Daniela stop—please," he whispered breathlessly.

I ignored his plea, springing upright, pushing him backward to the bed, quickly climbing on top, straddling his waist and holding his arms down. I thrust my mouth against his again, *hard*, biting the tender flesh of his lip. I felt so empowered! It was wrong and yet, so incredibly right!

"Daniela…Daniela…baby please—STOP!"

Immediately I halted; my body rigid with fear. Opening my eyes, everything now looked different. I was in my own bedroom. Looking down, I took in a startled breath.

"Robert!" I was straddled across him, holding his arms down, molesting my poor boyfriend! "Oh God, Robert, I'm sorry!" I said, letting go of his arms.

He gave me a gentle smile and then opened his mouth to speak, when both of us were suddenly startled as my bedroom door swung open and hit the wall!

We stared in dismay at a frazzled Becca, half asleep and in her pajamas, gawking at us, mouth open wide. Well, hell. I can't even imagine what it must have looked like. Middle of the night, me straddling Robert, him half dressed beneath me—and did I scream earlier? Ugh, the look on her face told me exactly what she thought was going on.

"Oh shit—sorry Dani!" she apologized, quickly pulling the door shut.

I looked back to Robert, who looked almost as surprised as Becca. Face in my hands I began laughing, which quickly turned to tears. Robert pulled me down to rest on his chest, wrapping me in an understanding hug.

"I'm so sorry, Robert. God, I'm a mess."

"You don't have to apologize, sweetie."

"Yes I do. Here you are just trying to wake me up and I practically rape you!"

Robert rolled me over to his side and gazed at me with tenderness. "Trust me, it wasn't that bad, and I much prefer being sexually assaulted than bitten any day," he laughed. I smiled sheepishly. "Honestly the only reason I stopped you was because I was afraid of feeding on you," he said with remorse.

"Thank goodness you didn't, I would have felt really bad then."

"Do you want to tell me exactly what you were dreaming about?"

My eyes became big and I swallowed hard. "No. I just want to lay here with you and forget about it," I replied.

"Okay."

Robert was good that way, never pushing to give up more information than I wanted. He respected my need to keep some things private. Though looking back now, I can see where a little more snooping could have helped head off certain events.

"Thank you for waking me up, I really do appreciate it," I said.

"No problem, but I really wish you would reconsider Michael's offer."

"I told you, I'm not sure about the whole blocking *thing*. Besides, I know I can handle this, I just need a little more time."

"You can't go on like this much longer. I'm seriously concerned about your health."

"I'm more concerned with what to tell Becca," I joked.

Robert glared at me with disapproval. "This is not funny. Your mind and body are very stressed out. If it wasn't for me projecting to you on a regular basis, you would be in a hospital right now—or worse," he said with graveness.

"Sorry, I didn't mean to joke about it. I know it's serious, but just try to see it from my point of view. There are a lot of things in this scattered brain of mine that are important to me. I have memories of Kimi, Becca, you…and other *things*," I said tensely. "And I can't chance losing any of them." Robert moved to argue, but I pressed, "Now, I just want to lay here and not think about it anymore; okay?"

Squeezing me tighter and with a submissive sigh, he replied, "Alright." I buried my face in the crook of his neck, inhaling his wonderful smell. Sexy. Warm. Sensual.

I tried to relax, but something was off. I lay still, trying to sense whether he was projecting to me. I couldn't tell, but knew I felt incredibly calm all of a sudden. "You'd better not be projecting to me right now," I accused.

"Hmmm?"

"Robert Elliot, I mean it, we had a deal." The only response I got was in the form of him snoring. Irritated, I poked him in the rib with one finger. "I know you're awake." He opened one eye and peeked at me playfully. "We made a deal, no projecting."

"Yes, I remember," he replied short.

"And?"

"And what? I remember the deal. Now, I'm really tired, so if you're not going to stop with this constant babble and poking me, I'm going back to my house where I can get some sleep," he threatened.

He had me. Robert knew exactly where to strike in order to silence my pestering. It was hard enough to let him go each evening when he would put me to bed and leave, but to have him in my bed and then be threatened with his departure was complete torture.

I tightened my arms around his tummy. "Okay, okay—I'll stop, just please, don't leave me."

He kissed my forehead gently and replied, "Never, my love."

Chapter Ten
Daniela

Monday started off well. I couldn't think of any nicer way to begin the day than waking up in the warm arms of Robert. However, my day seemed to go downhill from there as well as the rest of the week. Everyone had someplace to be (with the exception of me). Being shorthanded at the scrapbook store, Becca had to open every day and work until close. Robert and Miles both had very demanding jobs which also kept them unavailable throughout the day.

In the evening, Becca was usually too tired to talk much, going to bed right after dinner, and Robert was preoccupied with *Gran Conte*. I hadn't seen him for more than a few minutes on Tuesday when he stopped in to check on me. Luckily I'd *only* had dreams of the dark man all week, so nightmare intervention had not been called for. However, by the time Thursday night rolled around, I missed Robert so much I was ready to fake a nightmare just to get some quality time with him.

Friday morning arrived, but I lay around until close to noon, feeling there was no point in getting up. I took in a deep breath and blew it out with frustration, then stared out the window. I was going crazy from the solitude, which was strange for me. I'd spent the last five years isolated from everything, having no problem with it. Now, after the last few months of exploring the world and all of the wonderful experiences I'd had, it only took one week of mild loneliness and I was ready to commit myself to an institution.

"I gotta get out of here," I said aloud.

The last thing I honestly wanted to do was leave the safety of my house, but deep down, I longed for my freedom from these walls. I also wanted to prove to everyone else (and myself) that I was getting better.

At last I decided an outing was well in order. So what if I was by myself? It's not like I had never been anywhere alone before. I did live, work and occasionally shop for groceries for five years before all of this and was still perfectly capable of it now. I was just going to have to suck up all that fear and stuff it way down, deep inside.

I showered and dressed for the day, then nibbled on toast while anxiously awaiting a cab. It wasn't long before I heard the familiar *honk* of the horn, indicating the car had arrived.

I picked up my purse, then reached for the door, but suddenly stopped short of the knob. My breathing became heavy, heart raced and blood pounded in my temples. Many minutes went by and I was still struggling with my willingness to go. My hands were shaking, sweat forming above my lip.

The driver honked the cab's horn obnoxiously.

"You can do this Dani. Just open the door and step out—come on, you can do this," I said aloud.

At last I grabbed the knob, twisted it open and stepped out into the sunlight. The day was windy and cold. I shivered, pulling my coat tight. Locking the door, I turned around and stared at the awaiting cab. My throat felt tight. Slowly I walked the distance to the cab, took one more deep breath, opened the door and climbed in.

The driver of the cab looked irritated at having to wait on me for so long. I smiled nervously as I fumbled with my purse and coat to get situated.

"Where to?" he asked in a cold tone.

"I thought I would go to the Hobby Lobby, down on eighty-ninth."

"Yeah, I know where it is," he snapped, hitting the accelerator a little too quickly, causing the car to lurch forward with a jolt.

I watched out the window as we pulled away from my house, my stomach aching with fear. When I glanced up at the rearview mirror, the driver was staring at me with a vindictive grimace, eyebrows furrowed together angrily. I wondered how he could drive when his eyes never left me, and my heart pounded from the unbearable attention. I looked back at my house as we were about to pull onto the main road and suddenly felt sure I was going to vomit.

"Wait! Take me back please," I shouted.

He hit on the brakes. "Forget something?" he asked with irritation.

"No, I just changed my mind. Please take me back."

Reluctantly he turned the car around and drove back to my house, but his disapproval in doing so was all too clear when he slammed on the brakes hard, the car sliding to a screeching stop!

"What's the fare?" I asked timidly, digging through my purse.

He turned around in his seat, glaring at me with a sour expression. "A whole thirty-five cents! That's what I get for coming all the way out here. I wasted fifteen minutes sitting in front of your damn house, only to have you tell me you changed your mind. You think I don't have better things to do with my time than sit around waiting on some fruit loop who can't decide if she wants to go to a damn hobby store or not? Keep your thirty-five cents for the next cab. Maybe then you'll have enough to take a ride down to the corner and back!"

His anger was one thing, but the cruelty with which he spouted it was worse. My eyes filled with tears and I began shaking terribly, feeling at any moment he was going to attack. I reached in my purse, grabbed at the first bill I could find and threw it at him. Then, leaping out of the car, I ran for my door! I never looked back as I scrambled to get the key in the lock.

"Hey! Come back here!" he yelled. I could hear him getting closer as I fumbled nervously with the door. "Miss!" My chest hurt. I was cold, sweating, hands shaking. "Hey, I'm talking to you!" Oh God, I couldn't get the key in! Finally just as the cab driver reached my porch, the lock clicked! Rushing inside, I slammed the door, quickly set the alarm and then backed away.

He pounded on the door angrily. "Open up, I wanna talk to you!" he yelled. I remained silent, watching the door shake violently as he hammered on it, sure at any moment it would come smashing in. Finally after several minutes he stopped. "Fine—crazy!"

After he left, it didn't take long for the silence to become unbearable. Quickly I flipped on the stereo, turning the volume all the way up, then ran up the stairs to my room and hid in the closet. Even an entire floor up, the music was deafening. I sobbed uncontrollably, pushing myself as deep into the corner as possible, watching the doorframe through an endless cascade of tears. The loud beat of the radio became hypnotic, lulling me into a trance, until at last, fatigued and stressed from the terrifying ordeal, I passed out.

"Daniela..." A warm hand touched my face. "Daniela..." Two hands slid beneath me and my body left the cold floor. I opened my eyes, but everything was foggy, like a dream. Then, I felt the softness of my bed as I was laid down. Two hands cupped my face, the warm sensation of energy flowing into my skin which brought forth the sensation of happiness. I opened my eyes and was face to face with Robert. "Hi," he said softly.

I didn't answer, just slowly slid my arms around his neck and squeezed tight. The memory of the cab driver came rushing back and I began to silently cry again.

"What happened?" he asked gently.

"Nothing. It was stupid really. I tried to go somewhere and the cab driver was being extremely hateful. I guess I just freaked out."

"Did he hurt you?"

"No, just yelled at me."

Robert tucked a stray lock of hair behind my ear. I could tell he was upset. "I will call and file a complaint—"

"No, really, I'd rather just let it go. I'm okay now anyway, especially now that you're here." Then it dawned on me. "What *are* you doing here? What time is it?"

"It's a little after three o'clock," he replied.

"You're already done working?"

"No, I had to leave early because Mrs. Lang from next door could hear the radio and called me. I rushed over here as soon as I could."

"I'm sorry Robert. Jeesh, I am such a thorn. I still don't know why you bother with me, all I ever do is cause problems and—"

Robert abruptly covered my mouth with his, kissing me deeply, quieting my annoying babble. I instantly relaxed and gave over to his warm lips and the sweet exchange with pleasure. My mind was melting down with excitement. I knew it hadn't been four days yet, but was unwilling to stop him. Robert pulled back slowly, flashing a shy smile. I stared at him with delight and astonishment.

"When will you ever understand? You mean everything to me, Daniela. I don't '*bother with you*', I adore you, and intend to spend the rest of my life proving that," he exclaimed, his expression turning to one of sadness, "but it's killing me to watch you suffer from this fear and anxiety. I'm doing all I can to help you, but it's not working. The stress is killing your body *and* mind. I can't continue to stand by and watch you deteriorate. I'm begging you, if you care anything for my feelings, please reconsider the block."

Tears filled my eyes, I couldn't speak and all resistance melted away as I gazed at the pain of his expression. He was doing so much for me, yet I had continued to be stubborn and selfish by refusing to get help.

I threw my arms around his neck and hugged tight. "I will—I'll do it."

Robert pulled back to look into my eyes. Gently he wiped the tears away with his thumbs, "I'll make all of the arrangements. Daniela, everything's going to be alright, I promise—I love you."

"I love you too."

Chapter Eleven
Daniela

The weekend soon came and it was back to the job of painting. I had looked forward to it so much that it was depressing when the weekend came to an end so quickly. Miles, of course, had been a constant temptation, but I remained true, remembering this was a professional relationship. At least, that's what I kept repeating in my head every time he came within five feet of me. I really enjoyed the time with him though, and wished I wasn't restricted to only painting two days a week.

Robert had contacted Officer Kavenius, but he was out of the state on business and set to return in a couple of weeks. The arrangements had been made though, and as soon as he returned he was coming over to perform the block. This gave me a little relief, feeling maybe my nightmares were almost at an end. However, the days were getting worse and I was lonely most of the time.

I trudged through two more weeks of daytime isolation as best I could. At last Saturday came again, bright and early with a nice warm front and plenty of spring sunshine. This would be my fourth weekend of painting and I was feeling much more confident about my skills. Not only was the mural coming along beautifully, but I had attracted the attention of many people who inquired about my work, wanting to hire me. I had been inundated with so many job offers by the second weekend that Robert bought me an appointment book to keep up with them all. At the rate I was going, another couple of weekends and I was going to be booked through Christmas!

I was out on the balcony having morning coffee, when I heard the familiar sounds of Robert coming in and disarming the alarm. I looked out over the pond and smiled wide as I awaited his company. I was expecting him. He had phoned the night before, informing me he was bringing something by in the morning. My mind was occupied all evening trying to figure out what on earth it could be, but I didn't have a clue. However, I didn't let the notification go to waste and had risen early to shower (and shave), doing my best to look presentable.

It was only a few seconds before I felt his presence behind me. Our bond had grown so much, that I didn't hear him, but knew he was there. He stood still, silent for a moment and then sweetly placed a soft kiss on my cheek.

"Good morning my love," he whispered.

I turned in the chair, flashing a smile far too big, but was so happy, I couldn't help it. "Good morning to you too."

He lifted me out of the chair, sat down in my place, and pulled me into his lap. I wrapped my arms around his neck and hugged tight, taking in the wonderful smell of freshly applied cologne. Good gravy, talk about my favorite way to start the day!

"How did you sleep?"

"Good," I lied.

He swept a fall of hair from my face, running a thumb gently across my cheek. "You can't hide the truth from me you know. I see the toll it's taking on you every day. You look so tired," he said solemnly.

"I'm fine, really."

"Well, Wednesday will be here before you know it. Finally you can say goodbye to nightmares for good and start getting better."

"Yeah, it's funny, I was so worried about doing the block, but now I'm really excited about it. Well, maybe excited is the wrong word, more like…"

"Relieved," he finished for me.

"Yeah—relieved."

"I am too. The last couple of months have been hard. I'm happy to put them behind us as well."

"I'm sorry for all of the trouble I've been. It can't be easy giving me all of your energy constantly," I apologized.

Robert leaned his head back and gave a puzzled look. "That's not what I meant. I've enjoyed the exchanges just as much as you, sometimes maybe a little too much. I meant, it's been hard feeling your suffering and being helpless to stop it. Your nightmares have been very painful for me," he explained sadly.

"I know and I'm so sorry," I whispered, running my finger over his forearm. The bite mark was gone now, but the pain I inflicted was still fresh in my memory.

He took my hand, stopping me. "I'm not talking about you biting me either."

"I know—liked that did you?" I joked. He smiled brilliantly and then pulled me close, hugging my shoulders with a laugh.

I loved times like this with Robert, so easy and uncomplicated, like we'd been together forever. I knew I had a very busy day of painting ahead, but I was in no hurry at that moment to go anywhere. I was simply enjoying this precious time with him. It was time I hadn't had much of lately. Though I knew it wouldn't last long, I was determined to appreciate every last minute of this visit for what it was—a gift. Which reminded me; wasn't he supposed to be bringing me something?

"Have you eaten breakfast?" he asked.

I narrowed my eyes, certain he was aware of my curiosity. "Yeah, I had some eggs and toast, though I would have preferred one of your omelets; why?"

"No reason," he replied.

"So what was it you came by for?" I asked, trying not to sound demanding.

"Do you still have plenty of groceries or do I need to have the fridge restocked?" he asked, clearly avoiding my question.

"No, I have plenty of groceries, now what did you come by for?"

"Laundry soap; got plenty of that?" he asked playfully. The suspense was now killing me.

I took his face in my hands, bringing us nose to nose. As I brushed my lips across his, he took in a delighted breath. I ran my mouth along his jaw, and then made my way up to his ear, lightly nibbling at the lobe. He squeezed me tight, placing several kisses along my neck.

Finally, I whispered in his ear, "I know you have something for me."

He whispered back, "I don't know what you're talking about."

I sat back and narrowed my eyes at him with playful irritation. "You said you were bringing me something this morning, now what is it?" I whined.

He tucked my hair behind my ear again and smiled brightly. "Oh that—it's downstairs."

My eyes sparkled at his words and quickly I tried to jump up, but he had me firmly by the waist, restraining me. "Where are you going?" he asked.

"To see what it is!" I squealed, fighting against his strong hold.

"Oh, I see, you just want your gift, not me," he teased.

"No, I just want to see what it is," I said, prying his hands apart to free myself.

"Alright go," he said with a laugh, letting loose. I nearly fell to the floor, but quickly regained my balance and ran for the stairs. Robert was right behind me, eager to see what I thought of his present. Rounding the banister, I came to a screeching halt. Looking down at the living room below, I took in a large breath of excitement.

There, sitting in front of my door, looking up at me with the biggest brown eyes I had ever seen was a dog!

I threw my hands over my mouth, gasping with delight and then turned to face Robert. "He's mine?" I asked.

"Yes, *she* is yours," he corrected.

I began to walk slowly down the steps toward my new companion, unsure of how she would receive me. Immediately she stood up, a large white tail flopping around happily. When I reached the bottom, I sat down on my knees and clapped my hands together. Instantly, she came running, covering my face in a multitude of kisses.

"Well, I see I'm not the only one who wants to do that every time I see you," Robert laughed, bending down and giving her a scratch on the head.

"Oh Robert, she's wonderful! Where did you get her?"

"From the pound. She was actually on death row. Poor girl was scheduled to be euthanized today. When I met her yesterday, I knew you were meant for each other."

"When you met her? Can you tell what she's thinking?" I asked curiously.

"Somewhat. I can sense what she feels, like anyone. She was really scared, but what I like about her is her perceptiveness. She's far more discerning than the average dog." I looked at him with stark confusion. He smiled and stood up. "Here, I'll show you what I mean," he said, pulling me to my feet. Robert instructed me to stay there, then led the dog a few feet away and stopped. "I want you to remain still, but think about something really happy. Don't smile, just *think* about it," he instructed.

Finding a happy thought was easy, I was staring at the sweetest guy in the world, how could I not have a happy thought? Suddenly the dog's tail began wagging rapidly as if she sensed my happiness.

"Now, I want you to think about walking, either to your left or right. Don't say which, and don't move, just make your choice and think about it."

I did as he instructed. *Hmmm…I think right*, I thought to myself. Just as I did, the dog immediately stood up and walked a little to the right. *Okay, how about left,* I thought.   Again, as if reading my mind, she turned and took a few paces left.

"That's amazing!" I exclaimed, sitting down on the floor and motioning for her to come.

"I wanted you to have a companion here during the day, and also someone to keep guard. She'll be very good at sensing people's intentions."

"You mean, if someone wants to hurt me?"

Robert scratched the dog's ear, and smiled musingly. "Yes, she'll know if anyone wants to hurt you." I could see the deep fear in his eyes and my heart ached. I know how much I worried about him, and he was virtually indestructible. The giant target painted on me had to be horrible for him, knowing how much others sought my energy and that I was still just a fragile human.

"What's her name?" I asked.

"She doesn't have one yet. I thought I would let you have the honor," he said sweetly.

I looked at her thoughtfully, her giant chestnut eyes gazing back at me. She was absolutely beautiful. "What kind of dog is she?"

"The shelter had her listed as a Basenji mix—basically a mutt."

"Aww...my favorite kind," I said, patting her head. "Hmmm... what to call you. You know, my dad used to watch this show, Dr. Who. He had a companion named Teagan." Instantly her tail wagged as she placed several large, sloppy kisses on my cheek. "You like Teagan?" I asked. She got so excited, she nearly knocked me over!

"I like that," Robert approved. "Teagan it is," he exclaimed, pulling me to my feet. "Enough of that now," he scolded playfully, pointing at Teagan.

"She just likes giving me kisses," I defended teasingly.

He squeezed me tight, leaning his forehead against mine. "I do too." His voice was husky and low. I shivered and giggled childishly, biting at my lip. He leaned in to kiss me, but I immediately brought my hand up between us.

"Ah, ah, ah...you've already given me way too much of your energy today, no more," I insisted.

He watched me carefully and then shrugged his shoulders. "Fine with me."

"Fine with me t—" His mouth covered mine and I instantly quieted, awaiting the exchange—but it never came. Slowly his tongue found mine and I relished in the sweet taste of his mouth, like peppermint. As our tongues twisted together, I was all too aware of how dangerous this was, but was enjoying it so much I honestly didn't care if it killed me. I just wanted to kiss him forever and ever, and never stop. It wasn't a long kiss, but it was a *real* kiss nonetheless. At last he pulled back, smiling with great relief.

"That was unexpected," I breathed.

"Sorry, I couldn't help it. I've missed you this week and wanted to kiss you so bad—it just seemed like the right time."

"Yeah…I mean yes, it was—I'm glad you did," I stuttered.

It wasn't that he hadn't kissed me before; he had, almost daily as of late. However, this was one of only three kisses where he didn't project to me or nearly kill me. The exchanges felt great, felt unbelievable on an entirely different level, but I still preferred a real kiss. No mystical power, no exchange of energy. Just him and me—kissing.

I opened my mouth to say something else, but was interrupted by a knock at the door. Robert let out a long sigh of irritation.

"It's Miles, isn't it?" I asked. He didn't answer, just glared at the door as if it were a fungus. "I better go."

Robert squeezed me tighter. "Don't go—spend the day with me," he said.

"What? I can't. *You* have 'Gran Conte' and *I* have work."

"Forget Gran Conte, forget work. We haven't spent any time together in weeks. Spend today with me. We can go anywhere you want, or stay in if you prefer. I don't care, just please, stay with me," he pleaded.

Ugh, I was so torn. On the one hand I really wanted to stay with him, but on the other I really wanted to work on the mural (and see Miles).

"How about dinner tonight," I bargained.

"Not enough, I want the entire day."

I chewed at my lip. Lord, he was not making this easy. I glanced at the door, contemplating my answer, then just as I was about to speak, Robert abruptly pulled me to his mouth again, giving me another wonderfully satisfying kiss. Pulling back slowly, he waited confidently for my answer.

"I can't." The look of hurt broke my heart, but unfortunately, I was being so selfish, it did nothing to stop me from turning down his offer. "Dinner tonight, please?" I begged.

He let out a long breath of submission and nodded. I kissed his cheek, quickly gave Teagan a good head scratch, grabbed my purse, and opened the door.

"I thought I was going to have to break the door in again," Miles said with a brilliant white smile.

I rolled my eyes. "Don't even start," I scolded.

"Hey, a dog, I love dogs!" he said, squatting down to greet my new housemate. "Aren't you cute? And much better company than doc, definitely an improvement." He glanced up at Robert and grumbled sarcastically, "Oh, I didn't see you there."

Robert glared back with contempt. "Well, I adopted her because I thought she would be good at sensing evil—apparently I was wrong."

Miles glowered back with equal contempt. "Yeah, well your first clue should have been that she didn't bite you," Miles snarled, "Or did she?"

Robert puffed up, but I was immediately between them as usual, warding off another fight. "Guys!" I yelled. "Enough—this is stupid. Miles, let's go, please." I stepped up to Robert who still looked wounded by my choice. "I will see you tonight, okay?" He gave a weak smile.

I turned to go, but he caught my arm, pulling me back for one more kiss. That was three in one day! Though I knew it was only meant as a way to show up Miles, I still enjoyed it (thoroughly).

He let me go, shooting Miles a very challenging look.

"Someone learned a new trick," Miles remarked dryly. I turned around to face him. He looked irritated, but his expression quickly changed to one of delight as he took my hand. "Well, enjoy it while you can doc. Shall we my lady?" he asked, pulling me to the door.

I glanced back at Robert. "I'll see you tonight!" I shouted. He smiled, but couldn't hide his pain. I was making the wrong decision to go with Miles that day. I knew it too. Knew it and still did it. Ugh, this was going to cost me somewhere down the line, I could just feel it.

Chapter Twelve
Daniela

"Come on Dani, go to the mall with me," Becca pleaded.

"I told you, I don't want to."

"*Pleeeeeease*—come on, go with me," she begged.

I folded my arms stubbornly and turned away. "No."

"You know yer actin' like a toddler, right?" I didn't answer, only rolled my eyes with contempt, turning away again. "Awh! I know you dint just roll yer eyes at me," she said, walking around to face me. "Girlie, I invented the eye roll. Now, quit bein' like this. I know we've had this talk before, 'bout you isolatin' yerself; it ain't good for ya. Now all I wanna do is stay home an cry in my pillow, but I ain't gonna do it. Ya know why? Cause that ain't livin' Dani, it's just wastin' another day. Now get off yer ass, get dressed and come to the mall with me." She took ahold of my face and leaned in close, glaring at me eye to eye. "I *ain't* askin'."

I released a sigh of submission. If I knew anything, it was: *don't* cross Becca when she had her mind made up. I doubted there was a villain in the world as mean as her when she got angry. Though she didn't get upset often, standing between her and a day at the mall was enough to evoke a hissy fit of catastrophic proportion. That thought was funny, but did little to alleviate my anxiety about leaving the house. I toggled upstairs and got dressed, opting for several layers of clothes, my baseball cap and a thick, black pair of oversized sunglasses. No makeup, no frills, just plain boring, draw no attention to myself—Dani.

Slowly I made my way back downstairs. Becca nearly spit her drink across the kitchen at the sight of me.

"Muh gawd, Dani, what in hell are ya wearin'? Ya look like yer gonna mug somebody. We're goin' to the mall—you know—the *mall*? Not some gang fight."

"Well, this is what I'm wearing, so, either take me as I am or leave me here," I popped off, then held my breath as she looked me over with the evil eye. I was really hoping she would just leave me, but unfortunately it was only wishful thinking.

"Alrighty then. I guess it'll just have to do today, but next time, *I* get to dress ya," she said, heading to the door. I rolled my eyes at her back. "An ya better stop rollin' them eyes, 'for I roll 'em outta yer head, missy," she warned, never turning around. I smiled sheepishly. Crap, she knew me so well.

It was only Tuesday afternoon, so the mall was practically barren. We hit a few shops, mostly clothing. Becca needed an updated wardrobe to reflect her new attitude. I was proud of her. She was a lot stronger than I could have been having just lost her boyfriend. Technically I'd never had anyone break up with me. Ryan was my first love, but I broke up with him. After that, Robert was the first serious relationship I'd had. I shuttered at the thought of him ever leaving me. I admired her courage to push through the pain and continue on with life.

We ended up in the food court after a couple of hours, mostly at my insistence. This time I opted for a large order of chili cheese fries. With the regular exchanges, I was no longer worried about my figure. Though with Robert's increasing ability to kiss me without the need of them, *and* the block being put in place tomorrow, I was beginning to worry my weight could become an issue in the near future. Oh well, I was not going to stress over it. For now I would simply enjoy my super-duper-fattening order of artery-clogging-potato-goodness.

I'd been happily submerged in chili cheese, when as I piled a huge bite in my mouth, I nearly spit my fries! Right behind Becca, sliding into a booth, was Liz Beth. Just as she got settled into the seat, she looked up at me.

Hatred immediately flashed in her eyes. "Ah hell," she growled.

I rolled my eyes. "Hello to you too, *Liz Beth*," I pronounced clearly.

Becca turned in her seat to face the hateful hussy. "Hey Lizzy!" she exclaimed loudly. Liz Beth's lip curled up in a gruesome snarl. Then, looking around quickly, Becca asked with stark sarcasm, "Where's yer man?"

I honestly thought she was going to lunge at Becca, but to my absolute surprise, she didn't.

"He ain't my man anymore. I kicked him to the curb 'cause he wouldn't stop pawin' at me. Too needy," she said with vindictiveness.

I tried not to show my happiness over them no longer being an item. Though, for the life of me, I didn't know why it mattered. I was, after all, already seeing someone and had another waiting patiently for his chance. I had enough guy chaos in my life, the last thing I needed was to throw Ryan in the middle of it again. However, after her next statement, that rationalization did nothing to stop my look of sheer disappointment.

"Any way, he hangs out with some other chick now, Emily I think."

I realized after a few seconds, my mouth was hanging open. Quickly, I closed it and managed to utter, "Oh."

"Yeah, well, looks like a seat just opened up by the trashcan, so if you'll excuse me," she hissed, getting up and sashaying away.

"I still say somebody needs to suh-lap that bish," Becca grumbled with irritation. "So, baby-blue-eyes has a new girlfriend." I stared off in a haze. "D?" She waved her hand in my face.

"Huh?"

"Helloooo," Becca said, snapping her fingers, "earth to Dani."

"Sorry, what were you saying?"

"When was the last time ya talked to lover boy, Ryan?" she pried.

I began going through my purse, looking for nothing particular, just needing a distraction from the subject of Ryan. "I don't know—a month or so."

91

"Well, why don'tcha call him, see who this Emily chick is?"

I pulled out my mint Chapstick and slowly applied a thick layer, then in a cheeky tone answered, "Because it's none of my business."

Becca looked wide-eyed at me. "I beg to differ. He's still yer friend, right? An' what kinda friend wouldn't call to check on poor Ryan. Don't ever burn yer bridges Dani. Ya never know when ya might want to visit the other side again."

I was amazed at Becca's logic. Though she didn't know the entire story, she was right about needing to check on him.

"Can I borrow your phone?" I asked. Sporting an ear to ear grin, she handed it over. "Thanks." I knew the number, had dialed it a hundred times in the last weeks, but my mind went numb with the nervousness of talking to him and clumsily I hit the wrong number and hung up.

"Just breathe baby cakes. He's just a man, he ain't gonna bite," she joked.

I took in a harsh breath, and then rolled my neck around several times. *You can do this Dani, you **can** do this,* I assured myself. Finally I dialed again, swallowed hard and pressed '*send*'.

Ryan's sweet voice answered almost immediately, "Hello?" My heart was pounding, sweat forming on my forehead. I couldn't speak. I opened my mouth, but the only sound was stuttered gurgles. "Dani, is that you?" he asked.

"Um…yeah, its' me—sorry, I guess I had a bad connection," I lied.

"Well, I'm glad you called."

"You are?"

"Yeah, I've missed you, and I really need to talk to you," he said excitedly.

"What about?"

"So much has happened, and I just…" he trailed off, speaking in a hushed tone to someone else.

"Ryan—Are you still there?"

Several seconds passed. "Yeah, yeah, I'm still here."

"Who's that in the background?"

The line went quiet again. I could only make out the muffled sounds of him talking, but couldn't understand it. Finally he answered. "Look Dani, I can't get into it over the phone, but I can come to your house, have some coffee or something and we could talk then; what do you say?" I wanted to see him too, but knew a visit to my house was not the wisest choice at the moment. I was already dealing with the war between Robert and Miles, I honestly didn't need to throw Ryan into it, who for the time being had managed to fade into the background. "Dani?"

"Um...yeah...I mean no!" I took a breath and continued calmly, "What I mean is, I just got a new dog and she doesn't like strangers, so...how about we meet somewhere else."

"Yer dog don't like strangers?" Becca scoffed. "Freakin dog'll lick ya to death."

"Shush!" I whispered frantically, holding my hand up in her face. She slapped it away with an annoyed eye roll.

"Sure, we can meet somewhere else—hold on," he said, then continued with hushed conversation, this time I could clearly make out a female's voice. "Can you come out here, to my house?"

"Your apartment?"

"No, I moved a few weeks ago. It's a little ways out in the country, is that okay? Really, I don't mind coming there if you prefer," he offered.

"Uh, hold on." I placed my hand over the phone and then whispered to Becca, "He wants me to come out to his new house."

"Why?"

"I don't know, he says he needs to talk to me, says a bunch of stuff has changed or something. Can you take me?" I pleaded.

"Sure, just get his address an' good directions," she said.

"How about I let him give you the directions, you know how navigationally challenged I am."

"Good God, do I ever?" she huffed with another eye roll, taking the phone. "Kay babe, tell me how to git there." Once she had the address and directions, she uttered a, "*See ya in a bit,*" and abruptly shut her phone.

"Hey, I didn't get to say goodbye," I pouted.

"You'll live. However, that catastrophe you call an outfit, has got to go. So first off, we're gonna go back to yer house, cause I'm sure yer vicious, man-eatin' guard dog needs to go out," she stated with heavy sarcasm. "Then we're gonna getcha cleaned up and beautified." I opened my mouth, but she stuffed a hand full of fries in, quieting my attempt to argue. "An' I don't wanna hear none of this crap boutcha already havin' a boyfriend. NO bridge burnin'; remember? Besides, you should always look yer best when seein' an ex—it's protocol."

I lowered my shoulders with a submissive nod as I chewed the fries. Much as I hated to admit it, Becca, as always, had a very valid point. Plus, I can't say I didn't somewhat want to look nice when I saw him (somewhat). After all, Liz Beth had remarked that he was seeing someone, Emily maybe, and then there was the female voice I heard. That was enough to warrant a little makeup, a nice scarf and maybe a killer pair of skinny jeans at the very least.

At last I swallowed. "Alright, but nothing overboard; okay?"

Becca looked away mischievously. "Mmmm hmmm…"

Crap, this had *bad idea* written all over it.

Chapter Thirteen
Daniela

I stared at the address, trying to figure out where in the heck we were going. We were trying to find the Amanti Inn (Lovers Inn) Bed and Breakfast. Finding it took nearly an hour. I was relieved Becca was driving. Otherwise, we likely would've ended up in Texas somewhere. With winding country roads and several turns, I thought I would get turned around, but surprisingly, felt confident I would remember how to get here again just from the one trip. It was weird, like my mind was photographing the landscape as we went.

At last we pulled onto a long dirt road. The land was clear, open and light green with fresh spring grass. On the hill in the distance was an enormous, three story Victorian house. As we approached, my nervousness grew, realizing I was out in the middle of nowhere and had not thought to tell Robert where I'd gone. This vulnerability didn't sit well with me, but I tried to suppress the desire to freak out and barricade myself in the floorboard. *Relax Dani, you're just coming out here to visit Ryan,* I reminded myself.

As the car rolled to a stop, Becca looked over at me, "Alright, let me look at ya." She scanned over me, primping my hair a little here and there. "Well, ya definitely look better, and I was wrong earlier when I said the scarf didn't look good."

I smiled ear to ear. "Really, you like the scarf?"

"Yeah yeah, don't get a big head just cause ya picked out one thing that actually coordinates. Now, yer gonna have to let go of my car," she said, pointing to the deadly grip I had on the dashboard.

I pried my fingers from the car's interior. "I don't think I can do this. I feel sick," I said, giving a false heave as if to puke.

"Come on D, just go talk to him, see who this other chick is and then say, '*see ya!*' I promise you'll feel a lot better."

"Okay, okay," I agreed, getting out and closing my door softly. Becca followed, shutting her door with a loud *SLAM!* The sound echoed across the field, sending birds scattering from a nearby tree. I turned and glared at her, sure everyone in the house, along with people in Canada were well aware of our presence now. "Are you going to leave your purse?" I asked, pointing it out in the back seat.

Becca rolled her eyes. "Dani, we're out in the middle of nowhere. Who the heck is gonna take it, Grizzly Adams? Besides, it weighs about twenty pounds an' hurts my shoulder.

"Well at least lock your car," I scolded.

"Would you quite worryin' bout my purse, yer just stallin'. Git up there an ring the bell!" I glowered, but suppressed the desire to roll my eyes.

Starting up the front steps, I marveled at the lovely Italianate style of architecture. It was stunning, like something out of Victorian Magazine. Guests were welcomed by a long ivory staircase, leading up to a beautiful veranda, so massive it wrapped more than halfway around the bright white house.

A heavy crimson door with the words '*Amanti Inn*' was beautifully accentuated by two large planters of red anemone flowers on each side and several smaller pots stretching the entirety of the porch. They were exactly like the ones I'd picked out for my own house and reminiscent of my dreams.

Suddenly the air was filled with the musical tunes of Toby Keith. It was Becca's cell phone. The girl lived for Toby and had at least a dozen different T.K. ring tones, changing it every other day or so. "I'll be there in a minute Dani, I gotta call," she yelled, leaning back against the car.

As she chatted away at the caller, I turned my attention back to the anemones. The familiarity of ruby soft petals was eerie, but felt their presence was merely coincidence. I squatted down to admire them, running my fingers over the velvety flowers with longing and fondness, suppressing my desire to pluck one from the bushel and hold it to my nose.

"If you want some, just take'em, I don't mind," a husky voice said. I looked up to find a guy looking down on me with not only a warm smile, but a frighteningly gorgeous pair of bright! Emerald! Eyes!

Startled, I tried to bolt upwards to my feet, but lost my balance, tumbling backwards in a geriatric display of flailing arms, and crashing down on my butt with a loud *thump!*

"Ah hell, hold on missy, my friend just fell down," Becca yelled into her phone.

Immediately, the green eyed stranger was over me, lifting me to my feet as if I weighed nothing. "Are you okay, Daniela?" he asked, steadying me. I gazed at his beautiful face. He reminded me of someone. However, although familiar and very definitely attractive, he was without a doubt an emovamp, and currently held my hand.

I jerked it away quickly, whispering frantically, "You're…uh…uh…"

"An emovamp," he finished quietly with a half grin.

"Yeah…that."

"Don't worry princess, you're in no danger here," he whispered, glancing at the silver crested ring on my finger which proclaimed me a royal and family of the Oracle.

"Shit Dani, Can ya go a day without throwin' yerself down?" Becca asked sarcastically, scrambling up the steps.

"Sorry, it was my fault; I kinda snuck up on her. Honestly, I'm sorry," he apologized. I knew he was an emovamp, but he looked so young, more so than any emovamp I'd met before, other than Robert's baby sister. Even his mannerisms were not aged like those of Miles and Robert. With hands in his pockets, the way he rocked back on his heels and an adorable half smirk, he behaved

97

more like a true teenager. I had to wonder just how old he *really* was. "Are you okay? You didn't hurt yourself did you?" he asked.

I brushed myself off, flush with embarrassment that felt all too familiar, but I could handle this, could remain calm. So he was an emovamp. Not every one of them was out to get me, right? Sadly I wasn't entirely sure of that at the moment and continued to stare openmouthed and speechless.

"Uh, Dani?" Becca asked, waving a hand at my face. "Did ya hurt yerself?"

I shook my head. "Huh? Oh—yeah...I mean, no—I'm fine," I answered, turning my attention back to him suspiciously. "How did you know my name," I asked.

"Oh, Ryan said you were coming. We don't get many unannounced visitors out here, so I just assumed. I'm Colby, by the way."

I continued eyeing him with scrutiny. He winked, widening the half grin to a full smile. Scared as I was, his charm and good looks soothed my fear for the time being. Feeling confident I was unharmed, Becca went back to her call.

"Come on in," he offered, opening the door and motioning inside.

As we stepped in, my nose instantly filled with the marvelous scent of fresh baked apple pie. A lovely winding staircase cascaded down into a huge living area brimming with décor of Victorian pieces and modern art. It was a room overflowing with comfort and personality, soothing to my frazzled senses. Everything about the house was clean and inviting.

As Becca chatted away on her phone, Colby escorted us into a large parlor on the left. Painted in a deep shade of sunflower yellow, it was charming and every bit as inviting as the front room. Richly draped in heavy fabrics of butter cream and ivory, with multitudes of yellow roses, a large fireplace and toss pillows of white eyelet, it practically begged one to sit and have tea.

Torn

Suddenly, Becca tapped my shoulder. "Dani, we can't stay. That was work, an' one of the girls called in sick. I gotta go fill in."

"Can it wait at least fifteen minutes?" I asked desperately. I was so close to seeing Ryan and possibly meeting this Emily, I hated the thought of leaving now.

"I cain't, I gotta git. The other girl's up there and she shoulda left over two hours ago. She's freakin' out cause she's gotta git her kids in an hour. I'm sorry Dani, we gotta go now—unless you wanna call a cab?"

"No!" I blurted. I glanced at Colby and picked at the fringe of my scarf for a second. Regaining my composure, I began again, "No, I don't want to take a cab."

"I'm sure Ryan can take you home, and if he won't, I'd be happy to," Colby offered.

Good grief! All these options and none of them sounded any better than the other. I studied Colby carefully, trying to sense out any mal intent. It was right about now I was wishing Teagan was a tiny lap dog that could go with me everywhere. I was going to have to make the final call on this one. Maybe it was the calming smell of fresh baked pastries and cinnamon, but I went with my instincts (in other words, my overwhelming curiosity to see Ryan).

"I'll stay," I finally answered. "I'm sure Ryan won't mind giving me a ride."

"Ya sure?" Becca asked.

"Yeah, I'm sure."

"'Kay shoog, call me later an' let me know yer home safe."

"I'll see you out," Colby offered.

While he walked Becca out, I wandered around the large room, admiring the artistry and sheer brilliance in design. Whoever the interior decorator was, they had a great eye. Sitting on the mantle was a massive painting of a woman with thick black hair, full red lips and icy green eyes that filled me with fear. A beautiful painting, but like the red flowers outside, there was something hauntingly familiar about it, *the style perhaps*, I thought to myself.

The portrait was nestled against the wall with a multitude of glass vases, roses, knickknacks and candles, all of which were blocking my attempts at finding the artist's signature. However, with my track record of clumsiness, I was not about to touch any of it. My curiosity would have to go unsatisfied for now.

"Your friend's car won't start." Colby's voice startled me and I jumped, nearly taking out a flower arrangement nearby. "Sorry—you're a nervous little thing, aren't you?" he laughed. I let out a frustrated sigh. "Anyway, I'm gonna see if I can get it running real quick, but Ryan's room is just at the top of the stairs if you want to go on up."

"Yeah, sure…okay," I said, following him back to the front room.

"There're three floors, so just go all the way to the top. It's room 3C, second door on the left."

"Thanks, I'm sure I'll find it."

I slowly began the long walk upstairs, trying hard to think of what I would say when I saw Ryan. Knowing me, it would be something unintelligent. I was curious as to whether he knew Colby was an emovamp. He had too, it was obvious to me, but then I was getting better at identifying their kind. Some of that may have been the dead giveaway of emerald eyes, or perhaps due to the exchanges between Robert and I. Either way, I felt Ryan needed to be informed of the company he kept. Though I was aware their kind lived among us everywhere, and Colby seemed nice enough, it didn't change the fact that Ryan should be on guard.

Finally I reached the top. The door marked 3C appeared to stand out from all others. I stared at it, going over in my head what I would say, *Hey, what's up?* or how about, *Hey Ryan, did you know Colby's an emovamp?* I felt absolutely sick to my stomach.

"Ugh, this sucks. You can do this Dani, just take a breath and knock," I whispered.

Straightening my shoulders, I took a deep breath, and raised my fist to knock. Abruptly, the door swung open and I stared wide-eyed at a half-naked Ryan! He was dripping wet, holding a towel around his waist. In the background I could hear the shower going. Inappropriate as it may have been, I couldn't control my need to look over every inch of his glistening chest and arms. Unreserved, I scanned over each curve, every arch and chamber of glorious muscle. Oh my, he sure had filled out. At last I pried my eyes from his chest and focused on his face.

Instantly I gasped, covering my mouth with a hand. This wasn't possible. It couldn't be. *WAKE UP DANI!* I screamed in my head. Unbelievable, unexplainable, IMPOSSIBLE! They were all words that came to mind as I stared headlong into Ryan's deep, green, emerald eyes!

Chapter Fourteen
Daniela

I was immobilized by shock, unable to speak, unable to comprehend. Ryan smiled awkwardly at my realization, running a hand through his drenched hair.

"Um, Daniela—hi—I didn't think you were still coming," he said tensely.

I opened my mouth to seek an explanation, when I heard the shower abruptly turn off.

"Baby, who is it?" a feminine voice called from the bathroom.

I stared up at Ryan, who looked down at me with deep regret. Immediately, a woman stepped out, bereft of *any* clothing. The black haired beauty appeared unaffected by my wide-eyed stare. She smiled confidently as she picked up a bathrobe from the nearby, disheveled bed. Slipping it on and tying it lightly, she sashayed over, sliding her hands around Ryan's waist. Again, Ryan looked at me with remorse and horror.

"Who's this?" she asked, her icy green eyes glittering with interest.

My mouth hung open as he did his best with introductions. "Uh, Emily, this is Dani—Dani…this is Emily."

My mouth was like a sand dune, and tongue felt the size of a grapefruit, with no sound coming out. All I could do was stare. I didn't realize I was crying until the taste of salty tears collected in the corners of my mouth.

Emily looked at me with pity, then, after kissing Ryan on the cheek, she pushed past us. "I'll leave you two alone so you can talk."

I watched after her through glazed eyes as she walked down the stairs, disappearing after only a few steps. Turning back to Ryan, I was still unable to gather one coherent word in my head. "Do you want to come in?" he asked, stepping aside. Shutting my mouth at last, I simply nodded and entered.

Ryan began quickly straightening up, trying hard to discretely remove scattered pieces of ladies lingerie from around the room while I tried desperately to gather my thoughts.

I turned and stared at him again, unable to take my eyes from his, unable to pull myself together enough to speak. Suddenly, Ryan's face became distraught with regret.

"Dani, I'm really sorry. You shouldn't have found out this way."

"I don't understand how this is even possible," I choked, through an endless battery of tears. "I mean, I know what it takes to become one of them, so I know you must be truly in love with this woman, but…"

"It's hard to explain. It all happened so fast, I don't think there's any way to explain it, other than, we met, we hit it off and now I'm one of them," he explained (or *didn't* exactly explain). "Look, I know you're surprised, but—"

"Surprised?" I yelped, "Just surprised? If I woke up tomorrow with a third arm, I couldn't be more surprised! I am shocked!"

"I know you are, but—"

"You love her?" I blurted.

Ryan stopped, watching me carefully, contemplating the answer. He took in a deep breath, clutching the towel at his waist with frustration.

"Look, I really want to talk about this, but I can sense you're extremely upset. I need to get dressed, so, why don't you go downstairs to the kitchen," he said, taking my arm and leading me to the door, "It's right off the front room, to your left. I will be down in a few minutes and we can have some pie and talk; okay?"

I gazed at his concerned face, then lowered my shoulders and nodded, "Okay."

He guided me out and then gestured towards the stairs. "I'll be right down," he promised, closing the door.

I made my way back down to the bottom floor. I doubt Ryan even needed to tell me where I was going. The smell of cinnamon and apples was easy to follow. Walking into the kitchen, I was immediately greeted by Colby once more.

"Hey again," he said with a crooked grin. I smiled shyly, wiping the tears away with my sleeve, but didn't answer. "I know you really like the flowers out front, so I picked a few and bundled them up for you," he said, reaching over and picking up a small bouquet.

"Oh…that's really sweet. You didn't have to do that, but thanks," I sniffled, pulling them to my nose for a quick smell. "I don't know why I like them so much, I just do. I hope you don't get into any trouble for picking them."

"Well, I do all the gardening around here, so technically they're mine to give away."

"Oh, well that makes sense. Do you live out here also?"

"Yeah, my sister owns this place. I do the gardening and help out with…er…guests and stuff. In return she lets me stay here," he explained.

My senses calmed while I continued smelling the rich, red flowers, eyeing Colby with great curiosity. I still wondered how old he was. He smiled mischievously, as if aware of my question.

At last he let out a laugh, "Did you want to know something?"

Smiling sheepishly I answered, "Yeah, I was wondering how old you are."

"Twenty-five."

I rolled my eyes with a smirk. "Not your pretend age, I mean your real age," I scoffed.

He looked at me humorously. "That *is* my real age. I'm only twenty-five."

"Seriously?"

"Yeah, seriously," he laughed.

I suddenly felt a little foolish for my presumption. After all, it's not like they were born two-hundred years old. Logically there had to be lots of younger emovamps in the world. Out of embarrassment, I changed the subject. "So, you said your sister owns this place, I'd love to meet her. This place is amazing!"

"Thanks, and I think you already have, her name is Emily."

A painful lump formed in my throat. "Oh…that means Ryan's your brother-in-law."

Colby looked on me with sympathy. "Hey, you want some pie? I just took it out about twenty minutes ago."

Quickly, I wiped a tear from my cheek just as it spilled over. "Sure—but Ryan was going to come down and have some too; maybe we should wait for him."

"Psh! He can fight for his own piece, I'm gonna go ahead and dish up a couple for us. When the smell hits the house, it's not long before everyone comes running," he said with a half grin, causing my toes to curl in my shoes.

We continued to chat about different things while he sliced up the heavenly pastry. Being so close in age, it was easy to find lots of common interests. Colby was a few years older than me, but looked younger, it was an odd feeling. He was sweet, and very attractive. I found him easily likeable, but not just for those reasons. There was something about him, something I just couldn't put my finger on. I knew him, his smile, his eyes, even his mannerisms; they were all so…familiar.

"Ryan told me about your paintings, I'd love to see some of your work sometime," Colby said, sliding a huge piece of beautiful pie onto a crystal plate.

"Sure," I nodded shyly, still unable to embrace a compliment.

"Do you want ice cream too?"

"Are you kidding, is there any other way to eat it?" I laughed. "It smells wonderful; did you make it?"

"I did. I like to bake, it relaxes me."

"So, you garden and bake; I like that you're not afraid to admit that. Most guys would be embarrassed about exposing their softer side, when in fact, it's very attractive," I said.

He smiled warmly, scooping a large mound of vanilla and dropping it gently onto the pie. "You know, you're not like other girls I've met, Dani," he remarked.

"I know—my energy, it's different."

"No, I didn't mean that."

I swallowed hard. "What *did* you mean?"

"Just that you're very…" he paused and chewed at his lip, "real."

"Real?"

"You know, you don't hold back. You say what you feel," he explained.

I looked at him with confusion. "Don't most people say what they feel?"

Colby appeared very surprised by my question, and shook his head, "No, they don't. In fact, most humans rarely say what they really feel, they're too scared."

I held a look of surprise. "I think you've been sniffing too many flowers if you think I'm not scared to say how I feel. I am a complete fruitcake with no confidence. Besides, I thought I did a pretty good job of hiding my insanity."

He chuckled to himself. "I didn't say you weren't scared to say what you feel, but it doesn't seem to hold you back much. Ryan was right, you are different from most girls," he said, lifting my hand to his mouth for a kiss, "and beautiful."

"And taken." Ryan's gruff voice startled me and I jumped, jerking my hand away from Colby's mouth.

"Yeah, yeah, whatever—things change," Colby said with a sly smirk. Raising an eyebrow in Ryan's direction, he continued. "Too bad *you're* already taken, bro."

Ryan glared back. "Yeah well…" Tension immediately filled the air. I was no emovamp, but could plainly sense they didn't care much for each other.

Nervously I glanced around the room, my eyes falling on a clock above the sink. "Oh crap! Is it already 4:45? I have to get home! I promised Robert I'd have dinner with him tonight at 5:30!" I yelped hysterically.

"I can take you home," Colby offered.

Holding a black, gloved hand up, Ryan interjected quickly, "I don't think so—I'll take you home, it'll give us a chance to talk on the way."

I thought the gloves very odd, but then suddenly thought of little Maggi Hollin, Robert's baby sister. I didn't ask Ryan about them, but my guess was they were to keep him from feeding on anyone accidentally. Even though he was no toddler, he *was* a new emovamp and likely wasn't able to control his feeding yet.

I stared down at my untouched piece of pie with great longing, biting my lip and debating whether to stay and finish it since I was already going to be late.

"How about I wrap it up for you," Colby offered, taking the plate.

"Thanks," I blushed.

Flipping it into a bowl, he smiled sweetly. "It's no problem, just promise me you'll visit again so you can bring the bowl back to me; it's one of my favorites." He took my hand again, giving it a light kiss while shooting Ryan a challenging look.

Breathlessly I agreed, "Thanks, I will—I promise."

"Don't forget your flowers too," he said, handing me the lovely bouquet. Ryan let out a loud, aggravated sigh. Colby smiled, apparently happy to have gotten under Ryan's skin. "It really was nice to meet you, Dani."

I gazed into his dark green eyes with overwhelming familiarity and nodded shyly. "It was nice to meet you too, Colby."

As soon as he let go, Ryan had my hand, leading me from the house quickly. Odd as it was, he never let go the entire car ride home. I knew he was bonded to Emily, so this sign of affection had me somewhat confused. However, I did nothing to stop it (don't ask me why).

I'd like to say the ride home was informative, but other than Ryan confirming that he *was* an emovamp *and* bonded to Emily, that's just about the only thing I was sure of. Every time I pried for an explanation of how, why or whether they were actually married, Ryan managed to dodge the answers with ease.

Pulling up to my house, I had hoped to avoid Ryan and Robert crossing paths, unsure of how Ryan would be received. I immediately cringed when no sooner had Ryan's truck rolled to a stop, then Robert came walking out towards us hastily, a heavy look of concern.

"Crap! God Ryan, please don't say anything to start a fight," I begged, watching Robert approach.

"Relax, Dani, I can take care of myself. Besides, I'm not just some weak human anymore. I can hold my own against another emovamp with no problem," he bragged, getting out and coming around to my side.

When he opened my door, I glared at him. "Don't you dare start anything," I warned harshly.

"Okay, okay, I won't," he promised extending a hand.

As I took hold and slid out, I glanced up at Robert who was standing very rigid, eyes locked on Ryan with disbelief. He was close enough now that I knew he could sense Ryan was an emovamp. The entire situation suddenly became very awkward and I awaited the onslaught of jealous pain in my chest—but it never came.

Ryan smiled knowingly at Robert, who only stared back blankly. Incredible tension filled the air along with unnerving silence. I was about to speak, when suddenly Robert extended his hand to Ryan.

My mouth dropped open, when against all reasoning he said, "Welcome to the family, brother."

Chapter Fifteen
Daniela

After several long minutes of silently watching Ryan and Robert talk like old friends, Ryan finally turned to me with a big smile. "Well, I really need to get back to the house. So, I guess I'll talk to ya later, but the four of us should get together sometime, have dinner or something," Ryan offered.

"Sounds great. I'd love to meet Emily," Robert agreed.

I subdued the urge to roll my eyes, but they both sensed my disgust and looked at me. Hesitantly, I smiled and quickly changed the subject. "Speaking of dinner, I'm starving; can we go already?" I asked with annoyance, pulling Robert's arm.

"Sure sweetie. We'll see you later Ryan, and thanks for bringing Daniela home safely."

What the fire was going on? I was so confused over this behavior from both of them, I felt like I'd stepped into the Twilight Zone! Robert took my hand and casually walked me inside, where I was greeted by a very excited Teagan. Robert had already begun dinner and immediately went back to preparing the meal, all the while grinning to himself.

"Okay, you're going to have to fill me in on why you're being so calm," I said, scratching Teagan's head.

His smile widened. "Because, Ryan being an emovamp is a great thing."

"How is it a great thing? I thought for sure you'd be mad, or terrified he'd hurt me...or maybe even a little jealous. I never in a million years expected you to shake his hand and want to go to dinner with him."

With a relaxed laugh, he took a seat at the bar next to me. "Daniela, I think you're forgetting a very important fact about emovamps. When a human is turned, they are bonded for life to their mate, bound by true love. Ryan is bonded to Emily because he truly loves only her. Now that they're bonded, the only person he'll ever feel that for is her," he explained.

"Oh...yeah, I knew that." The words came out wounded and soft. It was hurt I couldn't hide from Robert. Indignantly I spouted, "Something doesn't add up. How could this happen so fast? I mean, what are the odds he would suddenly find an emovamp and then three weeks later be truly in love with her? It doesn't make sense—it's not right."

Robert looked on me with compassion, "Honey, I think with everything you've been through you're simply feeling a little paranoid. And that's understandable, but I promise you, there is only one way a human can be turned, and that is to possess true love for their mate."

"I don't care, something is off," I argued.

"Daniela, they are truly in love, that's why I'm not upset. Moreover, the fact that he loves you and would never allow anyone to harm you makes him a great ally."

"But you said he only loves Emily."

He tucked a lock of hair behind my ear. "No honey, he still loves you, the bond doesn't remove that, but his love for Emily is greater. The love he has for you now is more like that of a sister. You should be happy. I know how much you care about him. Losing him would be hard, but now he will be around for many hundreds of years, a friend you can always depend on," he assured.

I was happy for Ryan (in a way), and wanted to believe it was just as Robert said. Furthermore, crazy as it was, I had to entertain the notion that he was right. Considering I *was* suffering with terrible paranoia, how could I not be a little suspicious of everything at the moment? However, there was still something about all of it that just didn't add up.

"It's all going to get better, I promise. Michael's coming tomorrow to perform the block and all of this distrust and trepidation will go away. You can start enjoying life again," he smiled.

The very mention of this made my stomach ache. It's not that I wasn't looking forward to finally being rid of the terrible flashbacks and nightmares, I was, and had even made complete peace with it (for the most part). However, the process of having the block put into place still had me on edge and wishing I could simply abscond from my problems and once again hide from the world.

"So, are you ready to go?" Robert asked, snapping me from thought.

"Go where?"

He pulled out a picnic basket and began loading the food inside, finishing with a bottle of wine. "Just for a drive," he replied with a half-smile.

I narrowed my eyes with intrigue. "A drive where?"

He flipped the basket closed, then took my hand and pulled me toward the door. "Just a drive," he answered, offering no further detail.

When he said '*for a drive*' that's exactly what he meant. By the time we stopped, it was getting dark and the only lights visible were tiny specks, far away in the distance.

"Why'd we come all the way out here?" I asked.

Robert turned the car off, slid one arm around my shoulders and pulled me close. "I just wanted to be alone tonight. No TV, no Becca, no interruptions from anything or *anyone*. Only me and you," he said in a low voice.

I burrowed into him with an ear to ear grin. Oh yeah, I was in my happy place. We cuddled for a little while, eventually ate dinner, and afterwards, Robert threw a couple of heavy blankets in the bed of his truck and turned on the stereo. We had a little wine and snuggled under a quilt, gazing at the bright ocean of stars above, listening to, Delilah, play her awesome 80's love songs. He held me against him, running a hand gently through my hair as I traced little hearts on his chest with my fingers. The heat of his embrace was absolute heaven.

Nestled in the warm arms of the man I loved, with my best friend now safe, a great job and soon to be no more nightmares, I felt my life was finally coming together. It made what I had to talk to Robert about next, all the more difficult.

"What's bothering you sweetie?" he asked.

I dragged in a long, slow breath, and held it momentarily. Blowing it out, I answered, "I'm almost done painting Miles's office."

"I know, you already told me that."

I hesitated. "I know, but there's something I didn't tell you."

Robert sat up and looked at me directly in the eyes. He knew he wasn't going to like what I was about to say.

"And what would that be?"

Cringing, I exhaled a respite breath and replied, "Miles hired me to paint at his house also."

He looked off distantly, trying hard to maintain composure. His expression was a mixture of concern and frustration. "But you said you already had jobs booked for several months."

"I do—his *is* one of those jobs."

Robert pinched the bridge of his nose, irritated by this unwelcome news. "I don't understand; why are you taking on another project for him?"

I sat up, biting at my nails. "It's technically the same job. When he hired me, he asked me to paint a mural in his office *and* home. At the time, I wasn't sure I was up to it, so he said I could start with the one in his office and then if he liked it, he would have me paint one in his home," I explained.

"But that's not everything, is it?"

I chewed at my lip pensively. "No—Mr. Chadwick Sr. also hired me. He wants several murals painted throughout Chadwick Law—three to be exact. I know how you feel about me spending

112

more time around Miles, but I need you to understand how serious
I am about my work. I'm getting really confident about my
business now. I can't even describe how good it feels to know I
will be able to pay you back for all that you've—"

"Honey, I don't want you to pay me back," he interrupted, but I
quickly placed my hand against his lips.

"I know, but this is not about you, it's about me, and I *need* to
pay you back. It's just part of who I am. Try to understand that. I
don't like living off of someone, it's not in my nature and
something that eats at me daily. When I'm done with Miles and
Mr. Chadwick Sr.'s projects, I promise not to take any more jobs
with them; okay?"

I awaited his reaction, remembering the last time we had this
conversation. The explosive results still haunted me and I held my
breath nervously.

Robert suddenly relaxed his shoulders and smiled warmly.
"Okay."

"Okay? That's it? No argument, no nothing, just…okay?" I
asked in disbelief.

"Yes, just okay. I don't want to fight about this anymore," he
said, lying back and pulling me down with him. "Look, this is what
you do now and I respect that. There may be many times I don't
particularly like your clients, but I have to trust your judgment in
dealing with them. Otherwise, you're going to be constantly torn
between me and your work and I don't want that."

"I don't want that either," I said, shivering from the cold night
air. "So, now that we finally have it out of the way, I don't want to
talk about it anymore. I just want to lay here with you and listen to
Delilah," I said, nestling deeper into his warm chest.

Robert scooted down a little further, pulling a blanket over us.
The heat of his body filled the space around me, and I immediately
warmed. Lying face to face, he nuzzled my nose and smiled,
sweeping my face with the sweet mint of his breath. "I love you so
much, Daniela, I just want you to be happy."

"I am—more than I've ever been in my life."

"Me too," he whispered, taking my bottom lip into his mouth and giving a soft tug. I closed my eyes, breathing heavier with excitement at his willingness to once again kiss me without an exchange. Sliding a hand around my neck, he pulled me in, pressing his mouth over mine passionately. While our tongues twisted, my hands roamed free beneath the covers, mind racing with possibilities, but then he pulled back, breaking the kiss.

I let out a frustrated sigh, smiling impishly. Robert smiled back, running his thumb over my lips with deep longing. "Slow and steady my love, but rest assured, we will get there," he said. I had to wonder where '*there*' was, but felt it in poor taste to ask. "I better get you home, big day tomorrow and you'll need your rest. Michael will be doing all the work, but it's a long process and it will wear you out."

Though I didn't want our snuggle-session to end, I didn't argue. We packed up and drove back to the city. Whether it was the feeling of contentment, the hum of the engine or more likely the wine, somewhere along the way I dozed off. I scarcely remember being pulled from the car when Robert lifted me out. As he carried me in, I cuddled against his chest, breathing him in like a dream.

About the time we reached the door, I heard Becca's whispered voice.

"Oh good, I'm glad y'all showed up. I went to the store and now I cain't find my key, must've left it inside and my phone's dead too. Thought I was gonna be sittin' out here all night," she snickered.

I was so out of it, I barely cracked one eye open, opting to remain in my dreamlike state. "That's okay," he whispered, handing her the key, "I hope you haven't been sitting out here long."

"Na, just about ten minutes is all."

I dozed in and out as he carried me to the bedroom. Becca pulled the covers back and he gently laid me down.

114

"Thanks Becca, I got it from here," he said sweetly.

"Well, night then," she said, closing the bedroom door.

Robert removed my shoes and then sat down next to me. I knew he was about to leave, but was determined to keep him there. "Please don't leave," I mumbled, wrapping one arm over his tummy.

"I should go."

I squeezed tighter, "Please, just for tonight, I don't want to be alone, I'm afraid—please," I begged.

Robert brushed the hair from my face, then scooted down, and wrapped his arms firmly around me, "As you wish my love—only tonight."

Chapter Sixteen
Daniela

The next morning when I awoke, Robert had already gone, but was sweet enough to leave me breakfast and a note saying he would be back before Michael arrived. I was so nervous I barely picked at my food and what did go down I felt sure was going to come right back up. Afterwards I scrambled upstairs to take a shower. As Robert had explained, the entire procedure of placing the block was somewhat…intimate. This was one cause of my nausea.

I walked over to the bed and picked up the bikini top I had laid out earlier and let out a long sigh, swallowing down the lump in my throat. The process required a lot of skin to skin contact, hence the skimpy top. I would be wearing only the tiny red top and sweats, while Michael would have on *only* pants. We would sit on the floor, me in his lap, arms and legs wrapped around him, and my head against his bare chest. From start to finish, I was told it would take at least three hours.

I could practically hear what Becca would have said. *That's just plain crazy Dani!* Yes, I know, but placing the block was not some simple flip of a switch. It was a delicate process, one that required time, concentration and a whole lot of bare skin (I shuddered at the thought). Needless to say, I wanted to be clean (and shaved) before Michael arrived.

I turned the little radio on in the bathroom and cranked the water on high. Stepping into the shower, I immersed myself in the comforting flow, adjusting the temperature to the hottest setting I could stand. Trying desperately to not think about the impending ordeal, I began to sing loudly, lathering up with lots of soap.

Suddenly, I heard Becca's voice straining above the noise. "Dani, I'm about to leave, I gotta go in early today!" she yelled.

"Okay!"

116

I didn't catch what she shouted back over the rushing water and blaring tunes, only that it ended with, '*Have a good day, I'll see ya later!*'

Figuring it to be nothing of importance, I yelled back, "Okay, bye!"

The faucet gave a slight squeak as I turned it off and stepped out. I felt better—well, clean anyway. Clicking off the radio, I listened intently for any sounds of Robert. Hearing nothing, I moved ahead with getting ready. I blow-dried my hair, dabbed on a little make-up and then at last, dressed in my less than modest outfit.

Looking in the mirror at the tiny red top, I felt my breakfast once again creeping up my throat. I forced a tense smile, trying to suppress my gag reflex, but it didn't work and I gave up, rushing to the trash can.

"Nice Dani—well at least you threw up now, and not all over officer Kavenius," I remarked dryly.

After brushing my teeth (again), I examined the scar on my chest. Running a finger down the barely visible line between my breasts, I sighed with longing. From a distance I couldn't see it at all. I still wasn't sure of my feelings on that, but had avoided thinking about it since there was no point. It was going away and nothing would stop that now.

I was staring at the mirror in a daze when my ears were filled with sounds of Robert coming in and disarming the alarm. I immediately grabbed the bathrobe and slipped it on, tying it tight. As I strolled from the bathroom, I let out a laugh. There, sprawled out on my bed, paws in the air, was Teagan. She was flailed out on her back and appeared quite comfy.

Walking over, I patted her tummy lightly. "Well, don't let me disturb you, girl," I laughed. She made no effort to get up, barely cracking an eye to glance at me.

"Don't be mad, but I think I'll leave you to sleep while the nice detective is here—just in case," I said, closing the door. I snickered to myself, finding it funny that I was starting to talk to the dog.

Making my way down the hall, I suddenly became rigid at the sound of two voices. It was Robert and Michael. My stomach turned and I stopped, working up the nerve to emerge from behind the wall and make my presence known. *You can do this Dani, you can do this,* I repeated in my head. Hard as I tried convincing my feet to move, they wouldn't. At last I looked up and saw the sweet smile of Robert as he poked his head around the corner.

"You going to join us?" he asked. Feet still frozen to the ground, I smiled tensely. "Come on, sweet pea, everything's going to be alright, I promise."

Taking my arm, he gently pulled me toward the stairs. At last my feet gave up their grip on the floor and I followed quietly. Coming down the stairs, I kept my eyes lowered, feeling too nervous to look up, fearful I would vomit again.

At last, I could stand it no more and my eyes rose up slowly to meet Michael's.

He was standing at the bar, smiling softly. "Good morning Dani."

"Good morning."

"Sweetie, do you want some coffee or something before we get started?" Robert asked.

"No, I don't think it would be wise. I've already emptied my stomach, best not to fill it up again," I mumbled.

Michael laughed. "There's really nothing to be nervous about Dani. I've done this hundreds of times and haven't messed up yet."

"You must think I'm terrible. Here you are trying to help me and I'm behaving like a two year old. It's not that I don't trust you, it's just…"

"It's okay, you don't have to apologize. I know you're nervous and believe me, it's normal."

"Well, I'll try to relax then."

"Actually I have something for you that will help," Robert said holding out his hand. In his palm was a tiny white pill.

"What's this for?" I asked, taking the small tablet.

Michael handed me a glass of water. "It's just a mild tranquilizer, to relax you for the procedure. It's a very standard practice with what I do. The block takes a long time and you have to be very still while I do it. With the help of the sedative, the process will put you to sleep, enabling me to concentrate on the block rather than worrying about you moving or becoming fatigued."

I was determined to not over-analyze anything today. So, without thinking about it, I did as instructed. "Reasonable enough," I said, downing the pill. Even Robert looked a little surprised by my lack of resistance.

"Now, your friend is at work, correct?" Michael asked.

"Yes, she won't get off until at least 5:00 and I took her key just in case she comes home early."

"Smart—alright then, I already have everything set up, so I'm ready when you are," he said, motioning to a large, silver mat in the floor.

"Okay, so what's the silver mat for?" I asked.

Michael scolded Robert with a laugh. "Have you taught her nothing?"

"I have, just not about silver, at least not yet," he defended.

"What about silver?" I asked.

"It's the perfect conductor of energy, and the only material on earth capable of killing us," Robert said.

My heart fell and I gripped my chest with fear, "Silver can kill you?" I yelped. I was suddenly plagued with thoughts of all my jewelry. I only wore silver. It was my favorite. "Why didn't you tell me? If I'd known, I would have gotten rid of all my silver months ago."

Robert laughed, pulling me in for a hug. "Silly you, it's not kryptonite to us. It's only deadly when charged with energy."

119

"I don't understand."

Michael explained, "Silver is very soft, but if we charge it with energy, it becomes stronger than anything on the planet, virtually indestructible and capable of inflicting serious damage to one of us, even death. Just a small cut from something silver can scar us for life." He held out his arm, exposing a long mark down his forearm.

I cringed at the very notion, and immediately thought of the small crescent scar on Robert's collarbone. Though it explained what had caused the wound, I still didn't know the story behind it. However, now didn't feel like the right time to ask. "Okay, so the mat is silver because it's a good conductor of energy, which probably helps you with the block—I can see that—makes sense anyway."

"Alright, well now that we have that explained, let's go ahead and get into position before that sedative takes effect," Michael suggested.

I was doing okay right up until Michael started removing his shirt. With the undoing of each button, my heart sped up a little more. I was no doubt in love with Robert, but officer Kavenius was definitely easy on the eyes. With his clean, military style haircut and muscular physique, he was someone I could happily devote a lot of time staring at.

At last he pulled the shirt off, draping it over a nearby barstool. Unable to control my feelings, I turned away shyly, shutting my eyes tight. "I don't think I can do this," I whispered frantically.

Robert pulled me into his arms, leaning his forehead against mine. "Daniela, everything you are feeling right now is perfectly normal."

"No, it's not," I argued.

"Yes, it is," he assured. "I know you find Michael attractive. I've known it since the first time you met him. Michael knows it too. It's normal and completely understandable."

The very thought of this horrified me beyond words. "Doesn't it bother you?" I asked.

He smiled warmly, "No, it doesn't bother me. The attraction you feel for Michael is only physical, nothing more. It's only when it goes deeper that it bothers me," he said with irritation. He didn't have to say any names; I knew who he was speaking of. "Michael is just a friend, and I know you don't feel anything intimate for him, so don't worry about it. You're the bravest person I know—you can do this." I nodded my head, and then quickly stole a small kiss. He smiled widely, then reached down and took hold of my bathrobe belt. "Are you ready?"

"Well, I don't understand the difference, but I guess I'm as ready as ever—let's do this."

Robert slowly untied the belt, letting the robe drop open. His eyes quickly scanned down my front, sparkling with delight and a wide smile overtook him. Softly he ran his hands along the curve of my sides, taking in a deep breath and holding it momentarily. Robert had never seen so much of me, and to my satisfaction, I believe he was quite pleased with all of it.

Michael let loose a goodhearted laugh. "Dani, if you could feel what Robert is feeling right now, you would *clearly* understand the difference between physical and intimate attraction." I blushed slightly, but it was nothing compared to the lovely shade of red that flooded Robert's face. "Robert, would you prefer I be blindfolded?" Michael joked.

"I trust you to be a gentleman," he smiled, never taking his eyes from my body.

At last I placed my hand under his chin, lifting his face to mine. "I'm up here," I teased, causing him to blush once again.

"Sorry, I know, I know," he said, shaking his head.

He leaned in and gave me a quick, but gentle kiss. Pulling back, I instantly felt very confident. "I'm ready now Michael," I said, sliding the robe from my shoulders, letting it drop to the floor. Then turning around, I walked to the mat. Michael quickly came to me and sat down. Joining him on the floor, I scooted into position. Once in his lap, I wrapped my arms and legs around him.

"Now, just lay your head against my chest and relax, Dani," Michael said quietly, folding his arms around me.

"She's everything to me Michael. I trust you," Robert said. It was only then I realized how difficult this must have been for Robert. He was putting a lot of faith in Michael.

Within minutes of settling into position, the sedative kicked in and my body relaxed against him. Up to that point, he merely had his arms draped around me lightly. However, as my body became limp, he pulled tight, holding me firmly to him. His body was warm, his heart steady and strong, lulling me into a dreamlike state. Listening to it quietly, my eyes became heavy, body giving over to the seductive rhythm of its beat and the soothing heat of his embrace. I opened my eyes, momentarily gazing at Robert's sweet face. Just before falling asleep, I sent up a silent prayer, that when I awoke, I would still remember the man I loved.

Chapter Seventeen
Robert

Robert sat with arms crossed, watching intently. It had been nearly an hour. Daniela and Michael were sitting so still, they looked almost statuesque. His eyes scanned over Daniela again. She was so beautiful, flawless, like an angel.

He knew she held no intimate attraction to Michael, yet, while continuing to watch, he was overcome with feelings of jealousy. However, it was not Michael who had brought about these feelings of rivalry—it was Miles.

In his mind he visualized Miles holding her, and the very thought was unbearable. Well aware that her feelings went far deeper than physical attraction when it came to Chadwick, once again Robert revisited a thought he'd been having lately.

He hated deceiving Daniela, tricking her into believing he would make her into one of his kind if proof was found that a transplant patient had been successfully turned. It was proof Robert knew didn't exist, or more so, hoped didn't. Luckily, the burden of finding such evidence was on him, and unknown to Daniela, he wasn't searching for it.

He tried to reason that what he was doing was right, that there was nothing wrong with misleading her this way. He loved her, felt sure they could have a couple hundred years of happiness together. Much as he tried to convince himself though, he was inundated with guilt.

How could she honestly be happy? There would always be this barrier between them. He was still barely able to kiss her, and even the Oracle had warned it was the best he could ever hope for so long as she was human. Though she was content for now, it would not always be. Eventually she would want more, she would need more. It was a need he felt he couldn't satisfy. They could never *be* together, never make love—he could never give her a child. How could he be so selfish? Could he lie to the woman he loved, denying her these wonderful life experiences, and taking away her chance to be truly happy?

All at once, loud barking interrupted Robert's thoughts. Startled, he glanced at Michael and Dani again, both still completely silent in a trance-like state. Again, the room echoed with Teagan's cries for freedom.

Fearing the dog would disrupt them, Robert quickly followed the whines and scratching all the way to Daniela's room. Opening the door, a very excited Teagan came bounding out, jumping up and wagging all over. He bent down, giving her ear a good scratch.

Suddenly she froze, listening intently. Robert became rigid as he heard the click of the downstairs lock! Someone was coming in!

Immediately, he took off, the dog right on his heels. He rounded the banister, and in a split second had jumped the distance to the ground floor. But he was not fast enough. His feet no sooner hit the floor, than the front door swung open and in stepped Becca.

Her eyes immediately landed on Daniela and Michael with a *gasp*! Looking to Robert, she furrowed up her brow and asked, "What in hell is goin' on?"

Robert stood straight, a wide-eyed expression. He couldn't believe he'd been so careless as to let this happen, and was now faced with either trying to make up some strange lie, or at last coming clean to Becca about '*his kind*'. He glanced at Daniela and Michael; both remained unaware of Becca's presence.

Looking back to Becca, he made the choice. Lowering his voice, he said, "Becca, we need to talk."

She eyed him speculatively, and then walked over to Michael and Daniela, circling them with intense curiosity. "What are they doing?" she asked.

"Keep your voice down, they can't be disturbed."

"Why not?" she whispered.

"They are in a deep trance right now. Disrupting them would be really bad. I know you have a lot of questions, and I will be happy to answer all of them if you'll sit down and promise to remain quiet," he said motioning to the couch.

Becca narrowed her eyes, not sure what to make of the odd scene, but overcome with curiosity, she hesitantly took a seat. Teagan immediately jumped up, flopping down across her lap.

Once the dog was settled, Robert began. The conversation was odd, but Robert did his best to explain everything in detail. He told her of his kind, what they were, how they lived—what Alistair had done to Daniela. He considered not telling her about Tobias, but felt if he was to gain her trust and keep it, it was important to be as upfront and honest as possible. He told her everything, except that Tobias was now dead, feeling it was the one piece of information she wasn't ready for. Still, it was a difficult subject.

"So he was just usin' me?" she asked.

Robert nodded earnestly. "I'm afraid so. What he did to you is unforgivable and I hope you don't think poorly of our kind for the actions of a few. Most of my kind feel it's a terrible practice and would never do it."

"That's why Dani tried to get me to leave him. Y'all knew what he was."

"Yes, we knew."

"Well hell, now I feel really bad. Here she was just tryin' to protect me, an' I...well the thangs I said to her—if I'd known..."

"Don't feel bad, Becca, you had no idea and weren't yourself at the time. Daniela knows that. She loves you and is just happy you are away from him now."

"I guess so, but I still don't understand what her and this guy are doing half-naked an' huggin' on the floor," she said raising an eyebrow in their direction.

Robert quietly laughed. "Their not just hugging. Daniela, as you know, has been suffering from a lot of nightmares. They started when Alistair took her, but worsened after Tobias's attack. She's having so many flashbacks and nightmares she can barely tell what's real anymore. Many nights I have to come running over here just to wake her up. Michael is trying to stop them. He has a very special gift to block memories. When she wakes up in a little bit, she won't remember much about Alistair or Tobias."

"At all?" she asked skeptically.

"Only bits and pieces, more like a story she heard, or something from long ago, just fuzzy details. It will help if you try not to mention anything about them to her. You know, let her forget. The memories will still be there and can be triggered by just a word or phrase," he explained.

Becca nodded, continuing to pet Teagan, who was lying across her lap snoozing peacefully. Suddenly the dog's head snapped up, glancing in the direction of Daniela and Michael.

"What's a matter, baby girl?" Becca asked, petting her head.

"They must be about to come around."

Becca fidgeted nervously, "Well should I go or hide or somethin'?'

"No, just stay put. I have a feeling Daniela will be very happy that you know about everything now. It's been really hard for her not to tell you."

"Yeah, but this Michael, wont he be mad I'm here?"

"I've known him many years—I promise, he'll understand," he assured.

They both watched intently, waiting for any signs of movement. Several long minutes went by, when at last Michael opened his eyes and looked straight at Becca.

At first he looked very confused, but then a soft smile spread across his face. Quietly he asked, "Well, who are you?"

She smiled back shyly. "I'm Becca, Dani's friend. I kinda-sorta accidently walked in on y'all."

Immediately, Robert went to Michael and came to his knees. "Is she okay? Did it work?"

"She's fine, and yes, I believe it worked," he said, gently easing her back into Robert's arms. He lifted her from Michael, carrying her to the couch. "She's still out, but should wake up shortly. It was a pretty big mess in there, Robert. She's going to be very tired tonight, but should feel better by morning," Michael assured.

Robert cradled her, stroking the hair from her face. "Do you think you got them all?"

"I think so. There were several different bad memories, but I blocked a lot of nightmares as well. She's been dreaming of everything from Alistair, Tobias, to even hallucinating about a Tenebre."

"A what?" Becca interrupted.

"Tenebre. They're emovamps, but not any you would want to meet. Their eyes are solid black from the energy they live on, nothing but pure evil," Michael explained.

Robert shook his head. "It couldn't be a Tenebre. It has to be just a figment of her imagination. I've never even told her about them and if she'd ever seen one, it would have attacked immediately. No, it has to be from watching vampire movies or something."

"Well, I blocked them, so they shouldn't bother her anymore."

"And what about the memories of Miles?" Robert asked.

Michael took in a deep breath, holding it momentarily, "They are all still there, just as you asked. Though, I wonder if she would be better off forgetting about him. She's very torn between you two."

"Miles is an emovamp too?" Becca interrupted with huge eyes of revelation.

Michael and Robert looked at each other guiltily. "Well he can just be mad we told her," Robert defended. "She's Daniela's best friend and has a right to know."

"Man-o-man, this shit just keeps gettin' deeper an' deeper," she laughed.

"You have a very pretty laugh," Michael suddenly said.

Becca blushed, batting her eyes wildly. "Why thanks."

Michael and she continued to talk, while Robert remained focused on Daniela. Though he knew Michael was very good with his gift, he wouldn't rest easy until she opened her eyes and recognized him. He brushed her cheek with his hand, and traced the soft curve of her lips with a finger. Could he ever live without her? The very thought was worse than death.

Her fingers twitched, head moving side to side. She was waking up at last. He watched her eyes, waiting for them to open. When they did, she looked very confused. She furrowed up her eyebrows, searching Robert's face with intensity. Finally she opened her mouth, and quietly asked, "Who are you?"

Chapter Eighteen
Daniela

Ever had surgery? I have, several times. It's always the same. They put me out, but as soon as I close my eyes, I open them and the surgery is over. That's how it felt when Michael performed the block. It felt like no time had passed. I was sitting in Michael's lap one minute, closed my eyes, and then upon opening them, was staring into the face of the most gorgeous man I'd ever seen.

He looked so serious, so concerned. It's probably the reason for what I did next.

Scrunching up my eyebrows, I examined him with no recognition. At last I asked with stark confusion, "Who are you?" He looked horrified. Mean as it was, I couldn't refrain from having a tiny bit of fun with Robert. I let out a laugh, "Oh yes, I remember now—you're the man I love," I said, stroking his cheek.

His expression turned to one of relief and he smiled, kissing my forehead. "That wasn't very nice."

I grinned impishly, and then opened my mouth to speak, when I was cut off by the last voice I expected to hear.

"Yeah Dani, that was just downright mean."

I looked at Robert, my eyes like giant saucers. "Is that Becca?"

He nodded, helping me sit up to face my best friend. I stared in disbelief. "How long have you been here?" I asked hysterically.

Robert placed a hand on my arm. "It's okay, sweetie. She knows everything now."

I swallowed hard. "Everything?"

"Yes, everything."

"An' I'm cool with it babe. Yer man did a good job fillin' me in. Now ya don't have to hide it from me anymore."

Still in shock, I stuttered incoherently. "But when—why—how did this happen?"

Becca lowered her head sheepishly. "I walked in on y'all. You was all half-naked and looked like you was makin' out er somethin'."

"But how did you get in? You didn't have a key," I declared with confusion.

Again, Becca looked embarrassed. "I took yer key this mornin'. I told ya I was takin' it, shouted it at ya when you was in the shower—I guess ya didn't hear me."

Well, now I knew what that first part I missed was. "And you're okay with this? I mean, you believe all of it, just like that?"

"Dani, I knew somethin' strange was goin' on when I was with Tob—"

"What she means is, she's suspected something all along and now it all makes sense," Robert interjected.

Becca nodded vigorously. "Yeah, exactly, it all makes sense now."

Awkward as it was waking up to my best friend suddenly knowing all about the secret life I'd been living, more so I was relieved. It was just as she'd said—now I didn't have to hide anything from her.

In the coming months that made things a lot easier. I didn't have to conceal certain details and was now able to confide more in Becca about the struggle I was having between Miles and Robert. Just as expected, I gained little sympathy over the entire situation. *Emovamps or not, they're still men, Dani, yer gonna have to give one of 'em up.* Her words repeated in my head daily.

I knew she was right, had known it all along, but in my selfishness I tried to keep them both. At some point I was going to have to put an end to the relationship with Miles. We weren't dating, but that didn't matter. My feelings went far beyond those of friendship *or* professionalism. It was wrong and had to stop. I'd already made that decision, or at least that's what I told myself. Actually ending it was an entirely different matter.

130

The days of spring and summer went by quickly, with weekends painting in the charming company of Miles, and weeknights of movies, dining and many more midnight picnics with Robert.

Soon the first day of fall arrived. I had finished the mural at Miles's house and was almost done with the last mural at Chadwick law. I won't lie and say I didn't drag out the completion by quite a bit (around three weeks longer to be exact). I just wasn't ready to give up my time with Miles yet. I knew it, and he did too. When I look back now, there's no doubt Robert was aware of it also.

Inevitably, the last day of painting at Chadwick Law was here, and the depression I felt was obvious. I sulked all morning as I waited for Miles to pick me up, racking my brain for any possible way to add more time to the job. I even shamefully contemplated sabotaging my work just to buy me a few more days to fix it, but put the thought out of my head.

"This really stinks," I pouted to Teagan. She looked up at me with big brown eyes that offered little pity, only begged for the last of my breakfast. I handed her a piece of bacon, patting her head. "How did this get so complicated?"

The only answer I received was a knock at the door, indicating Miles had arrived. I sighed deeply, feeling such a mixture of excitement and gloom. I meandered to the door like a toddler and opened it unenthusiastically. In all of the time I'd known Miles, I'd never opened a door to him where I didn't find him smiling ear to ear—but not today. This day he looked as depressed as me.

"Morning sweets," he said quietly.

"Morning."

"Last day."

"Yeah, last day," I echoed solemnly.

He dragged in a deep breath, giving Teagan a scratch on the head. "I guess we'd better go then."

"Yeah."

The ride to Chadwick Law was the longest I can remember, and yet, didn't seem long enough. Neither one of us spoke, no happy conversation, no talk of the weather, not even one smartass comment from Miles, only the occasional sideways glance and sad smile. For months now Miles had been a gentleman, respecting the boundary I had set and maintaining his distance as I asked—but today was different. He had taken my hand as soon as we were in the car and hadn't let go yet. Every once in a while he would give it a light squeeze, caressing my skin with his thumb. I knew it was wrong, but did nothing to stop it. In fact, I encouraged it by occasionally squeezing back.

I too glanced over often, tracing the outline of his features with my mind. His nose, eyes, the soft curves of his lips, the way his hair had grown out again and now hung loosely in his face, grazing the tips of his dark eyelashes, tossing to the side occasionally with a flick of his head. Dear Lord, he was gorgeous. Aside from his charming personality, did he have to have so much sex appeal?

I had chosen Robert. He was everything I ever wanted and more. I felt certain he was my soul mate. So why is it then that I could take one look at Miles and question all of that?

Once we arrived at Chadwick Law, time flew by quickly. I was finishing up some minor details at one end of the mural and Miles was cleaning up at the other end. The mood was ominous. I tried to focus on what I was doing, but continuously peeked over. His expression tore me apart. It was unlike any I'd seen from him before—sad, hopeless, and heartbroken.

Suddenly he looked up, eyes catching mine. Overcome with heartache, I quickly looked back at the wall, letting my hair fall forward, trying hard to hide my face from his view. With a shaky hand, I raised my paintbrush to a flower, but couldn't see through my tears to complete the paint-stroke.

I heard his footsteps, and felt the heat from his body as he stepped up to my back. He wrapped his hand around mine, steadying it. Slowly he guided the brush over the picture, tracing

132

the outline of the small petals. My chest ached with tears that fell in waves. Miles gently swept my hair back, over my shoulder and laid a soft kiss on my neck.

"La mia belle," he whispered.

I opened my mouth, but no words came out, only the soft cries of my heart longing for our time to never end. Miles took the brush from my hand and laid it down. Taking my shoulders he turned me around to face him. I stared at the floor, unable to lift my head, to meet his heartbroken gaze.

Placing a hand under my chin, he lifted my eyes to his. "Daniela, our time doesn't have to end."

I looked at him with deep compassion, wishing it were true. In my heart though, I knew it did have to end. I didn't say a word, didn't have to, he could feel my response. He pulled me into his arms, holding tight. I hugged him desperately, my mind searching for anything that I may have overlooked, any detail in the paintings I might have missed—but could think of nothing. The job was done, and we no longer had any excuse to see each other.

Suddenly, someone cleared their throat loudly.

Startled, we both looked up at Mr. Chadwick Sr. standing in the doorway. "Sorry for interrupting, but I have something here you might like to have young lady," he said, waving an envelope in the air.

Miles let go, and I quickly began wiping the tears from my face as Mr. Chadwick approached. "What's this?" I asked, taking it from his hand.

"Pay day. Did you forget you get paid for all of this?" he laughed. "You've done a beautiful job, Dani. This old office building has never looked so nice. Now, I know what we agreed on for all three murals, but I really feel that's just not enough, so I added in a little bonus." Immediately I tore open the envelope and glanced inside. I nearly hit my knees at all of the zeros!

I looked up at him, eyes round as the moon. "Twenty thousand dollars?" I gasped. "That's like three times the amount I quoted! I can't take this," I said, stuffing the check back into his hand, "It's too much, it's just too much!"

He quickly grabbed my wrist, pushing the check back into my hand. "Dani, there's no sense in trying to give it back. Besides, I have ways of *making* you take it," he said with a smirk. "You did a wonderful job, were very professional *and* managed to put up with my son the entire time. You deserve every penny."

Miles leaned in and quietly advised, "Trust me, just take it and say thank you."

I held my ground only a moment, then lowered my shoulders and nodded. "Thank you, Mr. Chadwick."

He gave a slight nod, then turned and walked out, leaving Miles and I alone again. The mood instantly became gloomy once more as Miles and I stared at one another silently.

"Let me take you to dinner," he blurted suddenly.

"What?"

"Dinner—you know, food, wine, maybe a little dancing—dinner."

"I can't."

Miles stepped close. "Call it a celebratory meal—a congratulations for a job well done."

"I shouldn't, really." I tried to sound like I didn't want to, but deep down was bursting to accept his offer.

Miles took my hands, looking directly into my eyes. "Have dinner with me."

"No."

"Please."

I pulled my hands away. "Stop that—your persuasion isn't going to work on me, I can't."

Miles narrowed his eyes, and then arched one eyebrow. "You know technically you still owe me a date."

My eyes widened, throat went dry. "What?"

"My date, the date I won, I never got it," he explained.

I thought about it and realized he was right. He never did get his date. Though *why* was a little fuzzy. I tried to remember, but was unable to recall the exact reason. I stared at him, trying to think of an excuse, but my mind was bereft of any logic.

"I do still owe you a date, don't I?"

Miles beamed, knowing he'd found his loophole. "Call it a celebration, call it settling our bet, call it whatever you want, but have dinner with me. Don't think about it, don't overanalyze it, just say you will, please," he begged.

I chewed at my lip, seriously thinking it over. That crazy lady was back inside my head, screaming at the top of her lungs, *'DON'T DO IT, DON'T DO IT!'* But did I listen? No.

I looked him in the eye, and ignored her logical ranting. "Okay…I will."

Chapter Nineteen
Daniela

When the car rolled to a stop, Miles looked over with a huge smile. Now that he'd successfully found a way to prolong our time together, his mood was quite chipper.

"So, Friday night, six o'clock, and this time, please don't leave with anybody but me," he joked.

I gave a puzzled look, not fully understanding. "What are you talking about?" I asked.

Miles shook his head, "You know, because…er…never mind. I was just teasing. Anyway, *I* and only *I* will be here to pick you up; okay?"

"Okay," I laughed, still confused by his odd statement.

I went to open the door, when Miles caught my arm, "Wait, I have something for you." He reached into the back seat, playfully leaning too close as if to kiss me. I swatted at him, rolling my eyes. "Here," he said, plopping a large manila envelope on my lap. I'd already been given one envelope that day with more money than I'd ever seen in my life. Looking down at the one in my lap, I cringed at the possibilities.

"What is it?"

He smiled, exposing nearly every one of his perfect white teeth, "Proof."

"Proof? Proof of what?"

Taking my hand, he gave it a long, soft kiss. Then catching my eyes with his, he answered, "Inside that envelope is the medical history and all of the contact information for one Amie Ross, wife of Tim Ross, mother of three, emovamp pediatrician."

"Who is Amie Ross and why do I have her life and medical history? What, are we going to steal her kidney or something?"

He laughed, and then stroked his hand down my cheek. "You are so funny sometimes. Dani—she's a heart transplant patient."

His words skimmed over the mushy tissue of my brain, not fully soaking in at first. I stared at him trying to work out the meaning, to put together this tiny puzzle that was so simple—I couldn't comprehend.

At last it all clicked, and I covered my mouth, eyes huge and glazed with tears. "She's a…" I gasped.

"Yes."

"And she's a…"

"Yes."

"But that means…"

"Yes Dani. It means you can be changed, and there's no risk of your heart stopping because you're a transplant patient. It's just as the Oracle said, your emotions are bound to the heart. Doc should have nothing to worry about now," he explained with a sideways grin.

I threw my arms around his neck, squeezing with all my might! "Thank you Miles, thank you so much! I can't believe it, I just can't believe it! Where did you—how did you get this?" I asked, wiping the tears from my face.

"I have a lot of connections with what I do. I made a few calls, pulled a few strings, and then yesterday this arrived in the mail. Easy as 1-2-3!" he explained. I knew how hard it was for Miles to provide me with this information, knowing Robert should have no fear of turning me now. At the time, I saw it as a true sign of how much he cared. "Well, what are you waiting for, you better get in there and share the good news," he said shooing me with a smile.

I didn't argue, simply hugged him again. "Thank you Miles, you're a true friend." I climbed out and rushed into the house, never once glancing back.

Robert was sitting on the couch looking comfortable and extremely handsome when I came bursting through the door. Wearing a simple cotton tee and nicely worn jeans, my heart skipped a beat when he looked up and smiled.

"Hey sweetie," he said, turning off the TV. "How was your last day?"

I could tell Robert was overjoyed with my finishing the job for Miles and Mr. Chadwick. I couldn't blame him really, but still gave a small eye roll.

"Everything went great!" I said, flopping down on the couch next to him. I wanted to scream at the top of my lungs the news of Amie Ross, but was doing my best to control myself.

"You're awfully wound up, what's going on?" I glanced at the envelope in my lap, chewing at my lip with nervous excitement. "What's in the envelope?" he asked.

"Okay, I'll show you, but first I want to give you something."

Robert watched curiously as I picked up my purse and pulled out another smaller envelope. With a huge cheesy grin, I handed it to him. "This is for you."

"Okay," he said slowly, taking hold of it, "What exactly is it?"

I held onto it momentarily. "Before I let you have it, I just want to say—thank you. Thank you for everything you've done for me. For the place to stay, the food, the clothes—everything. You've taken care of every need I've had, never expecting anything in return, and for that, I thank you." Letting go of the envelope, I watched Robert excitedly. He looked at me quietly with a warm smile. "Well—open it," I laughed.

Carefully, he tore at the seal, and then pulled out the check inside. "What is this for?"

"It's everything I owe you. Every penny—well, every penny I could think of plus ten percent," I said proudly. He stared at it momentarily with a dazed expression, but said nothing. "It *is* enough, isn't it?"

Quickly he answered, "Yeah, yes, it's plenty—too much in fact." He drew in a frustrated breath. "Sweetie, I have no need for you to pay me back. I don't care about the money, I never have. I just want to take care of you and—"

"You have," I interrupted. "And I appreciate it, but this is something I have to do." Robert shook his head, but I wasn't about to let him refuse my payment. "Look, when I agreed to let you put me up here, you agreed to let me pay you back every penny. That's the deal we made, remember?" Robert gazed at me for a long time with endearment. At last the pressure became unbearable, and I blurted, "What?"

"I'm proud of you."

"Proud of me—why?"

Robert tucked a lock of hair behind my ear, and caressed my cheek. "Because you are true. True to me, true to your friends, but most of all, you are true to yourself." His words were sweet, but I couldn't agree with them. With everything I had put Robert through in the last several months, my unwillingness to let Miles go, my paranoia and jealousy over Ryan, '*true*' was the last word I would have used to describe me. I looked away, unable to respond without crying. Robert laid a hand against my cheek, bringing my eyes back to his. "I accept this compensation, but I will not keep it," he said sternly.

"What? But you promised—"

Robert quickly placed a finger to my lips. "Daniela, I only meant that instead of keeping it, I want it to go to a good cause."

I looked at him with a puzzled expression. "Okay, what did you have in mind?"

"I will donate it to the charity of your choice."

My eyes instantly filled with tears. "You would do that?"

"Of course. I know how much you want to help the needy, and this will go a long way in doing that."

I gently pulled him in for a hug, "Thank you."

"Now, what's this one?" he asked, tapping the large manila envelope in my lap.

Excitedly, I handed it to him. "Open it."

"What's in it?"

"Just open it," I insisted.

He narrowed his eyes and tore at the seal. As he pulled out the papers and began to read, I sat up on my knees, scooting close to read over his shoulder. Several long minutes went by and Robert remained silent, reading intently. Finally he stopped, looking at me with a blank expression.

"It's what you've been looking for, all the proof you need right there," I exclaimed.

Robert smiled tensely. "Yeah…what I've been looking for."

"Aren't you happy? I mean, this is great news! You don't have to be afraid of turning me anymore."

He pulled me in for a hug. "Yes, yes I'm happy. Of course I'm happy, I just…I didn't expect this," he said distantly.

I pulled back, feeling something odd in his behavior. Suddenly, it occurred to me. He wasn't upset about this news. He knew I had something else to tell him, something he wasn't going to like. I lowered my head with guilt. "I know what's bothering you," I said.

"You do?"

"Yeah," I nodded. "You know I have something else to tell you, something you won't like."

Robert looked confused, but urged, "Go ahead."

I pulled and twisted the end of my shirt nervously, then slowly began. "I sort of have…a…date."

Robert's expression quickly changed to one I'd seen before, cold, irritated and full of jealousy. "A date? Who with?" he growled.

"It's just a celebration—for a job well done," I explained, though it didn't sound quite as reasonable now.

"Who with?" he asked again.

I fidgeted anxiously. "You know technically I still owe him a date, so this is really just settling our bet," I reasoned. He only continued to glare. I lowered my head, speaking barely above a whisper. "It's with Miles."

I shut my eyes tight, awaiting the argument, the onslaught of accusations and jealous rage. But it never came. After several seconds I looked up. Robert was gazing off in the distance. "Aren't you going to say something?" I asked quietly.

He dragged in a ragged breath and then let it out slowly. "What do you want me to say? Don't do it? No? What would be the point?"

I sat back, guilt ridden. I was so selfish, so consumed by my own wants and desires that I was hurting the man I loved. Unfortunately, that realization didn't change my plans to go out with Miles.

I snuggled up to Robert, determined to ease his mind. "I promise this is the last time I'll see him. He's taking me out Friday and I will tell him then that I can't see him anymore." I took his face in my hand, turning it to mine. "I love you, and I want to spend the rest of my life with *only* you. After Friday we can both forget about Miles and just focus on you and me. We can make plans for you to turn me and we can finally be together—always."

Robert looked so torn. I understood this was hard for him to accept, but at the time, felt confident in my reasoning. Slowly he leaned in, pressing his lips to mine, pulling me so tight, I could scarcely breathe. He covered my mouth with the warmth of his, kissing me with desperation I'd never felt. He was hungry, needy, assaulting my lips with heated want and passion.

He broke the kiss suddenly, burying his face in my hair. The warm wetness of his tears spilled down my neck, and I hugged him tight, knowing the pain he felt was my fault. Foolishly, I was completely unwilling to stop it. My desire overrode all logic, my selfish wants tearing apart the man who meant everything to me. I was making a huge mistake.

I knew it.

Knew it and did it anyway. I reasoned that this was it, my final time with Miles. It was a choice that would have repercussions no one saw coming.

Chapter Twenty
Daniela

The week had passed with lightning speed, and it was now Friday. I glanced over at the clock. Five-fifteen. Not long now. I stared at myself in the mirror, once again speechless over the incredible job Becca had done with my hair and make-up. She'd applied my eye shadow flawlessly and pinned my hair up. It was very reminiscent of '*Breakfast at Tiffany's*'. Much as I liked it, it was times like this I wished she wasn't so darn good. My stomach let out a loud growl, complaining of hunger. I had tried to eat earlier, but as usual found it a near impossibility. What I did eat had come up shortly after.

I glanced over at the box sitting on my bed and sighed. It was a gift from the illustrious Miles Chadwick and had arrived this morning along with a note reminding me of our date tonight.

I pulled the packing tissue back and caressed the billowy fabric with admiration. "Oh Mr. Chadwick, if you only knew how upset Becca's going to be with you," I joked aloud. "Even Robert knows better than to cross into *her* territory."

Becca had gone through a great deal of trouble to pick out and accessorize my outfit for this evening, and I would have gladly gone with her choice, were it not for Miles's last minute gift.

I pulled the dress from the box and smiled ear to ear. It was a stunning evening dress. Strapless, black, form fitting and full length, it was the perfect dress for tonight. I held it against my body, looking it over in the mirror. Though the price tag was removed, the Christian Dior label stood out clearly. Of course, I expected nothing less from Miles, who was always dressed in the finest name brand clothing. I doubt the man had ever even set foot inside a Stalmart store.

I slid into the dress and the long black gloves that accompanied it, then spritzed a little perfume on my neck and stood back for a full view.

I looked down at Teagan who was watching me with intense curiosity. "Something's missing," I said. "Something…" Quickly, I rushed to the bathroom and opened my little silver trinket box. "There you are," I said to the marble necklace, lifting it out. I peered at it closely, again, admiring the tiny crystal in the center with fascination. Truly I had never seen a marble like this one, beautiful, petite—perfect for tonight.

Staring at the lovely necklace, a wave of sorrow swept over me. Though I had no doubt tonight was going to be wonderful, it was also sure to be one of the worst of my life. At some point I was going to have to make the break. Tonight I had to sever all ties with Miles. I took in a long heavy breath and held it, trying hard to choke back the tears which suddenly appeared.

A loud knock at the door announce his arrival. It was Miles!

Grabbing a tissue, I quickly dabbed at my eyes and then rushed downstairs with Teagan happily trailing behind. He was early, but honestly I didn't care. Just before answering, I paused, straightening my dress and taking in several calming breaths. Finally, I opened the door, revealing the ever impressive—"Robert?"

He looked at me with a mixed expression, confused, despondent, loving—heartbroken. "What are you doing here?" I asked, nervously glancing around.

He immediately pulled me tight, hugging with a neediness I didn't understand at the time. "I just came by to see you one last time before you go."

I gave him an odd smirk. "Well I *will* be back. It's just dinner, remember?" Robert only nodded, looking away. I placed my hand against his cheek, bringing his glistening eyes back to mine. "Hey, you have nothing to worry about. I know I'll be safe with Miles and he will be a perfect gentleman. After tonight, he'll be out of our lives. Then you and I can start making our plans." Robert gazed at me with pain so deep that I suddenly questioned the appropriateness of this date. However, one should never underestimate selfishness when it comes to matters of the heart. Though I knew it was wrong to allow this date, and knew it was tearing apart the man I loved—I didn't back out.

Teagan paced nervously and whined at Robert's feet, but he seemed distracted and paid her little attention.

"Come have breakfast with me in the morning. We can vegetate all day on the couch, maybe watch a little Hockey," I offered playfully. Robert only nodded solemnly, and then turned to go. He got about twenty feet away, when suddenly I was overcome with feelings of conflict. "Robert!" I yelped. He stopped and then slowly turned around. The words of the Oracle echoed heavily in my mind. *A heart divided between two seas, one with waters turbulent and exciting—one that is tranquil and calm. Each tide calls to you, but beware of the harbor you seek, for both are capable of drowning you.*

I bit at my lip pensively, so torn between what I needed and what I desired. "I love you," I said, regret in my tone.

He hesitated, saying nothing. Then, instantly he had bridged the distance and had me in his arms, longing and sorrow heavy in his eyes. He pulled me tight, covering my mouth with his, seeking out my tongue with hunger and heartbreak. The force of his kiss was painful, the strength of his embrace suffocating. Abruptly, he pulled back and stepped away. I stood taught, hand over my heart, trying to calm its quickened pace.

With one hand across his waist, and the other behind his back, he gave a slow, regal bow. Then, he turned and walked away.

I should have run to him, thrown myself on his mercy, and begged him to forgive me for only thinking of myself. I should have called off the date and never seen Miles again. I should have.

I *should* have…

Chapter Twenty-One

Robert

Robert scribbled something down, then quickly wadded up the
paper, throwing it with frustration. He picked up the nearby glass,
now half empty and stared at the amber liquid with despair.
Clothes wrinkled, hair untidy, he hadn't slept for days. He tipped
the glass back, finishing off all but the last sip of brandy, swirling
it around in deep thought. Sitting it down, he picked up the pen
once more.

Never in his life had he found something so difficult, never had
he been so torn. Should he tell her the truth? "No," he said aloud,
"I can't tell her the truth, she would know what a monster I am,"
he laughed. "She's going to think you're a monster either way,
which you are, so what difference does it make?"

He ran a hand through his hair, and then pressed the pen to
paper, holding tight, unable to move it, to form the words that
would destroy his world. "Will she ever forgive me?" he cried,
"Can I ever forgive myself?"

He sat the pen down, picking up the glass again. Swirling it
momentarily, he reminded himself of why he was doing this and
his blood was suddenly filled with guilt and trepidation. He tossed
the glass back, swallowing down the last of the brandy and then, in
a fit of rage, threw it! With a white-hot flash it shattered in the
flames. Gazing into the ominous fire with the weight of her life on
his shoulders, he wiped the tears from his face.

"I have to do this," he said solemnly. "I have to do it for her.
She will hate me, she will never forgive me, but I hope someday
she will understand that I did it for her—I just want her to be
happy."

He picked up the pen a final time and pressed it to the paper.
Taking a deep breath he began to write.

Torn

Dearest Daniela,
Please forgive me for what I am about to tell you…

The long strokes of his pen were labored, each word harder to write than the previous. He paused many times, struggling with his resolve to complete this arduous task. At last he finished, signing his name and then laid the pen down with defeat. Sliding the letter into the envelope, he closed it. Then, melting a small amount of red wax, he embossed it with his initials, sealing their fate inside.

A loud knock pulled him from his somber gaze.

Robert took in a ragged breath, then walked to the door and opened it.

"Damn, you look like hell man," Ryan said. Robert rubbed his eyes, but said nothing, simply gestured for Ryan to enter. "So what is it you wanted to see me about? Is it Dani, is she okay?"

"Yes, she's fine. I called you here because I need you to do something for me."

"Okay. What exactly is that?"

Robert flopped down on the couch, picking up the brandy bottle. He popped open the top and guzzled it back quickly, finishing it off. He gazed at the fire distantly, as if looking through it. "I'm leaving."

Ryan remained silent momentarily, a combination of feelings flashing through his veins. "You're leaving *her*?" he asked.

"Yes. Her—the state, I'm leaving it all. I can't be here…can't be with her, not anymore."

Ryan's blood boiled. He was furious with Robert for what this was going to do to Dani, but at the same time couldn't help feeling happy also. With Robert out of her life, he was sure she would return to him. "What do you need from me?" he asked.

"I need you to watch over her for me, keep her safe, stay close. I will meet with you in one week to make sure everything went as planned. After that, I will call you monthly to check on her. She will need energy. I'm afraid all of the exchanges have caused her to become dependent on it. However, she will be with Miles, so projecting to her yourself shouldn't be necessary; he'll take care of that."

Ryan shook his head with confusion. "And why is she going to be with Miles?"

Robert dragged in a long, painful breath again and retrieved two envelopes from his pocket. "Because, she loves him. And after she reads the letter I'm leaving her, she will run straight to him when I'm gone. This is a letter for Miles," he held one of them out, "It contains an explanation for my actions and all of the things I've put in place for her protection and wellbeing, including that you are watching over her. Give this to him tomorrow morning. Make it clear that he is the only one to read it. Daniela must never see this, she must *never* know." Ryan took hold of the letter. Robert hesitated letting go, but then slowly released his grip.

"I will do as you've asked, but not for you—for her." Robert nodded solemnly. Without another word, Ryan turned and walked out.

Robert sat down and placed his face in his hands—broken, defeated—and dying inside.

Chapter Twenty-Two
Daniela

I flipped the car's visor mirror down quickly, checking my makeup one last time, while Miles strolled around to open my door. A gust of warm air filled the car as he pulled it open. Technically it was now fall, but the balmy temperatures of summer still lingered. Even though I was ready for crisp, cool days and warm fires, in light of the strapless dress I was wearing, the heat made this evening far more comfortable. After all, it would have been a shame to have to cover up such an exquisite dress with a coat.

Miles extended a hand for mine, which I took graciously, trying hard to conduct myself as that of a lady. Once out of the car, he peered up and down my frame with excited eyes.

"Stop doing that, you're making me nervous," I scolded.

He shook his head. "Sorry, it's just, when I saw that dress I knew you would look amazing in it, and I have to say, I was right, as usual. Honestly, I should buy your clothes more often," he bragged.

I rolled my eyes. "Yeah well, a Christian Dior dress can make anyone look good," I scoffed.

Miles took my hand, giving it a long, slow kiss. "You're wrong princess; it's *you* who makes the dress look good."

My cheeks heated from his gaze. Playfully I swatted at him. "I said stop that—and quit calling me princess, I told you I don't like it."

Miles laughed, winding his arm around mine and leading me to the restaurant. He had brought me to Shoguns, a Japanese steakhouse in north Oklahoma City. I'd heard of it, but like most places, had never been. It wasn't the most high-end place he could have chosen, which surprised me. Miles always seemed eager to impress me with his taste for finer living. I wouldn't have been at all surprised if he'd flown me halfway around the world in a private jet, to attend the opening of an exclusive restaurant while surrounded by the world's most elite socialites—or something along those lines. However, I wasn't disappointed by any means, and in fact, was happy with this simpler choice.

Upon our arrival, a petite woman in a beautiful kimono greeted us. "Konbanwa, Miles-sama," she said with a gracious bow.

"Konbanwa, Kanako-chan," Miles replied with a return bow. I looked back and forth between them, not sure what to do, so I just smiled and waved. Miles gave me a clever grin, pulling me along as Kanako led us to our room. The restaurant was divided up into several individual suites, some large with three tables, some like ours, which held only one. Once we were seated, Kanako gave another bow, then stepped out and closed us in with a beautiful screen. The table was unlike any I'd ever seen, large, with a stainless steel midsection.

Displaying my usual childish lack of knowledge, I asked, "Do they cook on the table?"

Miles grinned amiably. "Yes, the table is basically a giant grill. It's called teppanyaki, a type of Japanese cuisine. I take it you've never had it before?"

I lowered my eyes with embarrassment. "No—I never did much dating before…well before now."

Miles lifted my chin. "The number of dates you've been on isn't important, only who you spend them with." Miles held my eyes, slowly leaning closer. "I'm glad you're with me tonight."

"Me too," I whispered.

Ugh, this was bad. I knew I was going to be cutting the strings tonight, but when was the right time? As we sat face to face, leaning closer with each passing second, I debated bringing it up now. It was a short debate though.

"Dani, I have to tell you something." His warm breath grazed my lips and I became still and quiet. "Dani, I—"

Kanako entered the room, pushing a cart which broke the stillness and Miles's concentration.

He let out a frustrated breath with a smile. "Well, dinner is here."

From the cart Kanako retrieved two mixed drinks and sat each one in front of us.

"What is this?" I asked, eyeing the creamy white drink.

Miles flashed an expert smile. "That, is a Shogun surprise."

I took a small sip. "Mmmm… Miles, it's wonderful," I exclaimed, taking another drink, much longer than the first.

"Whoa, slow down there princess. Those are sweet, but they still have kick." He raised an eyebrow, and then added mischievously, "On second thought, I'll order you another."

I rolled my eyes, "Whatever. And I'm serious, stop it with the princess stuff."

He didn't reply, only smiled teasingly.

The cart Kanako had brought in was loaded with a multitude of raw ingredients: chicken, shrimp, steak, and vegetables as well as a large bowl of rice. Honestly I think there was a little bit of everything.

"Can I get you anything else, Miles-sama?" she asked.

He was immediately on his feet giving another respectful bow. "Thank you, no, Kanako-chan."

Quietly, she pulled the screen closed, leaving us once more. I looked at Miles with an expression of confusion. He reached under the cart, pulled out a tall white chef's hat and then placed it on his head with a clever smile.

I nearly fell out of my chair with giggles. "You are so silly. Now put that back before the real chef comes in to kung-fu us out of here, "I scolded.

Miles looked at me with sheer orneriness. "I *am* the real chef."

"You are not. Now will you quit it—you're going to get us kicked out." He pulled the cart around to the opposite side of the table, and turned to face me. Pulling out a large knife and spatula without a word, he paused, grinning mischievously.

Tensely I whispered, "I'm serious, put that stuff down!"

Suddenly, he threw the knife into the air! It flipped several times, then made a loud *clang* as it hit the end of the spatula and went soaring into the air again. Repeatedly he hit the knife with the spatula, and vice versa, sending each spiraling in a mid-air ballet of cutlery! Abruptly, he stopped, and with the flip of his wrist, the knife twirled high again. Miles held his finger straight up beneath it. I gasped as it came down, the razor sharp tip landing exactly on the end of his finger. He held it there, balanced perfectly. If he'd been an ordinary human, we would have spent the rest of the evening in the emergency room having his finger sewn back together, but in light of his extraordinarily tough exterior, Miles didn't have a scratch. With a light push, the knife soared into the air once more and Miles caught it by the handle.

At first I only sat there with my mouth hanging open, but then slowly found the ability to speak again. "Miles—that was unbelievable!" I applauded.

"You think that was good, wait until you see the volcano I make out of an onion," he bragged.

Truly there was never a meal preparation I enjoyed watching so much. Miles sliced, diced and knocked my socks off with his amazing culinary skills. We chatted as he cooked, and he told me all about the family he lived with in Japan many years ago. Now when I say many years ago, I'm not talking about five, ten or even twenty years ago. I mean well before the 19th century. Additionally, it was no ordinary family he lived with, but a wise and powerful emperor. As a close friend to the emperor, Miles learned all about their culture and way of life as well as how to prepare food with Japanese tradition and style.

It came as no surprise to also learn that the emperor had a daughter. She was a very talented lamp-work artist, and no doubt, absolutely beautiful. I could tell by the way Miles spoke of her they were very fond of each other. But she was promised to another. Eventually, the emperor feared they were becoming too close and felt it best to send Miles away.

"It must have been very hard to leave," I said.

He smiled, but it couldn't hide the sadness that time had not erased. "The night before I left, she came to me and gave me a gift, told me that it was very special, something to be kept safe. She said that it would change my world and would someday lead me to my *true* love." He reached up and wrapped a hand around the marble dangling from my neck. My eyes widened with realization.

"When I saw it in your hand that day, I knew it was fate."

"You can't be serious. I didn't find the marble, it just happened to be the last one I picked up. There were dozens of marbles, it could have been any one of them," I argued.

"But it wasn't any other marble, it was this one," he said, giving it a light tug.

My cheeks heated under his intense gaze. The very idea that he was insinuating this marble somehow found me, and that it was an indication that I belonged with him, irritated me. "Well why did you have it out in the open in the first place?" I scoffed. "You were supposed to keep it safe, remember? You had it in a vase on your desk. That's not exactly the wisest place. If it was *so* special, *so* important, you should have had it locked up in a safe or something."

Miles's eyes glittered with excitement. "That's just it Dani—I did."

"What—what are you saying?"

"I'm saying the marble was locked up in my safe, and until that day, I had not laid eyes on it in more than one hundred years."

I shook my head, "No, no—I don't believe it. It can't be the same marble. They probably just look alike," I argued.

He stroked his hand down my cheek softly. "After you left, I went back and checked the safe. The case was there—but the marble was gone." He took my hands and kissed them, then captured my eyes with his again. "I don't know how, but that marble found its way to you. Against all odds, against all logic, bypassing all others—it found *you*."

My heart sped up and I felt sick. Suddenly, I jerked my hands back and jumped to my feet. Miles quickly had my arm, sending a warm current into my skin. "I'm sorry Dani, I didn't mean to—"

"Can we go? I need some air."

"Sure. I'd made plans for us to take a walk by the lake after dinner anyway. It's just across the highway. We can go now, if you're ready." I didn't resist, simply nodded. Though, for the record, this had '*bad idea*' written all over it.

When we arrived at the lake, Miles parked the car and then came around to get me. The initial shock over the marble was fading and I was feeling better. In my mind I tried to convince myself that it was just a trick on Miles's part. He probably had dozens of those little marbles that he gave out to women, telling them the same corny story. I just couldn't believe it. It was, after all, preposterous; right?

Miles took my arm, and began leading me down toward the shore. Very quickly I spotted a vast amount of warm light coming from up ahead.

"What's going on up there?" I asked, straining to make it out. Miles said nothing, only smiled and continued pulling me along. At last we were close enough to see and all at once I stopped dead in my tracks. "What is this?"

A man stood near the shore, a large blanket spread out at his feet, and a multitude of glowing candles everywhere. Miles glanced at me quickly then approached the man and shook his hand. "Thank you, Nate, for setting this up."

"No problem, Miles. Enjoy your evening." He tipped his hat to me and then quickly strolled off, disappearing into the dark.

I looked around at all of the burning candles with awe. The warm night air was perfectly still, allowing the flames to dance undisturbed. It was stunning, beautiful, and truly romantic. Ugh, I did already say this was bad idea, didn't I? Miles took my hand and led me the rest of the way to the blanket.

"Miles, we need to talk," I insisted.

He stroked a finger over my knuckle, spreading warmth across my skin, instantly quieting me. "How about a little wine first, and then we'll talk."

"Okay," I breathed. We sat down on the blanket and he handed me a tall, slender glass. Opening the wine with ease, he quickly filled my glass with the lovely golden liquid. I sipped at it tensely. He looked at me, awaiting my approval. "It's very good," I said.

"Thank you." Sipping at his glass, he watched me with delighted eyes. I tried to keep my eyes on the horizon in the distance, but glanced over often, smiling shyly. "Will you do me a favor?" he asked.

I fidgeted nervously. "What kind of favor?"

He grinned. "Nothing bad, it's just…would you let your hair down?"

I exhaled a breath of relief, then with a shy smile, did as he asked, letting the long, heavy locks fall around my shoulders. He scanned over me with intense desire, heating my blood with the sultriness of his gaze. "You're so beautiful."

I took in a long, hesitant breath. "Miles—"

"So what kind of car are you going to buy?" he interrupted.

His question caught me off guard, derailing my thoughts. "Huh?"

"What kind of car? With all the money you've earned now, I'm assuming you're going to finally get a new car."

"Um…I don't know. I hadn't really thought about it yet. Probably something used, something small, economical I guess."

Miles shook his head. "Aww come on Dani, where's the fun in that? You need something new, sleek—something fast!" he said excitedly.

Torn

"Easy for you to say, you can afford any car you want. I, however, have to watch my money. I have a new business now and I intend to put a lot of my earnings back into it. A used car will be sufficient for now. Besides, I don't need anything fancy, just need it to run."

Miles ran his finger around the rim of his glass. "Well I would be happy to loan you one of mine—hell, I'll buy you your own if you want. Just name it and it's yours," he offered.

"Well, as generous as that is, I'm afraid I will have to decline your offer, Mr. Chadwick, but thank you." He didn't press for an explanation, knowing I had my reasons. I gazed off toward the horizon again. The air was becoming increasingly cooler and a flicker of lightning danced across the sky in the distance. An unavoidable storm was coming. "Miles, we can't—"

Suddenly he was on his feet, a hand extended for mine. "May I have this dance?"

I glared at him with contempt. He was dodging the subject. I knew it, and continued to let him. "There's no music," I pointed out.

He took my hand and pulled me to my feet. "Sure there is." Drawing me into his arms, he held me tight against his warm body. "Just listen," he whispered against my ear. I shivered, listening intently, hearing nothing but the occasional wave splashing against the shore and the soft sound of his breathing on my neck. And my heart, which was pounding. He swayed back and forth slowly, and then softly began to sing.

"*When the rain is blowing in your face, and the whole world is on your case, I could offer you a warm embrace, to make you feel my love...*"

His voice was like satin, every note pure and soft. With a heavy heart I lowered my eyes as he continued.

"*When evening shadows and the stars appear, and there's no one there to dry your tears, I will hold you for a **thousand** years, to make you feel my love...*" He lifted my wet eyes to his, "*I know*

155

you haven't made your mind up yet, but I would never do you wrong. I've known it from the moment that we met, no doubt in my mind where you belong.

I'd go hungry, I'd go blind for you , I'd go crawling down the aisle for you, no there's nothing that I wouldn't do,
To make you feel my love…"

He spun us around several times and then dipped me back playfully as he hummed the chorus, then pulling me back up, he paused, gazing at me longingly.

"The storms are raging on the rolling sea and in a harbor of regret. The winds of change are blowing wild and free, but you ain't seen nothing like me yet…"

He paused, as if needing a moment to compose himself, then softly continue.

"I can make you happy; make your dreams come true, there is nothing that I wouldn't do, go to the ends of the earth for you— to make you feel my love…"

"To make you feel my love…" His words were whisper soft from lips which brushed over mine. I closed my eyes, my mind crying out to pull away, but my body failing to heed its warning. I could hear the Oracles voice. *A heart divided between two seas, one with waters turbulent and exciting—one tranquil and calm. Each tide calls to you, but beware of the harbor you seek, for both are capable of drowning you.*

Suddenly, a gust of cool air swept over us, extinguishing all of the candles at once. Miles waited, giving me the opportunity to close the gap, to give in to him. I had drawn the line, made it very clear he wasn't to cross it. So he waited, waited for me to do it, for me to break that barrier of my own free will—but I didn't.

He lowered his shoulders with disappointment. "It's going to rain soon—we should go," he said. I nodded solemnly. "But…I don't want to take you home yet."

"Okay," I agreed.

"We could go back to my place," he offered. I glared with disapproval. "I promise to be a complete gentleman. I just want to spend a little more time with you—please? What's the worst that could happen?" he asked in a husky tone.

I took in a cautious breath. "I can think of many things," I replied pensively.

He caressed my cheek and smiled softly. "Come on Dani; what are you so afraid of?"

I quickly pulled away and walked to the edge of the water. Staring up at the darkened sky through tear filled eyes, I awaited the inevitable storm. With a heavy heart, I took in a long, sad breath. The time had come for me to end this. No delaying any longer, no excuses—it was now or never.

A searing pain tore through my chest. Though my heart had already made its choice long ago, the inevitable pain of having to let him go was something I had avoided until now. But I could no longer afford to be selfish and keep them both. It wasn't fair to either of them and I loved them far too much to continue putting my own wants and desires first.

Suddenly, with a bright flash of lightning and loud crack of thunder, rain began to fall. Miles immediately gathered the blanket and shouted for me to come. I stood motionless, my back to him, allowing the soothing water to pour over me and soak deeply into my mind.

The heat of his body surrounded me as he stepped up slowly to my back and gently pulled my hair aside. His breath was warm on my neck and I shivered as he tenderly laid a kiss on my rain soaked shoulder.

"Miles…" His name quivered from my parted lips.

"Yes, la mia belle…" he cooed softly, continuing to run his kisses over my wet skin.

With his hands on my shoulders, a warm current slowly radiated down my arms, into my skin, spreading through my blood like flames. I closed my eyes and relaxed into him, taking in a quick

157

breath at the intense pleasure and laying my head back against his shoulder. As he pulled his mouth up my neck, I reached up and ran my fingers though his drenched locks. Wrapping one arm around my waist, he pulled me hard against his body. Though the rain was cold, I remained warm with the fire that was building in my veins. My body ached for him to take me and do as he wished.

He nuzzled my ear, biting at it eagerly, sending waves of heat and ecstasy pulsing deep within. We breathed heavily together—one motion—one rhythm—one storm.

I opened my eyes and looked out across the water once again, wishing to drown myself in the turbulent waves for the treachery I was allowing. Like a deadly tide, the trepidation of what I had to do came crashing in. Suddenly, I turned and pulled away, stumbling back.

Holding my chest, I cried, "I can't do this anymore! I can't keep being with him and being with you; it's not fair to either of you, and my heart…my heart can't take being torn between you any longer!"

"Then stop! Make your choice—you know it's me you should be with," he shouted over the rain.

Hands over my face, I sobbed. Miles stepped up and gently caressed my shoulders again, awaiting me to look up. Salty tears stung my eyes, and I fought to regain my composure. It was time—I could wait no longer. "I can't see you anymore," I said quietly.

"What?"

I slowly raised my face to his. As the rain mixed with my tears I repeated my words with clarity. "I can't see you anymore—*ever.*"

Miles let go and took several clumsy steps back, pushed off balance by my rejection. He stared at me, disbelieving. Determined, he shouted, "This is ridiculous! You and I belong together!"

"No, we don't. I know that's what you want to believe, but I belong with *him.*"

Torn

Miles rushed up and grabbed my arms, shaking me desperately, as if to shake another answer from my lips. "I know you love me, I can *feel* it! DAMMIT! You're so stubborn! Why can't you just admit it? SAY IT! Say you love me!" Miles demanded.

"I can't," I cried.

Abruptly, he pulled me into his arms, his lips brushing against mine as he spoke. "Kiss me, Daniela," he begged, "kiss me and then tell me you don't love me."

Shoving against his shoulders, I pushed away angrily, glaring at him and overtaken by tears. Though it had been many months since my birthday, the heat of his stolen kiss was still on my lips and my body longed for it again. Consumed by my self-centered desire, all logic, all reasoning, all resistance to deny my yearning vanished.

I threw myself at him, wrapping my arms around his neck and kissing him with desperation! "Oh God, Miles, I do—I do love you! God help me, I do!" I cried.

He blanketed me with his arms, pulling me tight against him, squeezing hard. His mouth beckoned me to open and accept his kiss, and I did so eagerly. With deep want, equally matched by mine, our aggression grew as we let loose the passion and hunger we'd held back for so long. Through rain and kisses, I wept loudly, my mind relishing in the heat of our desire, but my heart screaming out *STOP!*

Abruptly, I pulled back, taking several steps away, my hand held against my breaking heart. "This has to end," I sobbed.

Miles gritted his teeth, his tone cold and determined. "You belong with *me*."

"No...I belong with *him*."

"You say that, but I can hear what's in your heart and you want to be with me, you always have. Dani, from the moment I met you, I knew we were meant to be. I've never doubted it." He stepped closer. "You're everything to me—my world, my sun—the brightest star on my darkest night," he exclaimed with great passion. Pulling his rain-soaked shirt open he placed my hand against his bare skin, against his heart. "We have a connection, Dani, a bond I know you feel."

I tried to pull my hand away. "I'm not an emovamp, Miles, I can't feel anything."

"You're wrong. You don't have to be one of us to know how you feel. You *know*. Deep down, you know you love me…and you always have." Miles knelt down on one knee.

"*Please,* get up."

Holding my hands he looked up, his eyes full of love and determination. "Dani, I can't live without you in my life."

"Miles, don't," I pleaded.

"*Be* with me." I looked away, unable to glimpse his perfect face. "*Stay* with me." I shook my head desperately. I didn't want to hear this, I couldn't.

"If you love me you will not do this!" I shouted.

"It's because I love you that I have to."

"I'm begging you," I sobbed, "*don't* ask this of me…" My entire body trembled. "Don't," I whispered.

"Dani…marry me."

I'd never felt pain so deep, felt so much victory, and yet, so much loss all at once. I looked into his pleading eyes and within them could see the depth of his love. I couldn't believe what he was saying, couldn't believe it—and hated him for it. My heart was being ripped from my chest as I struggled to sever all ties with him, and yet, here he was, proposing, knowing how torn I was.

"Daniela Rose Moretti, I kneel before you as a man professing my undying love for you, and promising to protect, cherish and keep you with me forever—I love you. Please…be my wife."

As the rain continued to pour over his painfully beautiful face, I stared down into his eyes and my heart broke, fury building within. At last I jerked my hands away, "NO! Don't you understand! It's *HIM!* I pick *HIM!*" I fell to my knees, face in my hands, and continued to weep. "It will always be him," I cried softly. "I've made my choice—please, don't make this any harder."

Miles sat quietly for a long time. What more could he say? What more could either of us say?

Slowly, he stood up and held out a hand to me. "Come on—I'll take you home."

I refused his hand, keeping my eyes to the ground, and stood up. Wrapping my arms around my shoulders, I replied adamantly, "No, just call me a cab."

"Dani, this is ridiculous, just let me take you home," he insisted.

"No!" I snapped. "Please—just call me a cab," I repeated with eyes still on the ground.

Miles hesitated, but gave in at last and made the call. Like a gentleman, he waited with me until the cab arrived. Then, opening the door of the car, he made one final plea. "It doesn't have to be this way, Dani."

I never looked up, kept my eyes down and took hold of the door.

"Yes it does—please, if you care anything for me, you'll never contact me again. I'm sorry—goodbye Miles."

Chapter Twenty-Three
Daniela

Slowly, I stepped in and closed the door. Never had I felt so despondent, never so sad, like part of me had been severed—primarily my heart. Teagan was instantly at my feet, covering my hands in a multitude of welcoming kisses. I patted her head, thanking her for the sweet greeting.

"Oh Teagan, if only you knew how selfish I was, you wouldn't be so happy to see me."

I was soaking wet, freezing and mentally spent. After peeling the wet gloves from my arms, I removed my shoes, laying them out by the door to dry. I sulked to the kitchen and put a mug of water in the microwave for some much needed hot tea. Taking a seat at the bar, I took hold of the marble necklace and squeezed with great longing. "How did this become so complicated?" I asked. Gazing into the marble, I remembered what Miles had said about it. Could it really have found me? In my mind the notion was still absurd.

Suddenly, my eyes wandered beyond the marble, to a letter propped against the flower arrangement on the bar. Picking it up, I looked it over with curiosity. My name was written on it in lovely calligraphy. I would know his handwriting anywhere. On the back was a beautifully detailed, red wax seal with the initials *RH*.

Slowly, I broke the seal, ran my finger under the flap, then pulled it open and slid the note out.

Dearest Daniela,
Please forgive me for what I am about to tell you...

Torn

As I read the words over and over, my eyes filled with tears. Surely I was misunderstanding the message. Was this some kind of sick joke? My hands shook, chest labored for air and all sound was drowned out by blood pulsing through my ears. Frantically, I looked to the door and whispered, "Robert..."

Rushing outside, I ran towards his unit, next door, trying to focus on it through the pouring rain, looking for any signs of occupancy. At last I reached the door and pulled on the knob. Locked. "Robert! Robert, it's me! Please, open the door! Please, I know you're there, please open the door! I'm sorry, I'm so sorry!" I pounded desperately against the cold wood, feeling each second he didn't answer was an eternity. After several minutes, I went to the back door and mercilessly assaulted it, banging away, unwilling to give up. "Please! I'm sorry, forgive me! Please don't leave me!" I cried. I fell to my knees, sobbing against the door frame quietly. "Please—please don't leave me—I'll die if you do—I'll die..."

Quickly, I stood up and went to the window, hysterically clawing to get it open. Then placing my hands against the glass, I peered in, squinting through the dark for any signs of life, but there were none. Then, my eyes adjusted to the darkened room and I gasped in horror.

Empty.

It was completely empty, barren of all furniture, of all personal items, no signs that Robert had ever been there. Empty.

I rushed home and dialed his cell phone. '*Sorry, but the number you are trying to reach is no longer in service...*'

I don't even remember hanging up; just remember standing at the foot of the stairs, clutching the letter. No words—no sound—numbed by pain. I placed one hand on the banister and the other on my chest. Abruptly, searing pain ripped through my torso and I hunched over from the weight of it. It felt like my heart had just been torn in half. The room began to spin, growing hazy and dark—my mind was shutting down.

Instantaneously, I was blinded by a flash of light, the entire room lit up in a blaze of blue! Stunned, I looked down at the marble necklace still hanging around my neck. It was glowing and humming softly. Then, with one, ear piercing scream, I collapsed.

Ryan

Ryan sat on the edge of his bed, gazing out the window with great sadness. "I don't think this is right," he said.

Emily grabbed his face, harshly redirecting his eyes to hers. "Do you want her back or don't you?" she snarled.

Ryan's eyes widened, then he lowered his shoulders. "Yes, of course I do, but I just don't know if this is the best way to go about it."

Emily ran a sharp, red nail down his cheek. "Oh Ryan, ye of little faith. I've been on this earth a lot longer than you, and know a great deal more about a woman's heart. If you give Miles that letter, he will go to her and she will do just as Robert said—she will run to him. But if you don't…"

"If I don't, she will be heartbroken and all alone," he said gravely.

"Exactly."

"But what if she contacts Miles? Then it won't matter that he never received the letter, she will run to him anyway, and I know he won't refuse her," he argued.

Emily's mouth curled up in a vicious smile. "You saw the scene between them tonight. She made it quite clear that she never wants to see him again. It's over between Miles and Dani—trust me. And even if it isn't, I have a few ways of dealing with that," she snarled with delight. "As for now, when she finds that Robert has left her, she will be in just the emotional state we need her in."

"And that's where I come in," he said.

"No, that's where you must exercise extreme patience my love. If you go to her immediately, she will be too distraught. She will stay with you for a while, but then will eventually leave because you are not Robert. We need her to join with us, *permanently*. If you wait—let her suffer—make her feel abandoned—let her body go through withdrawal, then she will hate him," she hissed.

Ryan took in a deep breath. "But she'll get sick."

"Yessss…" she said excitedly.

"She'll be in pain."

"Yesss…"

"And she'll never want to see *him* again."

"Exactly. When that happens, then we make our move. She will no longer love him; she will only see *you*, and the opportunity we will give her. With your history together, she will see you as the only person she can trust. Throw in a little well placed fear and she won't be able to resist, I promise." Emily pulled his face to hers again. "This *will* work, if you do exactly as I tell you to." Ryan lowered his eyes and nodded his agreement. "Now, your gift of deception will be the key to pulling this off. When you meet with him in a week, you're going to have to convince him that everything went exactly as he wanted it to. If he senses for one moment that you're lying, everything will be lost."

"I don't know—I don't know if I can do it. You've had me practicing my other gift most of the time, so I haven't used deception much at all."

"Well then, we need to practice," she said seductively. Ryan stared at her questioningly. Suddenly, she sprang on him, throwing him back against the bed and straddling his waist. She covered his lips with hers and moaned into his mouth, "Tell me you don't love her."

"I don't love her," he breathed.

She slapped him hard. "Liar! Tell me you don't love her!" she demanded.

"I don't love her!" he yelled.

She kissed him forcefully, clawing at his chest and biting his neck. "Tell me you hate her!"

"I hate her!" he screamed, pulling her tight.

She leaned back, narrowing her eyes. Sadistically she commanded, "Tell me you wish she was dead."

Ryan's eyes widened. He pushed her back and sat up, staring at her with disgust. "I-I—I can't." He lowered his head in defeat.

Emily placed a sharp nail beneath his chin, raising his face to hers. Slowly, she ran her tongue up his chin and lips, chewing softly at his mouth. "Try again."

Ryan threw her back hard, springing on top of her, forcing her wrists deep into the bed. Her eyes flashed with excitement as she wiggled beneath his weight. He glared down into her face, and through gritted teeth, snarled, "I wish she was dead."

Her eyes sparkled wildly. She wrapped her legs around his waist and squeezed. "I love the way you lie—do it some more."

Ryan pushed his lips to hers, pulling her tight. All the while he thought of his first love.

He didn't want to deceive Dani, didn't want to hurt her, but he agreed with Emily. If he had any chance of winning her heart, *permanently*, it had to be this way. Later that night, he lie awake, unable to shake the guilt from his conscience, but greater was his longing to have Dani back.

Emily stirred in his arms, letting out a moan of satisfaction as she slept. He looked at her, overcome with admiration for her beauty, so torn between love and lust. He knew he didn't love Emily, but still had a bond with her unlike any he thought possible. Though his means of being turned was anything but traditional, the bond was still there, and Emily held a certain power over him, just like she did the others.

He wondered sometimes if it was only *his* bed that she frequented. Though she assured him that he was her only lover, he had his doubts. It mattered not though. He only truly loved one woman, and it was not Emily. He closed his eyes and pulled her tight, wishing it was Daniela who he held in his arms tonight.

Daniela

Wind swept over my face, and on it came a gentle voice. "*Daniela…Daniela…Daniela…*" it echoed.

I sat up suddenly, rubbing my eyes. Everything was brightly lit and it took many seconds for my vision to adjust to the dazzling sun. Finally, images became clear and I stared around in amazement. I sat in the middle of a huge field of red, with cluster upon cluster of red anemone flowers surrounding me for miles. They were the same flowers I had dreamed of so many times lately and had come to adore. The rich velvetiness soothed my skin, and I lay back, rolling in their comforting softness.

"*Daniela…*" someone whispered. I sat back up, looking around for the gentle voice, but saw no one. "*Daniela…*" she whispered again.

"Yes—I'm here."

"Remove your necklace child and hide it away…" Her voice carried over the sea of red like a gentle breeze, but there was fear in her command. The marble glowed brilliant blue, light so intense it was blinding. I did as instructed immediately and unclasped it, then held it tight. Searing pain engulfed my hand and I screamed, dropping it! I cradled the injured limb against my body, examining my palm. The skin was bright red, a small blister already forming from the burn.

"I can't touch it—it burns!"

Instantly, a vine sprung up from the ground and formed a beautiful white rose. In the blink of an eye, the petals turned into a white handkerchief. I took it and slowly ran my fingers across the delicately embroidered initials REH. *His* initials.

"*Place the necklace inside...cover it with the petals of the anemone...bind it with your hair and hide it away...*" her words were soft as wind, but frightened me deeply.

"Why?" I asked. But there was no reply. "Who are you? Why is this happening?"

"*Daniela my child, you know who I am...*"

I lowered my head, tears flowing down. "Yes, I know who you are—I'm so afraid. Please, tell me what to do," I cried.

"*Come to me, child...come to me...*"

Suddenly, a sharp pain erupted through my head, and cold set in. I opened my eyes and stared up at the ceiling. My body ached, teeth chattered. I wasn't even sure I could move. Finally, I managed to roll onto my side and sit up. A warm stream of blood trickled down my neck and over my shoulder. I'd hit the back of my head on the bottom step when I fell. Teagan immediately began licking my face. "Don't worry, I'm alive girl," I assured, patting her head.

I looked down at the marble necklace and gasped. It glowed brilliantly, just as it had in the dream, nearly blinding to my tear swollen eyes. I looked at my palm; it was burned as well. Then my eyes wandered to the crumpled letter on the floor and instantly my chest hurt. "Dear God no—*please*, no..."

I picked it up and read it again. This wasn't possible, it couldn't be, just couldn't be. Gazing at me with large, sad, brown eyes, Teagan let out a whine.

She knew.

I lay my head against the bottom step and sobbed into the rich wood. "What have I done?"

The light from the marble stung my eyes, and though it had burned my hand, it remained cold against my chest. I had so many things going through my head, but in spite of it all, I was compelled to do as instructed in the dream. It was as if my body had no will of its own.

Carefully, I reached up and unclasped the necklace, holding it by the chain, and then arduously made my way upstairs to my room. I opened my dresser, pulled from it Robert's handkerchief and ran my finger over the embroidery of his initials again. He'd given it to me one night while I was crying, and selfishly I'd kept it. A secret keepsake.

I placed the necklace inside, and then went to the balcony to retrieve the petals of the anemone. However, the blossoms had long since died, and all that remained now were the dried up remnants scattered in the bottom of the pot. "I guess these will just have to do," I said, gathering the wilted buds. The Oracles words echoed in my head. *Place the necklace inside...cover it with the petals of the anemone...bind it with your hair and hide it away...Hide it away...*

Like a zombie, I went through the motions, no control over my actions, simply following the directions. I went into the bathroom and retrieved a pair of scissors. Then, holding out a lock of my hair, I snipped it off. Tears fell onto the necklace in a downpour of sorrow as I packed it in the delicate cloth with the brown, shriveled petals of the anemone. Once it was full, I folded it up and wrapped the long lock of golden hair around it, binding it just as she'd said.

I went to my closet, and pulled down my keepsake box, then placed the fabric parcel inside, next to the gift from Kimi. Was it possible for such a small space to hold so much heartbreak?

I put it away and then returned to the bathroom. Looking in the mirror, I glared at my reflection. "What a fool, what a selfish fool," I scolded. I picked up the scissors and held out another lock of my hair. *Snip!* A small section fell into the sink. I held out another. *Snip!* And another. *Snip!* I clipped, pulled, and chopped away at the long length of golden waves with unyielding brutality.

I dropped the sheers and placed my hands against the mirror, wailing into the reflection. "Please...*please* God...let me wake up."

169

Chapter Twenty-Four
Daniela

I gazed out the window, hugging the pillow in front of me. I could feel the pressure of his body against my back and the warm sweet mint of his breath on my neck. Holding the collar of his shirt to my nose I inhaled deeply, searching for any remnants of his scent within the fabric. Pulling the blankets firmly around me I felt he couldn't hold me tight enough.

Suddenly, my bedroom door flew open, hitting the wall with a loud *bang!* I remained still. I knew who it was, but wasn't moving. I was with Robert right now, and refused to budge, to change positions, to leave the comfort of my fantasy and face *her*. She walked around to my side of the bed and glared down at me with disapproval. I glanced up at a very cross Becca and huffed, "What?"

She raised her eyebrows in surprise. "What do you mean '*what*'? You know darn tootin' well, '*what*'," she snapped.

"Leave us alone, we're spending the day in bed again."

Becca snarled, "*We*? Um, Dani dear, who is the '*we*'?"

I rolled my eyes. "Me and Robert of course," I replied, clutching my pillow tighter.

Becca stared at me with revulsion. "That's it, Dani! I love ya, but this has gotta stop." She yanked the pillow from my grip and ripped back the covers.

"Stop it!" I screamed, desperately clutching at the blankets in an attempt to cover back up. "What in hell is wrong with you?"

She jerked the blankets again, tearing them from my grip. "Dani, it's been almost two weeks and yer still in denial. Ya can't spend every day in bed, pretending he's still here."

"Shut up! Now give those back, I'm freezing!" I yelled, grabbing for the linens.

"*This* is not him!" she shouted, holding up the pillow. "You can put his clothes on it all ya want, but that don't make it him! You can't keep deludin' yerself—And it is like a hundred freakin' degrees in here—yer meltin' me with this heat!"

I curled into a ball, childishly plugging my ears, trying desperately to drown out the truth of what she said. "Leave me alone!"

Becca sat on the corner of the bed and placed a hand on my back. "Dani, I know what yer goin' through. When Tob...er...my boyfriend left me, I thought the world had ended. I didn't wanna eat, didn't wanna move, just wanted to curl up an' die; ya know? But I didn't. I got up, and I got on with my life."

I sat up and looked at her solemnly. "You don't have to hide his name anymore. I remember Tobias."

"What? But I thought that—the block—I thought the block worked!"

I gazed out the window, into my tortured past. Tears welled up and spilled down silently. "It did for a little while, but I remember everything now."

"Exactly *what* all do you remember?" she asked with caution.

"All of it—Tobias, Alistair—everything. All of the nightmares are back too," I said gravely.

Becca threw her arms around me, squeezing tight. "Oh-ma-gawd Dani, why didn't ya tell me? How long has it been?"

"Everything came back to me the morning after he..." My eyes immediately swelled with tears again and I choked on my words.

Becca stroked my cheek. "I know it hurts, shoog, but it'll get easier. Ya just gotta let him go. This stayin' in bed all day, every day has gotta stop. Ya gotta get up, get out and start over."

"I can't. I can't let him go. I try, but I'm dying inside. When I lay here, it's like I can feel him with me, feel his arms around me. Sometimes I think I can still hear him."

"Look, I know this ain't no ordinary thing yer goin' through. I know cause I been there. But fantasizin' about him ain't helpin'."

I squeezed my eyes shut, holding my gut and let out a loud cry, "Oh God, I can't take this, it hurts so bad!" Suddenly, I jumped up and ran for the bathroom. Becca followed, holding my hair back as I vomited. I hadn't eaten in days, not much at all since that night. Consequently, little came up. I had become accustomed to the energy exchanges and now my body was going through withdraw. In my life, I'd been through numerous surgeries, biopsies, nearly killed twice, and yet, none of it compared to the pain I was going through now.

"How long has it been since you took that last pain pill I gave ya?" she asked, handing me a cold washcloth.

"I don't know, maybe an hour or two. They're not really working much now anyway. The pain eases up for a few minutes, but then comes right back—I wish I would just die."

She grabbed my face, jerking it to hers. "Don't you ever say that, Dani, don't you *ever* give up. I know it hurts, but the pain will get better, I promise." Becca sounded confident, but she couldn't hide the fear in her eyes. Even she knew the withdrawal she went through from Tobias was nothing compared to mine now. "Call Miles, see if he can—"

"No," I snapped. "And don't ever mention his name again. After the way I treated him, I don't deserve his help. Besides, he was probably just using me too."

Becca nodded. "What about Ryan?"

"HA! No thank you. He's already got his hands full with his new wife, or whatever you want to call her—Emily. I'm sure he doesn't want me in the middle of all his marital bliss. A fruit loop ex-girlfriend is the last thing he needs right now."

"What about that cop, you know, Michael? He seemed like a nice guy, I don't think *he* was using you. Maybe he would be willing to try another block," she suggested hesitantly.

"I don't believe Michael was using me, but I can't be sure. For all we know they may *all* be like Tobias. I can't take a chance on getting hooked on another emovamp. I think it's better for both of us if we never speak of them again."

I don't think Becca agreed with me entirely, but she didn't press the subject. However, I knew it was only a matter of time before she brought it up again. Mentally I was not all together, and neither of us knew how long my mind or body could take it. Sadly I hoped it wasn't much longer. I wanted death—yearned for it more than anything. Not just because of the unbearable physical pain, but because being without Robert was a death sentence in and of itself. In my eyes, a life without him was pointless, even if it was only a life of being used. I would never love anyone like I did him, would never be able to trust again, never be able to *feel*. I was numb, my soul withering away more every day. Little did I know, the worst was just over the horizon.

In the coming weeks, pain took on an entirely new meaning. My body hurt in ways I didn't know possible. My hair became thin, dull, and stopped growing. My skin was dry and scaly, hands cracked and rough. I could never get warm and my nose bled constantly. No matter how many blankets, no matter how high I turned the heat, my body remained ice cold to the touch. Some of the effects were from the withdrawal, while others were from malnutrition. I had no desire to eat, and only did so at Becca's insistence. However, even if I managed to choke down whatever food she forced on me, it usually came back up shortly after. About the only thing that did stay down was water, and even that didn't always.

I didn't care though. As the days went by, death was all I thought about. In fact, I longed for it so much even my nightmares no longer bothered me. It didn't matter if it was Alistair or Tobias chasing me, beating me, or trying to kill me—I welcomed it now. The only thing that did bother me was waking up to find I was still alive—still alone—still without *him*.

I rarely left the house, and even then only at night. Becca didn't know it, but I was sneaking out and taking her car. I would drive to

Robert's old house a few miles away, but he was never there. Mostly I just sat and cried until dawn, then returned home and snuck back in.

The toll on my body was becoming evident. Becca was to the point of force feeding me, and threatening to call an ambulance or worse, my mother.

I pulled the mound of blankets tighter, shivering uncontrollably. The heat was on the highest setting and the fireplace blazed with a large amount of wood. I couldn't even feel my feet. I clutched the letter in my hand and cried. The words stung more each time I read it.

Dearest Daniela,

Please forgive me for what I am about to tell you. It is time that you knew the truth. I care for you, but cannot continue to lead you on any longer. It is now that we must part ways. I'm sorry for hurting and misleading you. I want you to be happy, and I cannot offer you that happiness. Furthermore, I can no longer stand in the way of someone who can. I know you love Miles, and he loves you. You deserve so much more than I can give, and it is selfish for me to keep you to myself any longer. Please know that I am sorry for all of the pain I have caused.

The house is yours for as long as you want to stay. There is a property manager who will see to any needs you have. As for me, I am leaving. I don't know where I'm going, just feel it will be better for you if I'm not around. Please do not try to contact me, just know that I am doing all of this for you. I know you will be happy with Miles, and he will protect and love you well. I wish you all the joy in the world.

Robert

A pain surged through my gut and I began to convulse. It was something I was used to, but it was no less unbearable. I crumpled up the paper in my fist, cringing and crying aloud, "Why? Why would you do this to me?" Once the violent shaking subsided, I became still again, gazing out the window with despair. "I thought you loved me…"

November arrived, and with it came Thanksgiving. It was a holiday I had honestly hoped to avoid. By avoid I mean, had hoped to have died by now. I'd managed to evade seeing my mother for the last two months by convincing her I had taken a painting job out of state. Though I called every few days to check in, there was no way I was going to be able to get out of going home for the holidays. I did make an effort to eat for the entire week beforehand, trying desperately to put on a pound or two before Thanksgiving Day, but my efforts were in vain. If I ate anything, most of it came right back up as usual. Truthfully, there was no reason I should have still been alive.

When at last Thanksgiving came, Becca did her best to make me presentable. I wore layers of frumpy, oversized clothes and drank several shots of butterscotch schnapps to warm my blood so that my constant shivering wouldn't be as noticeable. Though Becca did all she could to help me fool my parents, I think she wanted my mom to notice. She was worried about me, and well, she had good reason. When I look back, I still find it funny I thought my mom wouldn't notice my deteriorated state. I looked like the walking dead.

I didn't even make it through the door before mom was screeching at the top of her lungs over how gawd-awful I looked. It probably didn't help that I reeked of alcohol and had a full-blown nose bleed just as she opened the door either. She went into nurturing mode immediately, of course. After practically stuffing half the turkey down my throat, she insisted that I stay the night with her. I spent most of it vomiting up turkey and the other half fighting off a trip to the emergency room. She agreed not to make me go to the hospital, if I agreed to see our family doctor on Monday. I submitted, but had no intention of keeping the appointment. However, never underestimate a concerned mom. I went, but it wasn't without a good fight.

The doctor could find no physical reason for my poor health, and I showed none of the classic symptoms for heart rejection such as fluid retention, fever or heart palpitations. He was about to send me to the hospital for a battery of heart tests just to make sure, when my mother brought up the fact that I had recently been dumped. Instant diagnosis—depression. Since it was something I'd already been labeled with before, he easily concluded it was the case this time as well. I was put on a host of antidepressants, and sent home with my mother.

Over the next few months, she hovered, weighing me daily, and feeding me a high calorie, vitamin-rich diet. I still couldn't keep much of it down, but by some miracle managed to gain a few pounds—*three* to be exact.

By the time spring arrived I was up four and a half pounds, but honestly wasn't doing any better. I faked a smile for my mother, lied to the therapist I was forced to see, and was still sneaking out at night to sit in front of Robert's house. In my eyes it was all just a futile attempt to delay the inevitable—death. The strain was becoming too much though, and I was beginning to think of ways to end it myself, but couldn't bring myself to do it (I didn't understand why).

Chapter Twenty-Five
Daniela

"Daniela, we're going now."

I put on my best smile. "'Kay mom, have a good trip," I said.

My mother looked me over hesitantly. "Are you sure you'll be okay here by yourself?"

"Mom, I'll be fine. If I get lonely I'll get Becca to come over, and I have Teagan here, so..." She narrowed her eyes, still battling with leaving me alone for two weeks. "Mom, seriously, I'll be fine. Now will you just go before you miss your plane," I scolded, shooing her away.

She frowned and pulled me in for a hug. "Okay then. I'll call you as soon as we land."

As they pulled away, I waved, sporting a fake smile of health and confidence. Once I could no longer see them, I collapsed to the ground. The fatigue was getting worse. It had taken all of my energy just to walk outside that morning and stand there for twenty minutes while my parents loaded the luggage and said their farewells. The few pounds my mother had managed to put on me were gone too, but I'd been able to hide it by drinking huge amounts of water just before weigh-in. Of course, the hardest part was holding down the water long enough to get weighed.

Becca was gone too, out of state at a family reunion for the next week. With everyone gone, and nobody there to force feed me, three days passed and the only thing I'd eaten was the breakfast mom had forced on me the morning they left. In truth, my plan was to starve myself to death. It seemed easy enough to do anyway.

By day four I had taken my mother's car and returned to my townhouse at the Holloway Oak apartments, the complex Robert owned. It was the only place I felt close to him. All of my possessions were still there, everything just as I'd left it months ago. It was just one more indication that he hadn't returned, and wasn't going to. The first night there, sleeping in my old room, I dreamed of him. It wasn't uncommon, but this dream was so real, not a dream at all, but a memory. It was of the first time he had taken me for a truck-bed picnic in the country.

"Why'd we come all the way out here?" I asked.

Robert turned off the car, slid one arm around my shoulders and pulled me close. *"I just wanted to be alone tonight. No interruptions. Only me and you,"* he said in a low voice. We cuddled for a little while, and listened to Delilah play her love songs. He held me against him, running a hand gently through my hair as I traced little hearts on his chest with my fingers. The heat of his embrace was heaven. Nestled in the warm arms of the man I loved, I never wanted to wake up. *"Daniela, I love you."*

Suddenly, I bolted upright! The room was dark, and I stared around momentarily, trying to remember where I was. Just as I looked at the darkened balcony, my gut was instantly flooded with pain, and I grabbed my bedside trashcan and vomited. A flash of white lit up the room followed by the distant eruption of thunder.

Wind blew fiercely against the house causing the windows to shutter violently. Flipping on the TV quickly, I wasn't surprised to see Gary England warning everyone of the colossal storm headed our way and advising all to take shelter immediately.

I should have been frantic and wedged under the bed, but wasn't. Instead, I turned off the television, then daringly walked to the French doors and gripped the heavy bars that adorned them. Staring out at the approaching storm, I sighed with great longing, then quickly dressed and hit the road.

I knew exactly where I was going, except this time it wasn't to Robert's house. I drove out to the place I'd dreamed of, where he'd taken me many times. The wind was picking up and I had a hard time keeping the car on the road. I was driving head-on into the heart of the storm, but wasn't turning back. Veering off into a field, I plowed through, determined to reach the exact spot where we'd spent so many nights curled up together in the back of his truck. I drove with desperation, as if upon arriving I would find him there, but as the car came to a stop, I peered out into the darkened land with disappointment. It was just a barren field. He wasn't there.

No one was there.

I climbed out and walked toward the storm. The wind blew harshly against my face, drying the tears as they fell. Lightning flashed, thunder echoed across the land, and my heart grew heavier.

The storm was massive. I couldn't recall ever seeing one so large, but then, I didn't often stand out in the middle of a field and wait for one either. Gust after brutal gust of wind hit me, each one stronger than the next.

Then, in the distance, the unmistakable sound of tornado sirens blared through the dark, announcing to any rational individual it was time to take cover. My heart pounded and body shook. Not from fear, but from anticipation. I *wanted* a tornado, wanted a vast funnel with deadly rage. I wished for the storm to take me, to rip me from the earth and carry me away from all of this unbearable pain.

I walked faster into the heart of the gale, when abruptly the rain fell. Like a heavy curtain of ice it came down, soaking deep into my body, the wind so strong I could no longer walk against it. I fell to my knees, arms outstretched—waiting. Debris spiraled around me, water rushed through my clothes, and sorrow flooded my senses.

"What are you waiting for!" I yelled. "Take me! I don't want to be here anymore!" The rain blew against my face with such furry, that it burned my cheeks. "Please! Don't make me live another day—I can't do it—I can't!" I cried, collapsing to the ground, clawing at the mud and grass with hopelessness and frustration. "Why can't I just die!" Thunder shook the ground, arriving with an ear deafening *BOOM!*

I lay down and turned over, looking up into the torrential downpour, sobbing loudly, choking on the water as it flooded my nose and mouth. Softly I cried, "Please...*please*...I can't live without him...I can't..."

I don't recall how long I stayed out there, only that at some point I ended up back at the Holloway Oak apartments. I was freezing, covered in mud and lacking any further ability to cry. I looked down at my art caboodle, then opened the container and retrieved my paint brushes. With a heavy heart, I ran my muddy finger over the delicate silver handles with despair.

I missed Miles too.

Opening a bottle of color, I dipped the tip in, then turned to the nearest wall and began painting. It was the only thing I had left, the only part of me that made perfect sense, yet, made no sense at all. My desire to complete the mural was the only thing I thought of in the days to come. Along with the effects of food deprivation, my mind was out of control. I became obsessed with painting the mural, and spent every waking minute working on it. The only time I stopped was when I passed out from exhaustion.

Finally, after several days, I finished. This should have made me happy, but it didn't. I felt no happiness, no sadness, just something I couldn't put my finger on at the time. I stared at it all day. I stared at it the next day—and the next. In fact, that's all I did.

I still hadn't eaten, and couldn't recall the last time I drank anything. As I sat back against the couch, staring at the wall blankly, I suddenly realized it had been a week since I'd driven to Robert's house. What if he was there now? The idea that I could have missed his return terrified me beyond words.

Quickly, I jumped to my feet. Well, let me clarify. I slowly turned over and crawled up the side of the couch, then pulled and heaved until on my feet. Then, little by little, scaling the furniture with my hands, I made my way to the door. Somehow I managed to make it to my mother's car, but the details of getting there are fuzzy. Once behind the wheel, I laid my head back and rested, momentarily catching my breath. I started the car, and then blinked hard several times, trying to clear the fog from my vision. I couldn't see very well, but was determined to get to Robert's house. I pulled out onto the main street. Headlights of oncoming cars flashed across the windshield, temporarily blinding me each time. I struggled to stay on the road, veering over the yellow line several times. The hum of the car was soothing, and my eyes heavy.

Honk, honk, honk!

Suddenly I was jolted awake! "Shit!" I was on the opposite side of the road!

Cars swerved and honked as I pulled at the wheel hard. The car fishtailed, but by some miracle ended up on the correct side of the road. As I barreled away from the scene, I stared through the rearview mirror with panic. I was almost certain I'd seen the unmistakable markings of a black-and-white. Cars were scattered all over the road in my wake. I scanned over each one, but saw no sign of police. I continued to watch until I was well out of sight.

"Thank you God," I breathed with relief. I glanced up into the mirror again and cringed. There was a police officer right behind me! "Crap!"

HONK!

My eyes were blinded by light, ears filled with the screeching of breaks, tires and a horrifying *crunch*!

Chapter Twenty-Six
Officer Kavenius

The night had started out as any other, with Officer Kavenius beginning his routine drive of the city. It was only Tuesday, and wasn't a full moon, so he didn't expect too much in the way of trouble. *Maybe tonight will be uneventful; wouldn't that be nice?* he thought.

Several hours into his shift, he was pleased. He'd made a few routine traffic stops, taken one guy to county, but all in all he'd had no major trouble and was rather enjoying the ease of the night. However, just as he pulled back out onto a main road, he quickly caught sight of a small, white car going well over ninety, driving wildly and repeatedly crossing the center line.

He started toward it, but just as he reached to turn on the lights and siren, the car abruptly veered over the line again! Several oncoming cars swerved to avoid the out of control vehicle. Officer Kavenius himself was nearly plowed into, and had to quickly run off of the road to avoid one of the cars as it fishtailed and then spun out toward him. His car left the road and slammed into a small embankment! He wasn't hurt, but helplessly watched as the little white car fled the scene.

Hitting reverse, he punched the accelerator several times, but his car was caught up, unable to break loose from the small, grassy hill. Immediately he called for backup and then climbed out. With great frustration, and powerfully inhuman strength, he grabbed the front bumper and threw the car backward, freeing it with ease. Then, jumping back in, he hit the lights, and sped off, siren blaring, in search of the AWOL vehicle.

As he came up over the ridge, he no sooner caught sight of the car again, when it veered over the line once more. "No, no, no!" he shouted, as if his warning could somehow stop the inevitable. He cringed as the car plowed head-on into a large truck in the opposite lane. "Dammit!" he yelled with frustration. Quickly he radioed for paramedics, and then rushed out to check on both drivers.

"Are you okay?" he shouted to the driver of the truck. The man gave a dazed nod as he held a hand to his bleeding temple. Instantaneously the dark sky was lit up in a blaze of flames! Officer Kavenius ran towards what was left of the tiny white car which had flipped multiple times and was now upside down and on fire, roughly one hundred-fifty feet away. As he approached, he suddenly felt an emotional signature he knew very well. It was one that could only belong to one person, *one* woman.

"Daniela!" he cried. Falling to his knees, he tried to get a view of her through the crushed frame of the car. "Daniela, can you hear me!" he shouted. She didn't move, didn't respond. She was still alive, he could *feel* her, but her emotional signature was extremely weak. With flames growing larger and the car filling with smoke, she didn't have long. "Just hold on Dani—hold on!"

He looked around quickly. The driver of the truck was the only other person around. He had left his vehicle and was sprawled out in the grass, passed out from the concussion. Officer Kavenius placed both hands against each side of the crumpled door frame and pushed it apart, then pulled the mangled door open. He worked quickly to free her from the seatbelt, but her legs were caught up in the crushed floorboard. He pushed and pulled at the car's interior with great speed and strength, knowing he had only seconds before the car exploded.

Finally the metal gave under his superhuman strength and he pulled her free. There was no time to be gentle. He hauled her onto his shoulders and with lightning speed, fled from the car. They only made it a few steps though, when the car suddenly exploded into a massive ball of flames! Both were thrown forward, Dani's listless body crashing to the ground before him. Officer Kavenius rushed to her side and rolled her over. Immediately she opened her eyes, took in one, final, raspy breath—and then smiled when at last death claimed her.

Daniela

I sat in a field of red anemone flowers. It was the same field I had recently visited in my dreams. I liked it here. It was peaceful, quiet, soothing to my soul, which had been despondent for too long. I dusted a bit of grass from the white bodice of my dress, then happily plucked another flower and added it to my bouquet.

"Here are some more," Kimi said, handing me a lovely bundle.

"Thank you. They're so pretty, I just love them sis."

She giggled, tucking a strand of hair behind my ear. "I've really missed you," she said.

"I've missed you too, but I'm here now and nothing will ever keep us apart again." Kimi smiled warmly, but then her expression darkened. "What is it?"

She looked down and stroked the ruby petals of a nearby bud, then looked back up, sorrow heavy in her eyes. "You can't stay here, Dani."

"What? But that's ridiculous! We're finally together again and I will not let anything tear us apart!" I assured.

Kimi took my hand and gave it a light squeeze. "I know you don't want to leave, but you are not supposed to be here—not yet. You have too much life left, so much you haven't experienced—"

"I don't want any of it," I interjected. "There is nothing left for me now."

"Oh Daniela, there is so much more than you know, so much you will go on to do, so much love—"

"I want no more of love," I said coldly. She looked away, as if listening to a voice calling in the distance. "What is it?" I asked.

"Daniela, you have to go now."

"No! I'm not leaving you!" I pulled her to me, hugging with great desperation. "I will not be torn from you again!"

Kimi pried me from her, leaning back. "Sister—I am always with you." She took my hand and placed it against my own chest. "Any time you doubt it, just listen to your heart—*my* heart."

Suddenly, a searing pain erupted beneath my hand and I screamed! Kimi held her hand on mine, over our heart. "Remember, Dani—I'm always here with you," she cried. He words were miles away as another jolt of pain ripped through my chest! Again, and again, and again, fire exploded within the walls of my heart.

Instantly, my eyes jerked opened as I pulled in a harsh breath, choking on the salty, thick, iron fluid in my lungs. I gasped and flailed my arms. I could see a figure over me, but didn't know who it was.

They held my wrists, trying desperately to calm me. "Dani—Dani, settle down—relax, you've been in an accident," he said.

I knew that voice. "Michael?" My question came out gurgled and through a mouth full of blood.

"Yes, it's me."

"My chest—it hurts," I groaned, unable to breathe. It felt like I was drowning!

"I know it hurts, and I'm sorry. I had to shock your heart several times—I'm going to turn you on your side now." He began rolling me and I screamed; the pain so intense, I thought I would pass out. "I'm sorry, sweetie, but if I don't do it, you're going to drown in your own blood."

Once on my side, the dark red fluid poured from my mouth like a spigot. I was still dazed and in a terrible amount of pain. Michael placed a hand on my arm. Fearful he was projecting to me I quickly jerked away. "Don't touch me!" I shouted. As my vision cleared I glared up at his shocked expression.

"Dani…it's me, Michael—Officer Kavenius."

"I know who you are, and I mean it—don't touch me," I repeated coldly.

Michael shook his head. "Dani, what's wrong with you, what happened?" he tried to take hold of me again, but I slapped his hands away and screamed, "Leave me alone! Don't touch me!"

He put his hands up defensively. "Okay, okay—I won't, I won't touch you, just please tell me what's wrong. Where's Robert?"

The name stung and I began to cry, "He's gone."

Michael placed a comforting hand on me, but I jerked away again. "Dammit, don't touch me!" I shrieked.

"I'm not going to hurt you," he assured. "I just want to help."

"I don't want your help, or your energy! I don't want any projection, no exchanges!" I demanded.

"Alright—no projecting, I understand."

"You should have let me die!" I sobbed. "Why didn't you just let me die?" Michael said nothing, only sat quietly close by. How could he possibly understand when he was unaware of the events which had led to my downfall?

I lay passive on the ground, listening as the sounds of sirens rushed towards us. I knew Michael didn't understand my reasoning, but I didn't care. I wanted no part of *their* energy ever again, and was so terrified of becoming hooked on another emovamp, that I was willing to endure any amount of pain to avoid it. When the paramedics arrived, I made it very clear I didn't want to be touched. They accommodated me as best they could, but by the looks they gave, I could see a straightjacket in my near future. Though the sirens were loud, the rocking motion of the ambulance was hypnotic. I tried to keep my eyes open, afraid that if I fell asleep I would wake to find one of *them* touching me. However, I was pretty messed up, had lost a lot of blood and my mind was nearly gone. Needless to say, staying awake wasn't really an option.

Chapter Twenty-Seven
Becca

Becca sniffled, wiping her eyes with a small bit of crumpled tissue. It was soaked with so many tears that it did nothing to absorb the sadness still flooding her face. She'd come to the hospital immediately after Officer Kavenius called, and had remained all night.

Ever since she'd arrived home two days ago, she'd been searching for Dani, unsure if she was even still alive. When the concerned officer called, he sounded so upset, said she'd suffered serious injuries. Becca had no idea just how bad she was until she'd reached the hospital. Dani was worse than ever. Thin. Pale. Hollow.

Maybe that was the reason for what she did next. Dani didn't want *his* help, but at the same time, Becca knew, if anyone could aid her, it was him. He could at least project to her, make her feel better physically. Heal her, maybe. Dani was sure to be furious with her, but it was a risk worth taking. After all, Dani's life was on the line. She had to get better and soon. Becca had remained on the sideline, tried everything within her human capabilities to make Dani well, but it wasn't enough. Whether Dani wanted to accept it or not, she needed an emovamp—needed him. *Now.*

Though there were many emovamps available and willing, Dani wouldn't let any of them near her. Perhaps he would be different. Maybe. They had history, a connection. Dani couldn't deny their connection, could she?

Becca pulled out her cell phone and scrolled through numbers. At last she found his. Taking in a deep, hesitant breath, she made the call.

The phone picked up almost immediately and a surprised voice answered, "Becca—is that you?"

"Yeah, it's me," she replied, trying to suppress the distress in her voice. "Something's happened to Dani—she's been hurt really bad."

"Where are you? Tell me everything," he demanded. She gave him her location, and then began the account of hell on earth Dani had been through. When she was done, the phone line was dead silent. He took in a ragged breath, and replied, "I'm on my way."

Becca hung up, biting at her lip nervously. Had she done the right thing? Only time would tell.

"You look tired. When was the last time you slept?" A kind voice asked.

Becca looked up and couldn't control her smile. "Officer Kavenius—hi."

He sat down beside her. "Please, just Mike, or Michael if you prefer."

Becca batted her eyelashes shyly. "'Kay—Michael."

"So how's she doing?" he asked.

She shrugged. "I don't know. Nobody'll let me in there now. Dr. Hollin says she's real messed up." Her eyes flooded with tears again as she looked up into his face. "Is it true she died?"

Michael lowered his shoulders. "Yes, her heart stopped, but it was only for a minute. Luckily, I was able to get it started again. Though, it took nearly all of my energy. I had to shock her six times, and even then her heartbeat was very weak. That's why I was unable to heal her further," Michael explained.

Becca laid her hand on his arm. "Thank you for savin' her life. You're a real angel."

Michael smiled warmly, laying his hand over hers. "You're welcome. She didn't seem very happy about it though."

"Well, she's fried outta her mind right now. I know she'll be happy when she comes to her senses—*if* she comes to her senses," she cried, mooshing at the tears with her soggy tissue.

"Here," Michael offered, handing her a crisply folded handkerchief.

"Thanks," Becca squeaked. With her swollen eyes and little red nose, Michael found her adorable. "Hey, would you like to get some coffee or something?" She sat up straight, taken aback by his offer. Should she? What would Dani think? Well, she knew what Dani would think right now. She would totally freak with a capital *"F"*. Still, it was Michael. She had even admitted she didn't think he was bad. Plus, it was just coffee. It's not like he was asking her to marry him. She smiled at the thought.

"Becca?"

"Huh?" she replied dreamily.

He smiled a half grin that had her gripping the handkerchief excitedly. "Coffee?" he asked again.

She looked at him, chewing her lip while debating his offer. With a hesitant breath, she relaxed her shoulders. "Know what? Coffee'd be great."

Robert

As Robert sped towards the hospital, many things raced through his mind. *What in hell had happened?* All he knew was for months he'd been led to believe Daniela was doing very well now that she was with Miles. He'd met with Ryan one week after he'd left and was assured everything had gone as planned. He'd called to check on her monthly, and had even talked to Ryan just three days ago. Ryan reassured him she was doing well, thriving in fact. Now according to his father, she was beyond malnourished, run down, paranoid and emotionally broken.

What was going on? He thought he'd taken care of everything, thought he'd seen to it she would never suffer again. He pulled into the lot, threw the car in park, and then dialed Ryan's number, but once again there was no answer. He slammed his hand against the dashboard with frustration, denting it in. No matter. He would get answers later. Right now he just wanted to see her—*needed* to see her.

Stepping off the elevator, he immediately caught sight of his father, Dr. Henry Hollin. "Dad, where is she? Is she okay—what happened?"

Henry held up his hand, deflecting the onslaught of questions. "Not here. Come with me and we'll talk," he said, motioning to follow. Obediently, he did as instructed. Henry quietly led him down a lengthy hallway, along a series of corridors and then through a set of double doors. Robert glanced over often, feeling the deep concern and upset Henry held within. This only added to Robert's unrest.

"How did you know where to find me?" Robert asked.

"When you disappeared months ago, I didn't think anything of it. I just assumed you had taken Daniela on a trip somewhere. We're all accustomed to your spontaneous disappearances. You've been taking off without a word to anyone for decades. But when Michael called and said you weren't with Dani, I knew something was wrong, and knew if you were still alive, there was only one place you'd be. The lake house. It's where you've always gone when you're troubled—or running away from your problems," he muttered with a disapproving scowl. Robert lowered his head, ashamed to face his father's glare.

At last they arrived at the MHU (Mental Health Unit). "She's in here?" Robert gasped. Henry only nodded, then slid his key card and opened the door. Robert's heart sank. The thought of her in this place made him nauseous, and only added to his confusion as to what had happened to cause this.

Finally, Henry came to another door, slid his key card again, then opened the door and motioned inside. Robert knew immediately it was an observation room. A large, two-way window took up most of the wall at the far end. The only light came from the room on the other side of the glass. Robert was instantly overwhelmed with a terrible field of energy and started towards the window.

Henry caught his arm. "Son, you need to prepare yourself," he warned. "Daniela's been through a lot—she isn't the same girl you left behind."

Henry's words stung, feeling blame embedded in his tone. Robert pulled free, took a deep breath, and then walked to the glass. Nothing could have prepared him. No words, no warning, no description could have done it justice.

Daniela sat in the corner of the room, huddled in a tight ball, knees against her chest. Her hair was short, dark brown and thin, eyes sunken and dull. The chalky color of her skin was nearly the same as the white gown she wore. But worse was her energy. He'd never felt anything so terrible. An emotional signature worse than any he'd ever known possible. Like death.

He turned to his father with tear laden eyes and asked, "What in hell is going on? How did all of this happen? Was it the Tenebre?"

Henry shook his head. "No son, it wasn't the Tenebre."

"Then who, who is responsible for this—Chadwick? Did he do something to her?" The thought infuriated him. If Miles was to blame for this, blood would follow.

Henry shook his head again and laid a hand on Robert's shoulder. "No son, it wasn't him. Robert—it was *you*."

The accusation exploded in his head. He looked back at her and hit his knees. "How…I don't understand…"

Henry came to his knees beside his son. "That's what I've been trying to figure out myself." He pulled a crumpled letter from his pocket and handed it to Robert. "This is the only thing she had with her when they brought her in."

Robert clutched the note to his chest, recognizing it at once. It was the note he'd left for Daniela. Heartbreaking pain seeped into his skin instantly upon contact with the tattered paper. It was saturated in the worst, most unimaginable energy. Terrible. Painful. Agonizing. Everything she'd endured since his departure.

"Why would you leave her?" Henry asked.

"I had my reasons—"

"But you love her, why would you—"

"You know why I left!" Robert snapped.

Henry sucked in a frustrated breath. "You can't keep running from your past. Eventually you're going to have to face—"

"I have faced my past, and this is the consequences of it; a life of solitude, without love—without her. I can't give her what she wants and I will not deny her everything she deserves. I love her too much." He covered his face and sobbed.

Henry's heart ached, feeling the deep pain and regret which filled his son. "And what about Daniela?" Robert's eyes rose up to his. "Have you told her the truth?"

Terror filled him at even the thought. "No. I can't tell her."

"Don't you think she deserves to know the truth? Don't you think she deserves to hear it from you?"

"The truth doesn't matter. She deserves better than me, better than a killer."

"Son, you have to forgive yourself for what happened. It was an accident. You didn't mean to kill Sade. You were both young, you just—"

"Just carelessly disregarded every rule—and she died because of it—because of me. I will never forgive myself for that. It is my sentence, and not a sufficient one at that. When I stood trial, Johannes should have sentenced me to death—I wish now that he would have."

"He didn't condemn you to death, because you didn't deserve it," Henry argued, but Robert wouldn't hear of it.

"I did—and I still do. I don't deserve life, and I certainly don't deserve love."

"Even if that were so, she needs to hear the truth, and she needs to know that you still love her. She's broken, her soul torn apart." Henry rose to his feet and began pacing. "I can understand your reasoning for wanting to leave, but not for just taking off and leaving her unprotected and with no energy source. You knew she would get sick without you. What in God's name were you thinking?" Henry snapped.

Robert's eyes flashed with anger. "I didn't just take off. She was supposed to go to Miles!"

"Well she didn't! According to Rebecca, she's been alone this entire time."

Robert's mouth dropped open in shock. "What? But I…she was supposed to…why?" he stuttered.

"Go to him? It's *you* she truly loves." Robert couldn't answer. He was so confused. Why *wouldn't* she go to Chadwick? Something wasn't adding up. And why would Ryan lie? Ryan loved her; what could possibly be his motivation? Still, he hadn't spoken to Ryan yet, so he wasn't about to lay blame on someone else. As far as Robert knew, this was still his fault alone.

Henry placed his hands on both of Robert's shoulders. "Son, you have to go to her. You have to make things right between you. No matter what your past, no matter if you think it's right or wrong that you are together, she needs the truth, now more than ever. You owe her that."

"But how can I face her after the pain I've caused? What if she doesn't believe the truth? What if she doesn't care?"

"It doesn't matter. She'll have the truth, and that is what's most important. Look at her. Her life is in pieces, torn apart when you promised your love and then left without reason. Deception can cause destruction like nothing else in this world, but truth can bring forth forgiveness for even the gravest of trespasses. "

Robert's eyes swelled with tears again. "Why would she ever forgive me?"

"Because—she loves you," Henry smiled. "Go to her. Make this right."

Robert looked up again, seeking out the certainty in his father's eyes, those which held hundreds of years of wisdom and experience, many more than his own.

Torn

Robert turned to the glass once more. Daniela was now on her feet, pacing the room restlessly, arms gripping her shoulders tight, as if it was all that held her together. Suddenly she looked up at the window. To him it was a view into her world, to her, just a reflection of her ghostly self. She came straight to the glass, staring into it as if she could see through it, as if she could actually see him. Robert's chest burned with the anguish she held. He placed his hand against the glass, remorse flooding his eyes.

She continued to stare, seeking, agitated—desperate. Then her eyes filled with heavy tears and she placed her hand against the glass—exactly against *his*. After all this time, after all the pain he'd caused, could their bond still remain? They laid their heads against each other's, separated only by the thin window.

"I'm so sorry Daniela, I am so incredibly sorry," he whispered. She sobbed, stroking the glass, pawing at his unseen hand.

Suddenly, there was a loud disturbance just outside her room and she jerked her hand away, staring at the door with fear, crouching defensively.

"I said get the hell out of my way! I have every right to see her, so either move or *be* moved!"

And Robert knew that voice. Knew it like the smell of blood.

Chapter Twenty-Eight
Daniela

I sat huddled in the corner of the room, knees pulled tight to my chest. I'd been in that position for the last four hours. My back ached, neck and arms were stiff, longing to stretch and circulate fresh blood to my tired and sore muscles. I didn't want to move though. Didn't want to breathe. Didn't want to live.

I took in a long, deep breath and cringed. I had pain everywhere, even places I didn't know could hurt. Unbelievably, I had no broken bones, and because of Officer Kavenius, all of my major internal injuries were healing before the paramedics had even arrived to pick me up. However, I was so torn up when he found me, that even the huge amount of energy he used to restart my heart wasn't enough to repair me entirely. I was glad. Glad that I wasn't completely healed. Somehow, it felt easier to remain in a state of brokenness than it was to think of starting all over anew. That had been the worst part. Feeling so good, so complete, only to come crashing down. Broken. Alone. *Torn.*

There was a time when the thought of an exchange excited me beyond words, a time I would have welcomed emovamp pain relief. Not now. I'd gone mad, only able to comprehend pain. Pain had become my companion, something that never left me, never faltered. I could count on pain. It was always there, in one form or another. I could forever depend on pain. *It* would never abandon me.

At last the hurt in my back became unbearable. I slowly rose to my feet and began pacing, hugging my shoulders tight. I glanced around nervously at the room. The large mirror reflected a hideous, ghostly image of a girl I didn't recognize. *Dear God, is that me?* I thought. It didn't even look like me.

I remembered my reflection the last night Robert and I were in England. I was so confident then, so happy. What a fool I had been. To think I could ever mean anything to him.

Fool.

I walked to the mirror. It was as if I could feel him, like he was right there. Though I hated him, I still longed for him.

I placed my hand against the glass. He felt so close, but I knew that wasn't possible. It was only my desire for him, a trick of the mind. He wasn't there. Hadn't come. Didn't care. I cried into the haunted reflection of my eyes, pawing at the window with desperation. My eyes were deep, pale, and bereft of the joy that used to reside there. They weren't even my eyes anymore. Their blue and emerald sparkles had been replaced with a dreary, dull grey.

Lifeless.

I leaned my head against the smooth glass. I could *feel* him, I could. Right there in the room with me. I swear I could even hear him, I was sure of it. Of course I was also sure I had completely lost my mind—and I had.

Suddenly, a loud commotion stirred outside my room. I whirled around, crouching slightly, preparing for whatever orderlies came flooding into my room now. I had insisted no emovamps touch me, and even if I was sure they were human I protested and screamed at the slightest bit of contact. The hospital had been fairly willing to accommodate my unusual demand, but it was also why I was in the psychiatric ward. Seems they felt I was slightly unstable (I can't imagine why).

The disturbance was getting louder, someone was clearly yelling.

"I said get the hell out of my way! I have every right to see her, so either move or *be* moved!"

My body became rigid with fear. I knew that voice. But it couldn't be. It wasn't possible. How could he have found me?

There was a huge crash and the door abruptly swung open with a loud *BANG!* My eyes widened, mouth dropped open and mind cried out, *Miles!*

He stepped through the doorway, looking every bit as shocked as me. My heart raced, fear lodged in my throat. I was overcome with a combination of emotions. I was terrified, but at the same time was overwhelmed by feelings of happiness at the sight of him. I had missed him so much, but hadn't realized just how much until right then. On the one hand I wanted to run and throw myself into his arms, but on the other, I couldn't get past my fear and paranoia of his kind.

As he started toward me I shrieked, scrambling backwards. "Stay away! Don't touch me! Don't touch me!"

Miles took a step back, hands held up defensively. "Dani, sweets, it's me, Miles." He took another step forward.

I grabbed a nearby chair and pushed it in front of me as if to create a barrier, again screaming hysterically. "Get the hell away from me! Get away!"

"Dani, just calm down. I'm not going to hurt you." He stepped closer. "I'm here to help, just let me—"

"No! Get away! Get away!"

He continued forward, me screaming hysterically, him easing closer. All of a sudden, three large orderlies came flooding into the room. I recognized them at once, had seen them several times in the last 24 hours: Kurt, Ben and Justice. I thought at first they were going to come after me, but instead they went directly for Miles.

I watched with feelings of conflict as they attempted to wrestle him from my room. I didn't want Miles to touch me, but I didn't want to see him hurt either. However, Miles was no human like the orderlies, and he very easily overpowered them all, throwing them off one by one with little effort.

He came for me again, and I quickly climbed backwards onto the bed, but I was running out of retreat space.

Miles came to the edge of the bed, hands up in a deflective motion. "Dani, sweetie, come on. It's okay, don't fight this. I can hel—"

"No!" I yelled, tossing a pillow at him.

"Look at me," he said softly. "It's me. *Just me.* Miles." He began to climb up onto the bed. My eyes darted nervously to the dazed orderlies and then to the open door. Miles followed my gaze, knowing what I was thinking. "Don't do it Dani. Just sit down here and relax for a minute." Abruptly, I made a mad dash for my freedom! "Dani!" he yelled. I leapt off of the bed, but was so weak that I crashed to the ground with a painful *thud!* Quickly, I got to my feet. However, with my first step, I slammed right into Miles's hard chest.

Instantly, he wrapped his arms around me tight and I let out a high pitched scream! Just then, one of the orderlies had hold of Miles again. He let go of me momentarily to fend off the man.

Doing a frantic backstroke, I scrambled right into the arms of Kurt. "No! No! No! Leave me alone! DON'T TOUCH ME!" I screeched, kicking wildly.

"Nope. Now be a good little girl, or I'm gonna have to strap you down," he threatened, squeezing me so hard I could barely breathe.

"Please, your suffocating me," I gasped.

"Stop fighting me and I won't be so rough," he yelled. I bent my head and sank my teeth into his arm. He dropped me momentarily, and then grabbed me again, shaking me violently. "You bitch!"

Ben and Justice were now both on top of Miles, but it would take more than those two to restrain him. Effortlessly he tossed them off, and then lunged at Kurt! "Get the hell off of her!" he yelled, punching the man in the jaw, and then tossing him into the wall. Kurt crumpled to the ground, temporarily knocked out by the blow.

I rushed backwards and made it all of four steps before tripping over my own feet and falling onto the bed again. I kicked at Miles

199

frantically as he stalked me, coming closer every second. His eyes were so sad, yet focused. I knew that look. He was going to pounce on me! I shook my head back and forth with determination and pleading. "Please Miles, don't—"

"I'm sorry, sweets, but this is for your own good."

Instantly, he was on me. Only one blood-curdling scream escaped my lips before it was silenced by the tender passion of his kiss. He held my face carefully, filling me with the warm heat of his energy. Immediately I relaxed, melting into him. He pulled me into his arms, holding me tighter to him. I wanted to fight, wanted to push him away, but couldn't. It wasn't that I didn't have the physical energy to. I did. But the pleasure of the exchange had its hold on me. Again.

My body had hurt so terribly and for so long, nothing other than death could have felt this wonderful, this intoxicating—this freeing. My mind was becoming clear, the madness being pushed away, and giving way to calm. It was mental balance I hadn't had for a long time.

Finally, Miles pulled back slowly, never loosening his grip on me. I stared up into his soft emerald eyes with a look of awe and gratitude. He smiled warmly. "Everything's going to be okay baby. I'm here now, and I'll take care of you, I promise."

I didn't think I could speak. I was still dazed by everything that had happened. Was I dreaming? I couldn't be. It felt so real, everything clear for the first time in months. I reached up and placed a hand to his cheek, which he quickly covered with his own.

"Oh Miles, I'm so sorry. I—"

"Shhh…la mia belle," he whispered, "there is nothing to apologize for."

My eyes instantly filled with tears. "He left me," I choked. "He never loved me, he just used me!" I gripped his shirt, pulling him tighter, burying myself in the sanctuary of his embrace and wailed. "The pain was so terrible. I wanted to die, but I couldn't! I tried, but I couldn't!"

Miles squeezed me tighter. "I know, baby, I know. But it's over now. I promise *I'll* never leave you, and I'll never let him hurt you again," he said through gritted teeth. "*Ever.*"

Chapter Twenty-Nine
Robert

Robert watched Daniela with deep despair, guilt ridden over the pain he had caused her. He was about to go in and try to make things right, when there was a loud disturbance just outside her room.

"I said get the hell out of my way! I have every right to see her, so either move or *be* moved!"

"Chadwick," Robert growled.

Miles burst through the door to Dani's room, then immediately started towards her. Robert's throat tightened. His instinct was to rush into the room and tear Miles to shreds, but he paused. Her emotional signature had suddenly changed. She was terrified—but *happy*. She was happy to see Miles. And not just happy, she was uncontrollably ecstatic. He could feel it, her overwhelming desire to run to him.

Henry headed toward the door, on a mission to remove the unwelcome Miles. Robert caught his arm. "Dad wait. Just wait a minute."

Henry paused, a look of concern. "Son, you're not going to be able to work things out with her if he is here."

"Just wait. I want to see what happens. I need to see…"

Henry hesitantly took a place beside him and watched the scene as it unfolded. Orderlies being tossed about like rag dolls, Miles stalking Dani, and then at last, he jumped on her! "This has gone far enough!" Henry scolded, moving toward the door again.

Once more Robert caught his dads arm. "No, Wait! Look!"

Henry turned his attention back to Dani and Miles who were now locked together at the mouth. "I'll be damned, he's doing it. She's calming down, she's relaxing," he admitted.

Robert leaned his head against the glass, tears heavy in his eyes. "This should have never happened."

Henry placed a hand on Robert's shoulder. "I'll get security to remove him. I don't want you in it. All we need is for you two to get into a fight in the middle of the hospital."

"No, that's not what I meant. I meant, *this* shouldn't have happened. She never should have been alone, she never should have suffered. I thought I made sure of that, but I was wrong. I caused all of this, and now I'm going to make things right," Robert said coldly.

Henry stared at his son with confusion. "What are you saying?"

Robert dragged in a weary breath. "Give him complete clearance to her. She needs to be released into Miles's custody so he can care for her, get her well again. She needs him."

"She needs *you*," Henry argued.

"No!" he snapped. "I had my chance to do right by her a long time ago, and I blew it. This is the best thing for her. This is the way it was supposed to be in the first place. If I hadn't been so selfish to begin with, I would have let her go long ago and spared her this. She belongs with him." He turned and stared into his father's deep green eyes. "Father, I'm asking you, *please*, make this happen. Give him the clearance he needs, cover up whatever you have to, and get her out of this place," he pleaded. Henry's eyes were sad, but he knew his son's mind was made up. He nodded, and then turned to go. "And tell that damned orderly, Kurt, to never lay another hand on her again, or so help me, it'll be the last thing he ever does."

Henry nodded solemnly. "This is a mistake son, you know that."

"No. This is the first thing I've done right." Henry didn't argue further, simply gave another nod and walked out.

Robert fell to his knees again, hands against the glass, watching as his father delivered the news, releasing the woman he loved over to the man he felt had torn them apart.

He should have been furious with Miles, but he wasn't. The truth was Miles wasn't entirely to blame. In fact, Robert really owed him his gratitude. After all, if Miles hadn't found proof that a transplant patient had been successfully turned, who knows how long Robert would have carried on deceiving her. Though his motivation at that time seemed justified, he knew now it had been wrong to lie to her. He should have told her the truth from the beginning, informed her of the monster he was. No doubt she would have let him go without resistance then. But it was too late for that now.

It no longer mattered anyway. Daniela was where she belonged, with Miles. Looking at her cradled in his arms, Robert was sure they would never part now. He watched as Miles cuddled and held her, kissing her forehead the way he had so many times himself. Jealousy and pain boiled in his veins until at last it became too much to watch and he turned away.

Seeing her in Miles's arms had him wanting to rush in and sweep her away from him, tell her the truth and beg her forgiveness. But even if he did, even if he told her the truth and she forgave him, it was forgiveness he didn't want, because it was forgiveness he didn't deserve. Just as he knew from the beginning, he didn't deserve her.

"He left me!" she cried, "He never loved me, he was just using me!"

The accusation was more than he could stomach and her pain, much more than he could endure. Sure he wanted to come clean, tell her the truth. But he couldn't do it. He couldn't take her seeing him as a killer. *Far better that she think I am scum,*' he thought. The truth didn't matter now anyway.

Slowly, he rose to his feet, then kissed his fingers, turned back and placed them against the glass. One last farewell kiss. "Goodbye my sweet Daniela…I love you…I will *always* love you." With that, he turned and walked away.

He now had only one thing on his mind. Ryan Johnson. Where in hell was he, and why had he lied to him this entire time? Robert balled up his fists as he walked and thought of what he would do when he found Ryan. Angry as he was, it could very well end with one of them dying—or both.

Robert was determined to find out Ryan's motivation though, so he had to keep a clear head. He would question him in a calm, collected, mannerly fashion—then rip his limbs off and beat him to death with his own arms.

Miles

Miles clutched Dani to his chest, rocking her gently, all the while glaring at the enormous mirror on the other side of the room. He knew it was a two way mirror, and knew without a doubt that Robert was on the other side. He felt him the minute he'd entered the room. Miles clenched his jaw tight, continuing to watch the window with contempt.

Slowly, the three orderlies stirred, coming around and rising to their feet. They didn't look happy. Miles shifted Dani a little, preparing to fend off another attack from the unwelcome hospital staff. This was hard enough without them interfering. The three men cracked their necks and knuckles, clearly a little upset over having been tossed around. Miles wasn't afraid of them, just annoyed that he was going to have to kick their asses again.

Just as he was about to get up and face the disgruntled orderlies, a stern voice commanded from the doorway, "Leave him be."

The men immediately turned their attention to Dr. Henry Hollin. "Sir, this man is a danger to—" Kurt tried to argue, but Henry cut him off.

"I said leave him. I'll deal with this. You are all dismissed," he commanded. Kurt was irritated by his inability to seek vengeance, but didn't question the Doctor's orders. "And Kurt, don't ever touch her again, or it will be your job." Kurt looked stunned, but then nodded his compliance. Miles relaxed a little, but kept a watchful eye on the men as they exited the room. Henry walked over and crouched down to Dani's level.

Miles tensed up, gripping her tighter. No one was going to tear her from him without one hell of a fight. "If you think you're going to force me to leave, you better call them back to help you," Miles warned.

"I have no intention of making you leave. She obviously needs you." Miles had to suppress his desire to smile when he felt Dani slide her arms around his chest and squeeze tight. Henry looked at Dani with deep compassion. "You feeling better, young lady?" he asked. She only stared at him through tears and nodded, clutching Miles even harder.

"She can't stay in here. This place will only add to her illness," Miles said. "I need to get her out of here, *now*."

"I agree, but it will take a few hours to coordinate her release. In the meantime, I'll get you complete clearance and a security card to come and go as you wish. I'll arrange for her to be released into your care, if that's okay."

Miles was stunned by Henry's cooperation. "Yes—yes of course." Though Henry appeared willing for him to take charge of Dani, Miles sensed he wasn't happy about it.

"You'll need to come with me and sign some paperwork. I'll be at the front desk when you're ready," Henry said walking from the room.

Miles remained, holding her for a little longer. Once he felt she had calmed enough, he gently eased back and glanced down. She peered up with pleading eyes that wished for him to stay. "You are still so weak. If I'm going to get you better I need to feed. When I get back I'll give you some more energy, then we can get out of here. I won't be long; okay?" She clutched him tight again, hugging with fear, but then slowly released her grip, nodding in submission. He placed a long kiss on her forehead, then gently slid from beneath her, and urged her to lie down. He pulled a blanket up around her, stroking her cheek. "I'll be right back, I promise."

As Miles stepped out into the hall, he had barely closed the door when he took off down the hall. It didn't take him long to find his intended target.

Suddenly, feeling the burning sensation of hate at his back, Robert whirled around. Miles plowed into him, grabbing his throat and slamming him into the wall with such force the sheetrock caved in!

"You bastard!" Miles roared. "I'm gonna rip you to pieces you son of a bitch!"

Robert didn't even struggle, just dangled limply in Miles's deadly grasp. "Go ahead, I won't stop you."

Miles reared back and slammed his hand through the wall next to Robert's head, but he never flinched. "She trusted you and you destroyed her! You left her all alone knowing she would get sick! What, you'd rather she die than be with me? I should kill you for what you've done to her," he snarled.

"Then do it!" Robert yelled.

Miles seized Robert's throat with both hands, squeezing hard, sliding his body up the wall until his feet no longer touched the ground, but again, Robert put up no resistance.

Unexpectedly, Miles released his grip, dropping him to his feet. "I should kill you, but I won't. You don't deserve the mercy of death. You deserve to suffer, just as she has. She is sitting in that room," he pointed down the hall, "suffering more pain than any human should ever have to, and all because of you! I hope her agony haunts the eyes of every woman you look at for the rest of your days you coward."

Robert glared at Miles with contempt. "Don't worry, it will," he muttered under his breath and then growled, "If you're finished, I have important business elsewhere."

Miles stepped back, clenching his fists tight. Robert began to walk away, when Miles caught his arm. Robert glared at him, gritting his teeth. "Forget something, Chadwick?"

"Yeah, you *owe* her something." Miles tightened his grip and began drawing out Robert's energy as fast as he could take it. Robert stood rigid, allowing the exchange.

When done, Miles smiled, relaxing his shoulders and stepping back a half step, then abruptly swung, landing a fierce blow to Robert's jaw! Robert hit the ground, sliding several feet away. Miles was immediately on him, clutching the collar of his jacket tight, pulling Robert's face within inches of his own. A growl rose up his throat, then in a frigid tone, he warned, "You stay the hell away from her; you hear me? You don't talk to her—you don't look at her—and don't even *think* about getting back together with her."

Robert just stared back listlessly. "I have no intention to."

Miles released him again, snarling with disgust. Robert rose to his feet and straightened his clothes. He turned to go, and then quickly turned back. "I need to know something—when was the last time you spoke to Ryan?"

Miles shot him a look of confusion. "Never; why?"

Robert dragged in a frustrated breath. "Whatever you do, keep Daniela away from him, I don't trust him. He's up to something."

"Like what, what in hell are you talking about?"

"Just keep her away from him. I'll contact you when I know more." With that he turned once more and began walking away.

Miles called to his back, "Doc!" Robert turned and faced him one last time. "If you ever contact her again—I *will* kill you." Robert nodded gravely, then turned and walked away.

Chapter Thirty
Daniela

I lay curled on my side, gazing at Miles, who was gazing at me. He was sitting on the floor beside my bed, watching me quietly. I was calm and comfortable for the first time in—well, I couldn't remember how long. Though I was filled with a great deal of Miles's energy now, my body was hard at work trying to repair itself, and I was succumbing to the fatigue of it all. I didn't want to sleep, didn't want to close my eyes; afraid if I did I would wake to find Miles had only been a dream. Unable to fight the weariness though, I closed my eyes momentarily, and drifted off into a dreamless slumber. It felt as if I'd only been out for a few seconds when the warmth of Miles's hand caressed my cheek. I opened my eyes sleepily and looked up into his charming face.

"Hey there, sweets," he said softly. Immediately, I reached around his neck, hugging with great relief. I was cuddled in his arms, held tight in the security of his chest. I breathed him in, a fragrance so heavenly, I thought, maybe I *had* died. God, how I'd missed his smell. "How are you feeling?" he asked.

"Tired, but better. How long have I been asleep?" I yawned.

"Almost three hours."

"It felt like only seconds," I gasped. "How long have you been holding me?"

He smiled and let out a deep sigh of contentment. "Almost three hours," he repeated.

"What? Oh Miles, I'm sorry! You must be terribly uncomfortable," I apologized, trying to sit up.

His grasp tightened slightly. "Relax, la mia belle…" he cooed. A warm current seeped into my skin, pushing out my desire to resist him, and I settled back into his arms. He caressed my cheek and gazed at me with longing—longing he had held for me all of these months we'd been apart. "I've missed you so much, Dani."

"I've missed you too."

"I got something to make you feel better," he said, shifting me slightly to retrieve it from beside him.

"You didn't have to get me anything," I complained, but then quickly smiled at the sight of the bright yellow bag he held before me. "Chocolate covered peanut candies! Oh Lord, how I need those right now," I confessed, clutching the package to my chest.

Miles beamed down at me, happy that his gift was appeasing. "Do you need anything else?" he asked.

I shook my head. "No, I just want to get out of here. This place feels wrong—I can't explain it, it's just…weird."

He ran a finger gently across my eyebrow. "I know it does. We're just waiting for them to release you right now. It shouldn't be much longer and then I'll take you home where you can rest." Ahhh…the thought of my own bed sounded wonderful right then. "There *is* someone who wants to see you though, that is, if you're up to it," he offered.

I swallowed hard, panicking slightly at the thought. "It's not my mother is it?" I asked with dread. After all of this and the fact that her car was now a molten pile of crumpled steel, my mother was sure to go ballistic. I could just envision my next birthday gift. A pretty white coat with little buckles and extra long sleeves.

"No, it's not your mother," he replied with a relieved sigh.

"Really? I'm shocked. She should be pounding the door down to get in here right now." Miles smiled mischievously. I raised one brow. "Miles, what did you do?"

He let out a light hearted laugh, and then confessed, "Well, she was being a tad difficult, so—I had a little talk with her."

"A '*little talk*'? What kind of '*little talk*'?" I asked nervously.

"Nothing much. I simply explained to her that the best place for you right now is with me, and that I would see to it you were taken care of."

I looked at him doubtfully. "And she just went along with that?"

Miles smiled again, and then let out a respite breath. "No, actually, she nearly attacked me at first."

"What! Oh-ma-gawd Miles, what'd you do? You didn't brainwash her did you?" I gasped.

He kissed my forehead slow and tenderly, then replied, "No, I didn't brainwash her—at least not entirely. I just very delicately made her see it my way."

I narrowed my eyes at him. "You used your persuasion on my mother?" I accused.

"I had to, sweets," he defended. "I promise, she is as happy as a lark now, thinks it was all her idea in fact," he assured.

I wasn't sure how to feel about that, but for the most part it made me happy. It wasn't that I was just thrilled about Miles looking after me. Lord knows I was a nervous wreck about that, but at the same time, I certainly did not want to have to stay with my mother and her constant hovering. I much preferred my own place. Besides, she had her hands full with my oldest sister, Candace, now. She's who my parents had gone to visit for two weeks when I took my final plunge into madness.

Well, I say they went to visit her, when in reality they were traveling there to pack up her things and bring her home with them. All these years I knew something wasn't right with her, but had remained oblivious to her situation; just more proof of how self absorbed I could be.

Like the rest of my family, I thought her constant detachment and absence from family functions was due to her being a workaholic. However, just like everyone else, I was wrong. She'd kept us all in the dark, too scared and ashamed to tell anyone the truth about the abuse she'd been suffering at the hands of her husband.

I'm not sure when it had started, but it appeared to have been going on for many years. She'd done a good job of keeping her secret hidden, but that had all changed overnight. Seems her husband went a little too far, and this time she ended up at a local hospital. She'd finally had enough though, and called my parents.

Conveniently, now my mother had someone *else* to coddle and hover over. I was glad. Not that my sister had been abused, but that the situation had provided enough chaos that my mother was willing to go along with Miles's suggestion. If it hadn't been for Candace, I don't think my mom would have been so easily persuaded, even by Miles.

"So are you feeling up to a visitor?" he asked.

Pulled from my deep thoughts, I brought my attention back to him. "What?"

"A visitor—are you up for a visitor?" he repeated.

"Depends; who is it?"

"I'll give you a hint. She's about medium height, beautiful brown skin, a keen eye for fashion and the thickest Okie accent this side of the state."

My face lit up at once. "Becca!" I nearly squealed. "Yes, of course I want to see her!"

"Good," he said, sliding out from beneath me. He casually strolled to the door, then opened it and stuck his head out momentarily. "She's awake now." Immediately Becca's concerned face appeared in the doorway. She didn't rush in though. Instead she remained there, shifting timidly, not sure if she should approach. Miles placed a hand on her shoulder with a gentle smile. "It's okay Becca, she's better now. You can go on in. I'm going to go see what the holdup is on getting her out of here while you two visit."

She nodded her head, but never took her eyes from me. When he closed the door, the room became very still and awkwardly silent. Finally I asked, "How's Teagan?"

Becca's shoulders relaxed a little as she slowly approached. "Good, she's good. She misses ya, but other than that, she's good. I went by yer parents' house several times lookin' for ya, but after a couple days, I was afraid that since they weren't there either, she'd get lonely, so I took her on home with me."

"Thank you. I'm glad she's okay. I was worried. How are you?" I asked.

"Fine, tired's all. I hadn't got much sleep ya know," she scowled.

"I know, and I'm sorry. I shouldn't have just taken off like that, but—"

"I know Dani, it wasn't yer fault, ya didn't know what you was doin' with yer mind-melt-down and all. And I'm sorry for callin' Miles. I just didn't know what else to—"

"It's okay," I interjected. "You did the right thing."

"Ya sure?"

"Yeah," I nodded.

"Well, I'm just glad yer okay now—you *are* okay now, aren't ya?" she asked tensely.

I wasn't, but felt the need to reassure her I was, in fact, alright. "Yes, I'm fine now—never felt better," I lied. Truth was, even though I was feeling physically better, I was mentally a train wreck. My head was clear, but my feelings were a mass of confusion.

Sure, Miles seemed to be the answer to all of my problems, but in reality, he only added to them. I didn't want to be with an emovamp—*any* emovamp. Did I care for Miles? Yes. Had I missed him? Undoubtedly. But wanted to be with him? I wasn't sure.

I still felt in my heart that Robert had only been using me, and so I was naturally suspicious of Miles's intentions as well. However, there was no doubt that at this point I was very evidently dependent on him. I had to remain around an emovamp, or else return to the state of turmoil he'd found me in. I didn't like either choice, but going along with Miles for now seemed the lesser of two evils. My only hope was that I could somehow wean myself off of my dependency, but wasn't at all confident it was possible.

"Well ya definitely look better—'cept yer hair. Jeez Dani, I still cain't believe ya whacked all yer hair off. Ya look like Julia-freaking-Roberts when she played Tinker Bell in Hook. That disastrous style coulda damn near ended her career ya know," she scolded.

I rolled my eyes. "It'll grow back."

"Yeah, well it's been six months already and it ain't grown so much as one inch, and I cain't do diddly-squat with it till it does."

"You? Surely there is no fashion disaster you can't overcome," I teased. She rolled her eyes back at me.

Clicking her tongue, she reached out and pulled at a stubby strand. I could see the excitement of the challenge in her eyes. "Well, I may be able to do somethin' with it, but no promises—I aint Moses ya know. I cain't just wave my hand and make a miracle happen—Lord knows even Moses would be challenged with this mess." I smiled, loving the familiar badgering of my best friend. "Hey, there's someone else that wants to talk to ya, if ya feel like it—do ya?" she asked.

I stiffened and sat up in bed a little straighter. The list of people it could be was now getting shorter. "Who is it?" I asked nervously.

Becca patted my blanketed foot with a chuckle. "Only Michael."

"Michael who?"

She laughed again, "Kavenius, silly. You know, Officer Kavenius. Just how hard did ya hit yer head?" she giggled. "He's just worried. Said if ya felt up to it, he wanted to check in on ya. Feel up to it?" she asked again. I swallowed hard, and then nodded. "Relax Dani," she giggled again as she went to open the door, "if he wanted ya dead, he woulda just left ya in the burning car."

Her point was valid, but didn't ease my anxiety. I knew full well that few emovamps had anything to gain from my death. My energy would be gone then. I was a far more precious commodity if kept alive. Still, I couldn't help but brighten up a little when he entered the room in full uniform, carrying a paper bag and smiling softly. He and Becca came directly to my bedside. She sat down, while he remained standing.

"Well you look a lot better," he remarked.

"Yeah, I guess so," I sighed.

"You had us all pretty worried," he said.

"I know, and I'm really sorry. I never wanted to cause any trouble. Honestly, I would have preferred to be DOA."

"I know, but I hope you feel differently now," he said.

I looked down, unable to answer honestly. Instead, I simply nodded as if agreeing. "I hope you haven't been waiting up here for very long," I said, changing the subject quickly.

"I've come and gone a few times, just checking in to see how you were doing."

"Thank you, I know you're busy. Really, you didn't have to go through the trouble," I insisted.

He smiled again. "It's okay, I didn't mind. Besides, the company here is rather pleasant." He and Becca exchanged glances, ending with her biting her lip and looking away shyly.

Uh oh. I knew that look. The thought of Becca hooking up with any more emovamps terrified me. I could see another long talk about boyfriends in our future, and only hoped this one went better than the last.

With a tap at the door, Miles poked his head in. "We got the all-clear, sweets. It's time to go,"

"Thank God, I don't think I could take another minute in this place," I exclaimed.

"Oh, that reminds me, I brought ya some clothes," Becca said, taking Michael's paper bag and handing it to me.

"Your other ones were kind of destroyed in the accident," Michael explained.

I nodded with humility, still feeling ashamed at everything that had taken place. "Thank you," I groaned.

"Well, I'm gonna git, but I'll stop by and see ya tomorrow, if that's okay?" Becca asked.

"You've got the address right?" Miles asked.

I stared back and forth with confusion. "Address, what address? *Whose* address?"

"Mine of course," Miles replied very matter-of-fact.

I opened my mouth to protest, but was cut off by Becca. "Well, I know this is about to get real good, so we're gonna git. See ya D," Becca exclaimed over her shoulder, exiting the room in a hurry.

Michael gave a slight bow. "Take care Dani." Then, quickly he followed on Becca's heels.

As the door closed behind them, I turned my attention back to Miles. "I am not—" I began, but Miles quickly had my hand.

"It's only for a little while, just until you're all better," he assured.

I wanted to refuse, wanted to pull my hand away and say no, but I couldn't. Call it fatigue, call it a mental breakdown, call it whatever you like, but my ability to resist his persuasion was lost at the moment. Dreamily I replied, "Okay…just for a little while."

Ah crap.

Chapter Thirty-One
Present Day

As Robert's car came to a screeching halt, he glanced up at the *Amanti Inn Bed and Breakfast*. He'd only been here once, months ago, the day he'd met with Ryan to see that everything had gone as planned. At the time it appeared everything had, and Robert sensed no deception on Ryan's part. However, considering Daniela's current condition, he now knew he'd been misled. The only way that would have been possible, was if Ryan had the gift of deception.

Robert clenched his fists tight, struggling to suppress his temper. His instinct was to rush in there, beat the hell out of Ryan, and then drag the traitor to the hospital so he could see what he'd done to her.

"No, I have to keep my head clear. This is no time to lose control," he scolded himself.

He took a deep breath and then climbed from his truck. Within seconds he was at the door, knocking, using all restraint to not break it in. Almost instantly he felt the presence of *another*. The door swung open and a dark haired woman stood before him, full red lips turned up in a devilish grin.

"Welcome to the Amanti Inn. How may I help you?" she asked.

Robert straightened his tie and proclaimed, "I'm looking for Ryan Johnson; is he about?"

"Well, I'm not sure, but if you'll come in, I'll check," she said, taking his hand and tugging at it for him to enter.

Robert hesitated momentarily, but then stepped in. "Thank you."

"Allow me to take your coat," she purred, sliding it from his shoulders. Her voice was warm and husky, soothing to his weary senses. Robert didn't really want to remove his coat, he hadn't planned on staying that long, but he put up no resistance to her removing it either. "There, isn't that better?" she asked, stepping close and stroking a hand softly down his cheek.

"Yes…yes it is," he replied quietly. He stared down at her with awe. She was quiet beautiful—stunning in fact. Strangely, he couldn't seem to take his eyes from hers. She smelled of jasmine and heather, a fragrance he didn't usually care for, but on her he found it very appealing.

"I didn't get your name," she said, gliding a finger down his cheek. Softly. Slowly.

"My name?" he asked dreamily.

Stroking his cheek again, she replied, "Yesss…your name." The question rolled off her tongue like warm, buttery syrup.

Robert swallowed hard, trying to steady his breathing, which had increased considerably. "Oh…Robert—Robert Hollin—*Dr.* Robert Hollin," he clarified.

"Mmmmm…a doctor, how nice. I simply adore men in the medical field," she said, caressing a lock of hair at his collar.

Robert grinned boyishly, feeling overwhelmed with strange feelings for this new female. He shook his head which now felt foggy and light. "And what is your name?" he asked.

"Oh, I'm sorry; where are my manners?" she apologized, her eyes following her finger as she ran it slowly down his chest, caressing each button. Then, gazing back up into his eyes, she innocently replied, "I'm Emily."

Instantly, his lips tightened and he took a step back. "Emily—Ryan's wife?" he asked sternly.

"Girlfriend actually…that is we haven't made anything official yet," she clarified.

"I see." Robert's head was clearing. Determined to get back on task, he asked, "Well, is he here or not?"

Emily let out an aggravated sigh. "No, he's not here."

"If you knew that, then why did you even bother inviting me in?" he asked with frustration.

"I don't know, I guess I just *wanted* you—to come in that is."

"Well, do you know when he will be back?"

"Hmmm…nope."

She was toying with him and it was aggravating. Furthermore, he found it very odd that she was bonded to Ryan, yet was very obviously flirting with him. She was up to something. "Look, I don't have time for these games. I need to speak with him at once, so if you know where he is, kindly point me in the right direction. If not, I will be on my way."

Emily sauntered back up to him, running her hand down his cheek once more. "Relax. I'm sure he will be back in a bit. In the meantime, come and sit down with me." She took his hand and very easily led him to a couch. Again, Robert wanted to resist, but couldn't. He felt unexplainably powerless to deny Emily. As he sat down, she curled up next to him, snaking her arms around his shoulders and leaning in close. Stroking his face, she asked, "So, what are you a doctor of?"

"Uh…cardiology…" he said quietly.

"Mmmm…a heart doctor, how romantic."

Robert grinned shyly. "Yes, I get that a lot."

"I bet you do. I imagine it drives all the girls crazy," she whispered near his ear, while loosening his tie.

"I suppose so…" he breathed.

"Being a doctor, I bet you have very good hands too," she sighed, nibbling at his ear.

Robert closed his eyes, becoming consumed by the seductive power she had over him. "Good hands…yes…" he agreed quietly.

Robert felt the top button of his collar pop open under her fingers, then the next and the next. Slowly, she slid a hand inside his shirt. "I bet you can do many wonderful things with your hands; cant you?" she purred.

Robert tipped his head back as she began nibbling down his neck. He didn't understand it. He was overwhelmed with desire, his blood heated with fire and want for Emily. He struggled to remember what he'd come here for, but was unable to concentrate on anything other than her hands and mouth as they roved over his body, caressing and kissing. How could he allow this? Why would she be doing this when she's bonded to Ryan? As Ryan's named entered his mind once more, his head suddenly snapped up.

"Ryan," he snarled.

"What about him?" she groaned, planting another kiss on his chest.

Abruptly, Robert threw her back against the couch, springing on top of her. He grabbed her throat with both his hands, pinning her down and holding her against the arm of the couch. "Damn you! What game are you playing?" he demanded.

Emily's eyes flashed with excitement. "Oooo…forceful! I like that!"

Robert tightened his grasp on her neck. Leaning in close to her face, he growled, "Where is Ryan?"

"I told you, I don't know."

"You're lying. Tell me where he is, or—"

Emily's hand slid under his shirt once more, caressing the warm skin of his tummy and chest. "There's no need to get hostile. There are easier ways of getting information out of me." Robert's eyes closed and he relaxed his grip a little. She snaked her other hand around his neck and coaxed him forward to her mouth. He hesitated for a second, but then his lips parted, allowing her tongue to enter.

Her kiss was overpowering and he held no will to stop it. His weight relaxed onto her and she wrapped her legs around him, pulling him down tighter to her. He drew his mouth away and began biting at her collarbone savagely. She moaned and ground against him. "Yes, my love, yesss…"

Suddenly, Robert froze. He pulled back slowly and looked into her eyes. They were dark, nearly black with lust and desire. "What am I doing? *You*—you're doing something to me!" he accused. He began scrambling backwards when instantly the room was filled with a half-dozen emovamp men. All of them held silver, charged weapons to his throat.

Robert's eyes followed the tip of one sword all the way up to the face of Ryan. "You," he snarled. "You are behind all of this! Do you know what you've done to her? Have you any idea!" Robert knocked the swords aside and lunged at Ryan with full force, but was caught by several hands and thrown down to the ground, pinned with a sharp blade pressed to his neck. Robert glared up at Ryan, teeth bared, jaw clenched. "You were supposed to protect her—I trusted you with her life."

Ryan's eyes softened, pained with his own deceit. Emily interjected. "And she trusted *you* with her heart!" she sneered.

Robert immediately silenced, then staring wide-eyed at Emily, he pleaded, "What could you possibly have to gain by destroying Daniela's life?"

She stood up and straightened her clothes. "Everything," she smiled wickedly. "Now that she hates you—and trust me, she does," she hissed. "She will be easily persuaded to bond with me."

"But that doesn't make any sense. She can't bond with you, it's impossible," Robert argued.

Emily's smile widened. "I swear, some of you are so narrow minded. You focus too much on the old ways, never thinking how to grow and adapt to the changing times."

Robert blinked hard with confusion. "You're not making any sense. Adapt how? What do you mean?"

Immediately, the men jerked Robert to his feet, restraining him tightly.

"Sorry I can't be more specific right now, I have other things to see to—but what to do with you?" The large emovamp behind Robert pulled the blade tighter, causing a thin stream of blood to trail down his throat slowly. "Easy Ellis, I just had the carpets cleaned. I don't need his blood all over them," Emily scolded. She raised a brow, tapping her chin with one long, red fingernail. "I can't very well let you go, but at the same time I think you are far too valuable to kill—*yet*. I may still need you."

"Need me for what?" he asked pensively.

She sashayed up to him, snaked her arms over his shoulders and pressed her body against his. "Oh, I can think of many, *many* things." She brushed her mouth across his, biting at his lower lip. Dragging her tongue to his ear, she whispered, "We could be marvelous lovers you and I."

Robert's eye widened, and he became rigid with detest. "If that is your desire, kill me now. I would rather die than occupy the bed of a whore," he spat.

Emily reared back and brought her hand across his face with a loud *slap!* "I will forgive you for that comment today, but I will not forget. When Daniela is one of us, you will be begging me to be her lover, but you will have to prove yourself to me first. I will enjoy your groveling then."

Robert's mouth tightened. "I will kill you first!" he yelled, trying to struggle free, but his efforts were in vain. He was not strong enough to overpower so many others.

"Take him underground and lock him up," she ordered.

Robert immediately began to struggle again, but instantly he was gagged and a black cloth bag lowered over his head, blocking out all light.

Chapter Thirty-Two
Daniela

"Come on Dani, this is ridiculous. There's no reason for you to stay here anymore," Miles said.

"Yes, there is, I happen to like it. Besides, all my stuff is already here, and this place makes me feel safe."

"Safe? You're kidding, right?" he scoffed. "Safe—? Here? I know you have your memories back, so I shouldn't have to remind you that Tobias nearly killed you right where you're standing."

I rolled my eyes. "No he didn't," I stepped two paces to the right, "he nearly killed me right here," I corrected.

Miles let out a long, aggravated sigh. "Look, I understand you don't want to stay at my house anymore, but there are a lot of other places you can live—places much closer to me specifically."

I flopped down on the couch and propped my feet on the coffee table. "It's not that far of a drive for you. Besides, I've already paid the rent for this month and next." I flipped open a magazine, pretending to peruse articles.

"Rent, my ass, you shouldn't pay anything for this dump after what he did to you," Miles growled under his breath.

Instantly, I sat up and turned on him sharply. "We agreed to never mention *him* again."

Miles rushed to my side, taking my hands and giving them an apologetic kiss. "I'm sorry. I didn't mean to upset you. I just meant that—"

"I know what you meant. Just—ugh! And stop trying to persuade me!" I jerked my hands away with annoyance. "This is my house, and I don't want to leave—and it doesn't matter who owns it, because he's never coming back anyway; okay? So just drop it. I'm staying and that's final." I crossed my arms in a juvenile manner and turned away.

Miles remained quiet momentarily, then scooted up close, lowering his voice to barely above a whisper. "I'm sorry. If this is where you wish to stay, then I'll just deal with it." I felt the warm sensation of his skin as he gently glided a knuckle over my forearm. "I just want to keep you safe is all, and that's hard to do with you so far away."

I turned and gazed into his deep green eyes. "You can't keep me safe. No one can," I said soberly.

His face became tense, his tone calm and sure. "*I* can. I promise you, I will never let anyone hurt you again."

I understood he felt certain of that, but at the same time, had heard those words uttered before, and to me, they were a lie. Besides, in truth, he could be living right next door and it wouldn't matter if someone marked me. And then, what of my heart? Could he keep my heart from being broken again? It was a redundant question anyway. My heart was already broken, and in my opinion, was beyond repair. Could a heart be broken twice? I didn't wish to find out.

He reached up and stroked my cheek, sending a warm simmer of comfort into my skin, easing my anxiety. "I know you don't believe me right now, but in time I will prove myself to you."

"Please don't."

"I *will*. I know you've been hurt and that you're afraid to trust me, but I love you, Dani, and I'm willing to do anything to prove that." I stared into his eyes. They were filled with such confidence. He leaned closer, his breath sweeping over my lips, sweet and warm.

"Miles, I..."

"Yes..."

My body gave a small shiver, when suddenly I jerked back and stood up. "I have to feed Teagan," I said, quickly heading to the pantry to get the dog food.

I was determined to maintain my distance from Miles as much as possible. After just one week of staying with him, I'd grown extremely dependent on his energy. But I had drawn a line in the sand and asked that he not cross it. Though he obliged my request as much as physically possible, I still required constant handling to keep my body at a certain emotional level. This had required several mouth to mouth exchanges per day for the first few days and then just simple 'touching' at least once a day thereafter.

Because of this, I had no choice but to spend some degree of time with him. Not that I minded. On the contrary, I thoroughly enjoyed my time with Miles, always had. Furthermore, the mouth to mouth exchanges had been mind blowing. I'd found it extremely difficult to not give in and enjoy them longer than necessary.

However, things were different now. I no longer trusted his kind entirely. This caused a great deal of hesitance on my part in allowing him to get too close to me, hence, my desire to remain in my townhouse at the Holloway Oak apartments. At least, that's what I chalked it up to at the time. Truth was I didn't want to leave, because this was the only place where I felt close to Robert. I hated him, yes, but longed for him just the same. Secretly, I felt he would return any day now.

Additionally, something had changed in me. I was feeling, different. Cocky. Arrogant. Entitled. Crap, I was acting like Miles. Funny as that sounds, it made perfect sense to me. Miles was all of those things and was projecting it to me every day. It only stood to reason he would rub off a little. Weird as it was, I kind of enjoyed it. Though, I was beginning to think Miles himself was finding it a bit problematic.

Reaching the pantry, I grabbed the bag of kibble and poured a small amount into Teagan's bowl, the one that was already full. Miles looked at me cynically.

"What?" I snapped. "She eats a lot." Teagan sat, gazing up at me, tail wagging back and forth across the tile with a soft *whoosh, whoosh, whoosh.* I looked back to Miles, who was sporting a knowing grin. "What? Well, she does."

He held up his hands, surrendering to my ridiculous reasoning. "Speaking of food, I'm starving. What do you say we go grab some dinner?"

"Um, I'm not really hungry right now. I'll probably just make a sandwich later or something," I lied. Truthfully, I was so hungry at the moment, I was eyeing Teagan's overflowing food bowl. She looked up at me guardedly as if sensing the madness of my thoughts. I peeked at Miles's face as I pushed past. He was smiling that half grin that made my toes curl.

"I wasn't really asking," he replied, catching my arm and pulling me back. His voice was deep, low and full of command. He leaned in close, bringing with him the fragrance of him; musk, spice, sexy man smell. I took in an excited breath, unable to pull away from the exotic scent.

"Really?" I breathed. He nodded slowly. I arched a playful brow. "What are you going to do, hold me down and force-feed me?"

"Hold you down, now there's an idea." He grazed his lips across mine and I stilled immediately. Oh. Dear. God.

I closed my eyes momentarily, indulging in the sweet comfort of his masculine presence. It was something I had been without for so long now, and had missed terribly. The scent of a man. The sound of a man. The sheer presence of a man. Why did I long for it so? Why does any woman? It's a caustic curse of which we have no means to resist. Damn you irresistible men!

I let out a sigh of longing, but with it came a breathy reply, "Please..." It was only one word, but it carried with it a cry for mercy. I wasn't ready for this. For him. My body felt better, my mind clearing, but my heart? My heart was still torn to pieces. I was healing, but far from well, far from being over Robert.

I didn't have to say anything else. Didn't have to pull away, or explain. Miles understood exactly. Slowly he let go and eased back. "I'm sorry. I was just foolin' around," he apologized. "Come on; let me take you out for dinner. There's nothing edible here, and you need to eat." I gave him a scrutinizing glance. "Hey, I promised your mother I would take care of you, make sure you ate. You wouldn't want to make me a liar, would you?"

I took in a deep breath, and let it out submissively. "Okay, but just dinner, something simple, then you promise to bring me right back here."

He groaned his disapproval, rolling his head back and stretching his neck. "Fine, I'll even let you pick," he said, pulling my hand to his mouth for a quick kiss. The unmistakable heat of his energy pulsed into my knuckle at the point of contact, and my shoulders relaxed again. Lord, how I hated the affect he had on me. Loved it—but hated it.

After dinner, Miles did as promised, and delivered me back to my house. I knew he wanted to come in, but if that happened, I would surely find it very difficult to get him out later without it being awkward. No, I felt the best way to deal with it, was to just halt the evening right then.

"Thank you for dinner," I said quickly, turning to face Miles just as I stepped onto the porch.

He stopped abruptly, catching the shortness in my words. "You're welcome," he replied cautiously. There was a long pause, neither of us sure what to say.

Finally I blurted, "Well, I guess I'll see you tomorrow then."

He raised his eyebrows in surprise, and then his features changed, softened, and seemed almost sad. With a slight bow, he tugged my hand to his lips for a quick kiss. "Goodnight then, my lady."

He turned to go, when suddenly my mouth opened and a small yelp escaped. "Miles!"

He spun around instantly, a look of optimism. "Yes?"

I didn't want him to go and, in fact, really wanted him to stay. I don't know why. Perhaps it was loneliness, or just fear, but whatever it was I wanted him there with me. If I asked him to stay, he would, no doubt. However, I couldn't allow it, couldn't allow myself to indulge in the comfort of his company any more than necessary. To do so opened up the possibility of getting too close. Still, my chest hurt just at the thought of his departure. I couldn't allow him to stay with me, but I couldn't go long without seeing him either. By morning I would be going nuts for sure.

Miles smiled warmly at me as I stood there speechless, unable to think of anything to say. So, he spoke for me. "Dinner tomorrow night," he asked, "my place?"

I smiled way bigger than intended, nodding vigorously. He beamed brightly, then turned and walked away. I stepped inside, and slowly began to close the door. Just before it shut, he called over his shoulder, "By the way, you're cooking!"

I groaned with a half-smile and closed the door. Leaning my back against it, I let out a frustrated sigh. "God, I need a cold shower."

Chapter Thirty-Three
Daniela

Emerging from the bathroom, I smelled head to toe of tangerine and orange flower. Becca had slipped a body wash into the bag of clothes she'd given me at the hospital. *She sure knows how to make a girl feel better,* I thought to myself.

I turned off all of the lights, then crossed to the window and pulled the curtain back just a little, enough to peek outside undetected. The sun was now gone, but Miles's car glimmered in the moonlight below. I knew he would still be there, watching over me from a distance. It wasn't in his nature to just leave me alone. I felt bad for him. The arduous task of my safety now rested in his hands. It's a challenge he may not have fully considered when he took it on. I had assumed he would only stay an hour or two, and then go on home, but upon waking the next morning, I found he had slept in his car the entire night. Or maybe, *not* slept.

This, of course, brought on a host of guilt. I felt terrible. I'd been such a crud to him the night before, while he was, as always, sweet and patient. I decided right then I would invite him in for breakfast. I rushed downstairs and flung the front door open. But by the time I got there, he was gone.

"Crap." With a deep sigh, I closed the door and sauntered over to the kitchen to start coffee. That's all there was, just coffee. No sugar, no milk or cream. Everything that was in the fridge had expired months ago, and I hadn't made it to a grocery store to stock the house again. So, this morning it was straight black coffee for me.

I took one sip and… "Bleh! No thank you," I sneered. "If that's all there is, I'll just do without it today." My tummy let loose a terrible growl. I rubbed at it, and then glanced down at Teagan sitting patiently, waiting for any part of my breakfast, but I had none to offer. "Sorry girl," I said patting her head. "Think I'm going to be skipping breakfast this morning."

I got up and with slouched shoulders, started towards the stairs.

Unexpectedly, there was a tap at the door. I stopped, my body becoming rigid at once. There had been a time when I would have opened the door to anyone—and then a time when I would open the door to no one. Now, I only stared at the door with uncertainty. I should have been scared, at the very least, concerned for my safety, but I wasn't. Instead, I felt apprehensive for an entirely different reason. What if it was Robert? The possibility did unfathomable things to my mind and body. I stared at the door, unable to move my feet, to pull myself in that direction.

Suddenly, Teagan gave a deep, throaty growl. "What is it girl?" she watched the door with intensity, growling again.

"Dani, I know you're there, I can feel you."

"Ryan?" I yelped, quickly grabbing the knob and pulling the door open.

Teagan immediately went into a frenzy of barking and snarling!

"Teagan!" I scolded. "Stop that, it's okay girl," I shouted over her, but no amount of scolding calmed her down. Quickly taking hold of her collar, I pulled her into the pantry and closed the door.

"Sorry about that, she's usually really friendly, but she just doesn't know you like I do," I apologized. I stopped, a tiny smile curling at the corners of my mouth. Instantly, Ryan pulled me in for a hug, giving me little time to say anything else. "God Dani, I'm so glad you're okay. When I heard you'd been in an accident, I went up to the hospital, but they wouldn't let me see you. I've been so worried. "

Goodness, my senses went into overdrive. He smelled and felt so good. Incredibly familiar. Instantly, my defenses went down. Yes, he was an emovamp, but this was Ryan, my ex-boyfriend, Ryan. He loved me long before he was an emovamp, and I was entirely confident he would never hurt me. Furthermore, he was bonded to Emily, which meant I didn't have to worry about him from a romantic standpoint. He was just a good friend now. Safe.

Immediately, I pulled him the rest of the way inside. "Come in! How have you been, and how did you know I'd been in an accident?"

"Oh…your mom told my mom," he replied casually. Suddenly, he pulled me in for another hug, this time holding much longer than the first. "Mmmm…you smell like oranges."

"It's tangerines," I giggled childishly, "from my shower last night. I'm surprised you can still smell it."

"Heightened smell," he reminded.

"Oh yeah—I forgot." Stepping back, I looked at Ryan with new eyes. He had really filled out. Not just since we were kids, but even more since he had been turned. I didn't think that was possible, considering he was already very well built before. Still, eyeing him now, I had an even greater appreciation for his physique, which was impressive, even by emovamp standards.

"So, how are you doing?" he asked, his tone suddenly very concerned.

I glimpsed his face quickly, but kept mine averted. "Fine, good, I'm good—great in fact," I lied.

Ryan didn't buy it though. "I heard what happened between you and Robert."

Defenses went right back up, and immediately my tone was sharp and flooded with hurt. "I guess that makes you pretty happy, doesn't it? After all, you said he was just using me, and you were right." My face instantly stung with salty tears, and I turned my back, walking towards the kitchen.

He caught my arm. "Dani, I'm not happy. I'm really sorry he turned out to be a jerk. I never wanted you to get hurt."

I turned back and gazed solemnly into his beautiful green eyes. They were stunning. However, in that moment I wished they were still the familiar blue I once knew, those of the human boy I'd given my heart to long ago.

"Are you hungry? You want to maybe go get some breakfast or something?" he asked.

He had my hand, brushing his thumb gently across my knuckle. I glanced down and realized he was not wearing gloves as he had in the beginning. "No gloves," I remarked, caressing the top of his hand with a finger.

"No, I only had to wear them for a few months, just until I learned to control myself."

"And now? You don't have any problem controlling yourself now?"

Ryan gave a shy smile. "No, I don't have any problem now."

"Not even with me?" I asked quietly.

He lowered his voice, it was husky and warm. "No, not even with you. I could touch you all day and never have a problem with it." He held my eyes for several long seconds, then finally asked, "So—do you want to go get some breakfast—with me?"

The room stilled as I thought about his offer. Should I? "Uh...I—"

Suddenly, the front door swung open! "Morning, sweets," Miles announced, strolling in with two deli bags. "You didn't really think I would let you go without breakfast did you? It *is* the most important meal of the day you know." He flashed me an arrogant grin as he brushed past, paying little attention to my other visitor. Sitting down the bags, he began unloading to-go containers onto the counter. "Coffee?" he asked, pulling a large 'Wholly Grounds' cup from one of the sacks. "Extra cream and sugar, right?"

Sensing the awkwardness between him and Ryan, I quickly rushed towards the cup. "Oh-ma-gawd, coffee! Yes, I so need that!" I squealed, brushing past Ryan. With my cup in hand, I sipped tensely at the rich brew, glancing back and forth between the two massive men as they glared at each other.

Miles draped a possessive arm around my shoulders. "So Ryan, how do you like the change? I know it's hard to adjust to when you're not *born* an emovamp," Miles remarked with a superior tone, "but don't worry, you'll get the hang of it eventually. Like I tell all the newbies; just give it a hundred years or so—you know, baby steps." Ryan didn't answer, only glared back disdainfully.

Crap. Now I had this to deal with? Quickly, I spoke up on Ryan's behalf. "He's doing really well so far—in fact, he doesn't have to wear his gloves anymore," I pointed out confidently, though both looked a little aggravated by my meddling.

All at once, Ryan was at the door, seeing himself out. "Well, I see you have breakfast covered, so I'll leave you to eat, but will you call me later?"

"Oh—sure, okay." I started towards him for a hug, but he was already outside, pulling the door closed.

I turned on Miles, a look of disapproval. "You know, you didn't have to be rude to him. He was just worried about me."

Miles made no attempt to apologize. "I don't want you seeing or talking to him anymore."

My eyes widened with surprise. "Excuse me? That's not really any of your—"

"I don't trust him, Dani. There's something about him. I can't put my finger on it, but I don't trust him and I don't like the way he looks at you."

He claimed there was something he didn't like about Ryan, that he just couldn't put his finger on it. Well, I knew exactly what it was. I looked at Miles with a knowing smirk.

"What?" he asked.

"You're not jealous of Ryan are you?" Miles looked aggravated by my accusation.

Momentarily avoiding the question, he walked to the pantry door and let Teagan out, then came back to me and replied pompously, "That makes no sense. Ryan's bonded to someone and shouldn't have any interest in you romantically."

I raised one eyebrow. "He *shouldn't* or he *doesn't*?" I asked with intrigue.

Miles glowered back. Choosing not to answer, he quickly looked to Teagan. "You need to go outside girl? Outside?" Immediately, Teagan started into a whirlwind of ear-flapping-tail-wagging-jumping-up-and-down excitement. "Res rou do! Res rou do!" Miles encouraged in his best Scooby-Doo voice. He grabbed her leash from the counter, then snapped it on and looked to me. I eyed him playfully. "Come on, grab your coat and let's go walk your poor mutt before she bursts."

He was dodging the subject, something he was rather good at being an attorney and all. I could have pressed the matter, but felt it was a simple case of unnecessary jealousy. Even though he was an emovamp, he was *also* a man.

Chapter Thirty-Four
Daniela

"So, what are you making me?" Miles asked.

"Dinner," I replied curtly.

"I know that. What are you making for dinner?"

"Food."

He let out an annoyed sigh. "What kind of food?"

I took in a long breath, dragging out the answer. "Edible food," I teased.

"You're killing me. You do know that, right?" he asked wrapping his hands around my waist and laying his chin on my shoulder.

I giggled, nudging him away. "I can't concentrate with you breathing in my ear. Now go away before you make me burn something," I scolded playfully.

He gave a quick squeeze, a peck on the cheek, and then strolled off into the living room. I was so nervous about cooking for Miles. Not that I didn't know how to cook. On the contrary, thanks to Robert I had become quite skilled in the kitchen, but had never cooked for Miles. The idea both thrilled and terrified me. I wanted to impress him. But impress him isn't the right word really. I wanted to knock his socks off!

For tonight's meal, I had chosen an unusual dish of orange sherry pork chops. I had seen it on a cooking show and it looked simple enough. Having no car, I hadn't been able to make it to the grocery store to get all of the necessary ingredients. However, Miles's kitchen was more than adequately stocked, making it easy to find everything I needed. I had seared the pork, and was starting on the sauce which called for sherry. I opened the cabinet that held all of the vinegars and such, but there was no sherry. I then checked the liquor cabinet, but again, there was none.

I poked my head around the corner, seeking Miles. He was sprawled out on the couch, legs propped up on the coffee table, hands behind his head, eyes closed. Gracious, he looked good. "Hey—do you have any sherry?" I asked.

"I think I'm out. Do you need me to go to the store and grab some?"

I chewed at my lip. I needed it now. I'd already begun the sauce, and really didn't have time to wait. "Um…no, that's okay. I can just use a substitute."

He sat up and looked at me questioningly. "You sure? It's no problem, really."

"No…no it'll be fine," I waved the offer away.

Going back to my pan, I pondered, *hmmm…what to use?* Quickly, I grabbed the nearby carton of orange juice and measured out the amount I had needed of the sherry. "That should do it, nice and citricy!" I exclaimed quietly.

I was proud of myself. There was a time when I would have been nervous about cooking, terrified to stray even a little from a tried and true recipe. But now I was learning to improvise, go with my gut and take chances. Honestly, I was excited to see how everything would turn out. To go with the pork chops, I made a couple of vegetable side dishes and some canned buttermilk biscuits.

I popped the biscuits into the oven, covered the side dishes with a little foil to keep them hot and stirred the bright orange sauce again. As I waited for the sauce to reduce and thicken, I peeked around the corner again, spying on Miles. He had resumed his original position, laid back and relaxed. The stereo was on, playing a lovely selection of classical music. In the last week of staying here with him, I found he liked to listen to it often. I thought it odd for him, but also a charming characteristic.

With my head leaned against the door frame, I'd been dreamily watching him for some time, scanning over every part of his gorgeous body, when suddenly he opened his eyes and looked at me (sensing my stare no doubt). His gaze was intense, fixed, drawing me in, and not allowing me to look away no matter how hard I tried. I smiled shyly, feeling like such a juvenile for gawking. How could any girl help herself though? I mean, he was absolutely beautiful.

Almost instantly my nose was filled with a smell I knew well. Something was burning. "Oh crap!" I exclaimed, rushing to the oven. I pulled the pan out, waving my hand over the blackened rolls, fanning the smoke. I let out a frustrated sigh. "Great."

Just then, my attention was caught by the splattering mess of orange sauce as it bubbled wildly, coating everything nearby in speckles of citric goo. "Freaking hell!" I whispered hysterically, grabbing several paper towels. Wiping at the sticky mess was pointless, and made worse by the fact that the paper towels stuck to everything.

"Babe—you okay in there?" Miles called from the living room.

Swiftly, I stuck my head around the corner. "Yeah—yes, everything's fine—just peachy!" I exclaimed with a strained smile. I went back to the mess at hand, scolding myself quietly. "Well, not so much peachy as it is orangey."

Once I had everything clean and sparkly again, I turned my attention to the food. It was a disaster. Well, except for the vegetables. "Okay Dani, you're just going to have to do some creative garnishing," I told myself. I plated the food, arranged a few small sprigs of parsley, some orange peel and then sprinkled the top with fresh chives. Looking at the gloppy sauce and burnt biscuits, I let out a groan. "There is no garnish in the world that is going to help this mess."

And I was right.

Miles sat staring at the plate. He tried to look excited, but I could see the dread tugging at the corners of his mouth. "What is it?" he asked cautiously.

Torn

"Orange sherry pork chops," I replied with poise. "Well, since you were out of sherry, then I guess it's just orange juice pork chops."

He raised his eyebrows, giving a nod of interest and uncertainty. "Well, they look just, um…well, they seem…they smell just, um…" he stuttered. After a long pause, he managed, "The orange peel was a nice touch."

I smiled my gratitude for his kind words. Truthfully, as I eyed my own plate, I wondered how anyone could eat it. It looked as if an orange had vomited on the pork chops and given birth to hockey pucks.

Miles cut a section of pork, and raised it to his mouth. He looked at me hesitantly, but then slowly bit down on the slimy orange bite. As he began to chew, he tried to maintain a smile, but I could see detest in his eyes.

"How is it?" I asked. Really this was a redundant question. I knew it was bad. I'd gotten a little of the orange sauce on my finger while dishing up the plates and made the mistake of licking it off. The taste was beyond dreadful.

I could have told him I had already called for pizza to be delivered, but didn't. I wanted to see just how much I could torture him before he gave in and admitted they were terrible.

He continued to chew, then took a long drink of wine and swallowed. The look on his face was priceless, like he'd swallowed a frog. I tried to hide the laughter in my eyes, but couldn't.

He squinted at me. "What?" I asked defensively.

"Aren't you going to try it, dear?"

"Oh—I will in a minute, I just like watching you."

"Well, by all means, don't let me be the only one enjoying this wonderful creation. Have some," he insisted, gesturing to my plate.

Crap! He knew he'd been had. "You know, I filled up on bread while I was cooking, so maybe in a little bit."

He stood up and came to my side of the table. "Oh, I'm sure you can manage one bite. You know, just a taste," he said, forking a piece of the slimy pork and raising it to my mouth. The smell alone was enough to make me gag.

"No, really, I'm so full, I just couldn't—"

"I insist," he said as he plunged the bite at my mouth. Immediately, I closed my lips together, which resulted in orange sauce going all over my face. Miles looked down and snickered with an apologetic smile. "Oops—I'm sorry, Dani, I didn't mean to—"

Instantly, I silenced his words with a handful of the sauce, smearing it from his forehead to chin. He looked stunned, but then a huge, evil grin spread wide on his orange covered face.

I can't explain exactly what happened next, only to say that it ended with me straddled on top of him, smearing a combination of orange sauce, butter and cream corn in his hair! We laughed so hard, and for so long, that finally, I collapsed with exhaustion, curling up in his sticky arms. He turned on his side, scooting down so that we were face to face. We were still giggling quietly.

He gently rubbed his thumb across my cheek, wiping away a glop of orange. Our laughter died down as our stare intensified. "You're so beautiful," he said. His tone was hushed and soft.

I gazed into his emerald eyes, admiring the topaz flakes within them. Slowly, the distance between our faces lessened, his breath becoming warm on my lips. Miles was so focused. He knew what he wanted. My heart pounded, chest ached, and body shivered uncontrollably. Tenderly his lips bumped against mine and they parted ever so slightly, welcoming his mouth. Miles saw the invitation, and moved to accept it, when suddenly, the doorbell sounded.

I bolted upright. "Pizza's here!" I exclaimed with relief.

Miles sat up with a look of frustration, but then he smiled. "Why don't you go take a shower and get cleaned up while I get the pizza," he offered. I nodded happily, and then sprang for the bathroom.

The hot water poured over me as I shampooed away the last of the orange goop from my hair (and the anxiety from my mind). I was so relieved that the pizza guy had interrupted us. "Lord Dani, what are you doing?" I asked aloud. "You cannot allow this to happen, you can't get involved with him romantically," I scolded myself.

"Dani—I brought you some extra towels and one of my shirts," Miles called from over the rushing water.

I froze. He was right there! The only thing between us was a set of glass shower doors. Though they were etched and painted with a beautiful abstract design which allotted some cover, it didn't make me feel any better. I could still see the dark, hazy figure of him with a certain degree of detail. "Thanks!" I yelped.

"Do you need anything else?"

"No, thank you," I shouted tensely.

"I could wash your back," he offered playfully. Suddenly, his figure moved closer, and the shower door began to open slightly.

"NO!" I exclaimed with a giggle, grabbing the door and holding it closed.

"You sure?" he teased, jiggling the door again.

"Yes!"

"Yes, you *want* me to wash your back?"

"NO! GET OUT!" I laughed, holding the door as firmly as possible. I could still here him laughing as trailed off down the hall.

Later, when I emerged from the shower, I found several fluffy towels and one of Miles's long dress shirts on the vanity. I dried off and slipped into the fresh cotton shirt. I wasn't petite by any means, but Miles, like so many emovamps, was very tall and exceptionally wide in the shoulders and chest. I could practically swim in his clothes. My hair was still quite short, so I towel dried it, leaving it messy and scattered. I wanted to look as unappealing as possible.

Walking back into the dining room, I expected to find the gloppy orange mess waiting for me to clean it up, but Miles had already taken care of it. *Where is he?* I wondered. I checked the kitchen, then the living room, but he wasn't there. The pizza box sat untouched on the coffee table, along with two glasses and a bottle of wine, but no Miles.

I curled up on the couch, pulling his enormous shirt over my knees, tucking them against my chest. My skin was still slightly moist from the shower and I had become chilled almost immediately after leaving the warmth of the bathroom.

I was eyeing the bottle of wine and debating helping myself to a glass, when suddenly, Miles bounded over the back of the couch, plopping down beside me and throwing a very warm arm over my shoulder. "Ahhhh....Now we're both all nice and clean," he exclaimed.

I let out a girlish giggle (I couldn't help it), and looked wide-eyed at him. He was wearing only a pair of pajama bottoms, his hair and chest still damp from the shower he'd taken.

Muh. Dear. God.

All I could do was stare, like some stroke victim, with gargled sounds my only means of communication.

He pulled me tight to his side, wrapping both arms snuggly around my shoulders. I had been cold just moments before, but had not been shivering. Now, I was more than adequately warm, but trembling terribly.

Miles's bouncing around on the couch had caused my shirt to ride up slightly, and I nervously pulled it back down, attempting to cover my feet as well. Miles was quick to sabotage my efforts though. "You're cold—come here and I'll warm you up," he offered. Before I could refuse, he took hold of my waist and pulled me into his lap, causing my legs to come loose from beneath the shelter of the shirt.

Cuddled in his arms, mere millimeters from his face, I knew I was in big trouble. I giggled and resisted at first, squirming slightly, but the heat of his body felt so good, the fight didn't last long. It seemed that wriggling around was of no help anyway, he only tightened his grip with each movement. At last I gave up and relaxed into him. How was I to resist? After all, he *was* very persuasive.

"There now—isn't that better?" he asked.

For him? No doubt. For me? Well, let's just say, the crazy woman in my mind had been resurrected, and was already in a full uproar.

I leaned my head against the crook of his neck and let out a submissive sigh, "Yes, it's better." He smelled only of soap, and him—warm, clean and sensual. It was a combination I liked more than I wanted to admit. Tilting my head down a bit, I peeked at his chest and tummy. His skin was kissed gently by the sun, and looked almost velvety. I nearly had to tuck my hands between my legs to keep from running my finger tips over his smooth chest.

Miles on the other hand was not so reserved with my skin. His hands wandered skillfully, uninhibited, gliding softly over my knee, down the length of my shin, around my ankle, then slowly back up, caressing my calf. All I kept thinking was, *thank God I shaved my legs!*

Suddenly, his hand slid all the way up, finding the underside of my thigh, under the hem of his shirt! Instantly, I had hold of his hand, halting its ascent. I sat back and looked at him with pleading eyes, ones that wished him to keep going, but also begged him to stop.

"I'm sorry," he apologized.

I fought hard to withhold the tears, my voice quivering from the strain. "Please Miles—my heart—it's just not ready for this—*I'm* not ready for this."

"I know, I understand, and I can be patient."

"That's just it. I don't know if I'll ever be ready. I feel like my soul has been shattered. I don't know if I will ever heal and I don't want you hanging onto me because I've somehow misled you into believing—"

Miles placed a hand against my mouth, then softly traced my bottom lip with the pad of his thumb. "You have in no way, done anything to mislead me. In time your heart *will* heal, and I will be here, as always. I have nothing but time, my love."

I caught his eyes and held them firmly. "But *I* don't."

He gently glided the back of his hand down my cheek, and whispered, "Well, I hope to change that some day." I had no reply. I only sat there silently, thinking, contemplating—hoping. Could it ever be? Would the day ever come when my heart would heal and I could finally, truly love again?

"Dani—where's the marble necklace I gave you?"

His question brought all thought to a sudden halt. "What?"

"The necklace I gave you, where is it?" he asked again.

I swallowed hard. The question made my throat tighten up. "Why—why do you want to know?" I asked defensively.

He looked at me oddly. "Did you lose it again?"

"No."

"Then where is it?" I chewed at my lip nervously. I knew exactly where it was, and although I should have had no reason not to trust him with its whereabouts, something deep in my gut told me I shouldn't. *Hide it away...* The Oracles words echoed in my head. "Dani?" Miles waved his hand before my face.

"Huh?"

"Are you going to tell me where the necklace is?"

I looked him in the eye, took a deep breath, and then calmly replied, "No."

He raised his eyebrows with disbelief. "And why not?"

"Why do you want to know? Why now, why all of a sudden is it so important?" I blurted, as if accusing him of something.

"Easy, sweets, I was just curious. I like to see you wearing it, that's all," he defended gently. "What's going on? Your acting really strange and you're emotional signature just went nuts. Is there something wrong—did something happen?"

Several long seconds went by. "Miles—I think I'm supposed to see the Oracle."

His expression was instantly staid. "Why do you think that?" he asked, his tone equally serious.

"I dreamed of her."

"What did she say?"

"She said, '*come to me child.*' And I keep hearing her in my head, all the time. I feel like I am being pulled to her," I explained. I knew it sounded ridiculous. It was, after all, just a dream and the ranting of my mind, which had not been sound for quite some time. It wasn't exactly enough to convince him I should travel thousands of miles away. In fact, he should have been laughing at me—but he wasn't. He was staring at me with calm and seriousness.

"The necklace has something to do with it, doesn't it?" he asked.

"I think so."

He didn't hesitate, didn't ask for more information, and didn't scrutinize my reasoning. Instead, he simply took my hands, gently kissed them, and replied, "Then I shall take you to see the Oracle."

Chapter Thirty-Five
Daniela

"Miss Moretti, so good to have you back," Andrew exclaimed as Miles and I approached the check-in desk.

I returned his smile quietly, trying hard to hide my horror of being back at the *Bath Priory Hotel and Spa*. This was the same hotel Robert and I had stayed in while here before. A fact Miles was aware of, but failed to inform me of until we were nearly here.

Miles had insisted on getting me to England as fast as possible. Consequently, it meant taking whatever was available, which at the time wasn't much. Somerset was in the middle of its annual food festival. With the Oracle nearby, and massive amounts of tasty food, the place was overflowing with emovamps. As I was informed, this was one of their most cherished yearly events.

The only reason he'd even been able to get us a room anywhere, was because a colleague of his had already secured reservations. He and his wife had planned to attend the local food fair for their 200th anniversary. Miles said it had been very hard to talk him into giving us the reservation, but in the end, his friend was '*persuaded*' to help us out. I have a feeling the man's wife had not been as understanding.

Miles had pointed out that I could have just waved my ring in the direction of almost any emovamp and probably gotten my choice of places to stay, but I hated the thought of exploiting it, and did not feel entitled to any special treatment the ring might allow. I was not royalty and did not wish to be treated as such.

So this left us here, at the one place in the world I never wanted to see again, a place which held many memories of Robert and me, memories I wanted to forget. Standing here now, Andrew bubbling away with happy English greetings, I wanted to just throw up all over him.

At least we weren't in the same room Robert and I had stayed in previously. Instead, we were in the Magnolia suite, one floor down. It was a splendid room, divine by anyone's standards. Delicate bee motifs blended elegantly into cornflower blue walls, complimented by dainty floral curtains. The feeling was calm and relaxing. It was a large, brightly lit room, which donned a spectacular view of the garden. Nearly in full bloom, it was a view I wanted nothing to do with, and would avoid at all cost.

It was late when we arrived, and so Miles had ventured off downstairs to rustle-up some dinner for the two of us. In the meantime, I unpacked the last of my clothes and placed them in one of the dressers. Seeing as how I didn't have to go through the council to see the Oracle this time, I hadn't packed nearly as much, just a few days' worth.

Hesitantly I walked to the window and peered out into the darkened garden. Deep anguish filled me, and I quickly stepped away.

Just then, Miles returned, pushing a cart inside that was brimming with several silver hooded trays. "Room service," he announced. Immediately, he looked at me, his smile vanishing. "Dani, what's wrong?"

"Nothing, nothing, I'm fine?"

"No you're not, you're crying," he said, bringing me a tissue.

I hadn't even realized I was, but when I did, the tears fell in waves. "Thanks," I said, dabbing at my eyes.

"How about some dinner," he said, lifting the lid from one of the trays. The food looked and smelled heavenly, but I honestly had no appetite at the moment.

"You go ahead and eat without me. I'm suddenly not very hungry."

Gently, Miles took my hands and gave them a kiss. "How are you feeling? Do you need a little extra energy, maybe a little pick-me-up kiss?"

"No, I'm fine." He narrowed his eyes. "Really, I'm fine," I assured.

"You're sure? You look extremely worn out and I *am* here to serve your every need. You have but to ask." He swayed forward slightly, his breath tickling the top of my lips as he spoke.

I smiled, but then pushed back gently. "No—seriously, I'm fine," I insisted. "I think I'm just going to take a shower while you eat, if that's okay?"

"Of course, princess," he said with a slight bow.

I rolled my eyes and swatted at him playfully. "For the last time, stop calling me that." He only laughed, then took a chair and started into the food.

After my shower, I dried off then slipped into my night clothes. Frumpy sweats and an oversized t-shirt with coffee stains on the front (intentionally placed coffee stains). When I'd packed for the trip, I was very careful of the items I chose. Specifically, I picked unappealing clothes that were sure to repel Miles. At least, that was my plan. I messed up my stumpy hair, scrubbed all the make-up from my face, then put on a big thick pair of wool socks, and casually walked out of the bathroom.

The look on Miles's face said it all. He'd been expecting a regal, sexy princess, but instead found a catastrophe of a commoner. I struggled to keep from laughing, maintaining a nonchalant demeanor.

"Shower's all yours," I announced.

Miles let out a sigh of disappointment, then jumped up and headed into the bathroom. Within seconds the sound of rushing water filled the suite, followed by loud singing. I sat down in one of the chairs, and smiled distantly, gazing towards the darkened window, remembering back to the last night Robert and I were here.

"*You dance beautifully,*" Robert said.

"*Not really, you just happen to lead really well,*" I corrected. Robert gave me an endearing smile, shaking his head. "*What?*"

"*Nothing—it's only, I find it funny that you can't take a compliment,*" he remarked.

"*I can so take a compliment—when I think it's true.*"

"*That's the problem, you never believe it's true, even though it is. For someone so beautiful and talented, I just don't understand why you have such a low opinion of yourself.*"

"*It's not that I have a low opinion of myself. I just don't think there's anything all that exceptional about me. You say I dance beautifully, but in reality, I'm just keeping up with you and have managed to not trip and fall yet. That doesn't make me a beautiful dancer.*"

"*You'll just never see it will you?*" he asked.

I looked at him questioningly. "*See what?*"

"*How exceptional you are.*"

The pain of remembering Robert was too much, and I broke down crying again. "Damn him," I sobbed. "Exceptional? Yeah, I see just how '*exceptional*' I am." Angry tears stung my face, anger matched only by the hatred building within the walls of my chest.

Suddenly, the sounds of the shower quieted, as well as Miles's obnoxious singing. I quickly grabbed some tissue and attempted to clean up my face, but no amount of Kleenex was going to remove the red puffiness around my eyes. Within minutes he came strolling out of the bathroom, wearing, of course, only his pajama bottoms. I needed another shower just looking at him.

Miles flexed and stretched, then shook his head creating a shower of water everywhere. Taking in an excited breath, I bit down on my lip nervously. He caught my eyes with his, well aware of just how much I was enjoying the show. He had an unfair advantage, one that allowed him to know what I was feeling. It's a

248

terrible thing to be betrayed by your own feelings. With a smile, I let out a long sigh, accompanied by an equally long eye roll.

He returned my smile with a devilish grin. "Dani, sweets, you have no idea how much I've looked forward to this all day. So, how do you want to do this," he asked, eyeing the bed, "are you a snuggle-first kind of girl, or just a go-right-to-sleep type? Personally, I like a long, slow back-scratching first, then a little snuggle time, followed by—" I threw a pillow in his face, hard, knocking the wind from his words. It was followed by an extra blanket.

"*You'll* be sleeping on the couch," I clarified.

He glanced at the divan with contempt, then back to me, not seeing the joke. "Good night," I said with an arched brow.

He gave a surrendering smirk and bowed slightly. "Good night then, la mia belle."

I quickly climbed into bed and pulled the covers around me, my back to him. Though I couldn't see him, I could hear his disapproval as he settled down into the petite sofa. He tossed, turned and let out several groans and sighs of discomfort. I remained still though, back turned, eyes closed, and eventually drifted off to sleep.

I had expected to have a dream of the black-eyed man again, but didn't. In fact, I didn't dream at all, which left me a little disappointed. I awoke in the middle of the night, restless and worried about the coming day. I didn't know what I was going to say to the Oracle, and was apprehensive that she would find me discourteous for wasting her time. She would want the ring back no doubt.

I tossed and turned a few times, and then sat up. As my eyes adjusted to the dark, I peered towards Miles. He was stretched out on the couch, his long massive frame cramped, and feet hanging over the edge. I felt terrible, and debated waking him with an invitation to share the other half of my bed.

"Can't sleep?" His question came softly through the dark.

"No—you?"

"No."

"Are you nervous about tomorrow?" I asked.

"No—you?"

"Yeah," I admitted.

He sat up, stretching to ease the discomfort caused by the small sofa. "Don't be. Everything will be okay. I'll be with you the entire time, I promise."

I smiled warmly, then pulled back the covers and gave the mattress an inviting pat. Even in the dark, I could see the brilliant white of his teeth when he smiled. He quickly accepted my invitation and climbed in. "Just—behave yourself," I warned, turning on my side. He scooted up to my back, draped a warm arm over my waist, and pulled me against him. I should have resisted, but didn't. It felt good to be in his arms. Felt safe. I snuggled into him with a smile, and immediately fell asleep once more.

Chapter Thirty-Six
Daniela

When we arrived at the castle, I didn't know what to expect. I wasn't even sure the Oracle would remember me, let alone take the time to talk. She was, after all, a very busy woman. Besides, I was Daniela Moretti, the jobless, hapless, hopeless nobody from Oklahoma. So, to say the welcome I received was surprising would be a huge understatement.

There were dozens of emovamps gathered all around the castle grounds when we pulled up, visitors for the festival who had come to experience the Oracles incredible energy or perhaps get lucky enough to get a glimpse of the regal woman. Everyone was moving about the grounds, conversing blissfully amongst themselves when Miles took my hand and pulled me from the car.

All of a sudden they stopped with eyes wide, each one focused entirely on me. Then, like something from a fairytale, everyone bowed their heads respectfully. Miles straightened his shoulders proudly, and with a wide grin, escorted me towards the castle.

As we approached the main doors, I was overcome with a feeling of peace and serenity. Instantly I recognized the tranquility of the Oracle. I had felt her energy here during my first visit, but it was nowhere near as strong that day. Today, I didn't even have to touch anything; her radiance was humming throughout the property with great strength.

When we reached the entrance, immediately the doors swung open and two massive guards stepped forth. Both bowed down on one knee, lowering their heads. Right away Christy was there, greeting us with a long, courteous bow as well.

I should have been excited or flattered by these royal greetings, but looking down at the jeans and t-shirt I was wearing it was very evident I was honestly nothing more than a commoner. There was nothing special about me and certainly nothing royal (unless you count my being a *royal* pain in the ass). I didn't like being treated as someone of importance. '*Important, royal, worthy*', all words that did not pertain to me, and precisely the reason I had decided to give back the ring.

"Good day, Your Highness," Christy exclaimed. "Her Highness, Terézia, awaits your presence."

My eyes widened. "But how—I didn't…" I turned to Miles, "Did you tell them we were coming?"

He shook his head with a knowing smile. "Nope."

"Then how did she—"

"If you will, follow me please," Christy instructed, never answering my question.

As we walked through the castle, we were again greeted with a bow from every guard we passed. Some gave only a slight tip of the head, while others fell to one knee. Though I endured it all with a convincing smile, they had to have sensed how much I disliked it.

We were taken to the same parlor as before. When we arrived, the two massive guards looked down on me, then stepped aside and knelt. I stifled the urge to roll my eyes as Christy opened the door and motioned for us to enter.

On my previous visit here, the room had been dark and stuffy, a fire burning, heating the room to almost an uncomfortable level. Today though, it was just the opposite. The parlor was brightly lit, with all curtains and windows open, a breeze drifting in, sweetened by the smell of hyacinths from the gardens below.

"Daniela!" Terézia's voice sounded almost strained with relief as she immediately rushed up, embracing me in a warm hug. "Oh, sweet child, I've worried so."

Something about her tone brought forth a wealth of emotion I'd been holding back, and instantly I clung to her tightly, sobbing into her shoulder. She hugged me a little longer, then leaned back and looked on me with fondness. Her eyes glittered brightly with deep emerald hues, even prettier than I had remembered. Her hair was silver, shiny, like spun silk, and skin much smoother than was last I saw her. She looked healthy, more vibrant and much younger.

"Your Highness," Miles greeted, extending a bow to Terézia.

"Mr. Chadwick," she replied short, "thank you for bringing my daughter, but your company is not required for the duration of the afternoon. If you like, you may return to your hotel and I will have her escorted back."

Miles and I both exchanged shocked looks. Well, I did more so than Miles. Number one: I was astounded that she would refer to me as her daughter. Two: I was floored at her abrupt dismissal of Miles. He appeared more wounded by her cold treatment than shocked, and I can't say I blamed him.

"Can he not stay with me?" I asked quickly.

With no explanation, she replied, "No."

I opened my mouth to argue, but Miles interjected politely. "It's alright, Dani."

I went to him immediately. "But you promised to stay with me."

"I won't leave the castle grounds, I promise. When you're done, I'll be at the front, waiting," he assured.

Impatiently Terézia scolded, "Let him go, we have no need of his company today."

Her demeanor was so different this time, not quite the warm and inviting woman I remembered, at least, when it came to Miles that is. By the look on Miles's face, I knew he'd picked up on it as well.

Miles gave me a confident smile, but I could still see the rejection and hurt in his eyes. With another bow to us both, he turned and walked out. Immediately Adalmund and Godwin, the Oracles two closest guards, materialized out of nowhere and stepped out of the room, followed by Christy, who bowed and then closed the doors, leaving us completely alone.

I turned to the Oracle. Her face was kind, smiling, but held a sense of regret. "My apologies for dismissing your friend so callously, but I've no time for him, and have many important matters to discuss with you. Details he cannot know—*no one else can know*," she stressed.

A violent chill rushed up my spine and I suddenly felt nauseous with fear. "What sort of matters?" I asked tensely.

Instantly, her features softened and she took my hand, giving it a pat. "Come daughter—let us have tea," she said, leading me to a plush, cozy sofa.

Again, I was taken aback by this affectionate term. "Why do you call me daughter?" I asked.

She smiled warmly. "Does it bother you?"

"No, of course not. I just don't understand why you would call me that."

Terézia gestured to the tea set on the table. "Pour us some tea, and I will explain." I nodded, and did as instructed. "Being Oracle is —" she hesitated, "a very demanding station. Children require a great deal of time and energy not often afforded with my position as it is."

"You never had any children?" I asked with surprise.

With a deep sigh, she looked away with great sadness, then quickly turned back with a gentle smile and wet eyes. "You could say I have been blessed with several children. Over the years I have come upon a few individuals whom I felt a great connection to and deemed them family—in a way, I adopted them as my children."

I stared at her blankly, "And you chose me as one of them?" I asked with surprise.

"Yes. I knew the moment I met you, we were family."

"How many children do you have then?" Now that I knew she picked her children all the time, I didn't feel so overwhelmed by the labeling. Being the oldest emovamp in the world, I imagined she had hundreds of adopted offspring.

"Including you, only four." I smiled taunt, trying to suppress my sudden urge to vomit. Terézia's hand was on mine quickly though, and all desire to purge vanished. "What is it, my child?" she asked.

I lowered my head, unable to look her in the eye. "I'm sorry, Your Highness, but you've made a mistake. I am not worthy of such an honor," I said, removing the ring from my finger and pressing it into her palm.

She lifted my chin. "Your worthiness is not a matter for you to decide. I chose you as one of my children. Regardless of what you do or say, you are now my family. You will never be looked at or treated the same, no matter if you return the ring or not. Word of your being one of my heirs has spread throughout our society. You are a princess, of the House of Galbraith, and I would no sooner remove that title than remove my own hand." Gently, she slipped the silver band onto my finger. "Keep the ring and wear it proudly. You are going to do many great things in your lifetime, and deserve the title and benefits of my lineage—trust me Daniela, I am never wrong."

Her statement was controversial, and though I wanted to debate it further, I chose not to today. Today, there were more important things to discuss. Besides, something told me it would have been a pointless argument anyway.

"Now, let's have our tea before it gets cold; shall we?" she asked.

I smiled, handed her one of the cups, then picked up mine and took a quick sip. The taste of apple cinnamon and chamomile danced across my tongue bringing forth a sigh of discontent. It was yet another reminder of the previous visit with Robert.

"Such pain," Terézia remarked. I gazed at her through heartbroken tears. "In all my life, I have scarcely ever encountered such a broken heart as yours."

"It hurts so much—all the time. It's been more than six months and I still can't move past it." Suddenly, I was spilling my guts to her, explaining everything that had happened between Robert and me, barely taking a breath between sentences and using up half of her tissues. Kindly she listened with the patience only a mother possessed, never once interrupting or appearing uninterested. She was attentive and highly focused on every detail of my story.

When I came to the part about the necklace glowing, she suddenly stopped me. "Your soul has been torn," she remarked.

I nodded. "Most days I don't even want to go on living."

"Ahhh, but you must. That's what life is. It's enduring all things, good or bad, struggling, pushing and hurting. If it was all perfect, it wouldn't be life—it would be death."

"But how can I go on living without love?"

"Sweet Daniela, you have love, an abundance of it, so much that you cannot possibly imagine."

My voice stiffened with hurt. "Not *his* love. His is the only love I ever wanted. I thought I had it, but I was a fool."

Terézia sat up straight and took in a deep breath. "Daniela, what do you know of our history?"

"Only that you were created by an ancient civilization thousands of years ago—that you were created to purify humans."

"Well, that's one *theory* among the Pulire. However, that is only a fragment of our true history." She looked around the room. "Come, help me close all of the windows and curtains," she instructed. I did as told, feeling like we were sneaky teenagers about to do something we weren't supposed to do. Terézia sat down, then lit a large candle on the table and I turned out all of the lights. Once all curtains were drawn, I took a seat beside her again. She turned to me and extended her hands. Without hesitation I laid my palms against hers. "Good—Daniela, I have many gifts, and today I am going to share one of them with you."

"Okay."

"I'm going to share my sight with you, allow you to see the visions in my mind. What I am about to reveal, no other human has ever seen. Very few of my own kind even know our true history. It

256

has been hidden away for nearly two thousand years," she explained.

The entire prospect of this terrified me. I should have been on the verge of vomiting, but for whatever reason, was completely calm. "I'm ready," I replied quietly.

She took a deep, cleansing breath, and closed her eyes. Suddenly it was as if fire shot into my hands! Instinctively I tried to pull away, but she held tight. Almost as quickly as the pain began, it ended, and calming pleasure seeped forth, pushing out all discomfort. I closed my eyes, instantly filled with visions, images of a time long ago.

A warm wind swept over me, and I could hear the rustling of grass in the pasture before us. Terézia's beautiful and unique English accent sounded clearly in my ears as I watched the story unfold.

"A great many lifetimes ago, there lived a noble man, Ceredig ap Cunedda, son of King Cunedda ap Edern. According to legend, Ceredig arrived in what is now known as Wales, with his father's family. Immediately upon their arrival, they were called to help ward off Irish invaders. Ceredig accepted the call without hesitation, and they were, of course, successful. As a reward for Ceredig's bravery, his father gave him the southernmost part of the territories in northwest Wales, re-conquered from the Irish. The realm came to be called the kingdom of *Ceredigion,* after him."

I could see the spectacular kingdom in perfect detail stretched forth for miles. I wanted to reach out, caress the lush grass of the meadow which was beautiful, hilly, green with life and absolutely breathtaking.

"The kingdom of Ceredigion prospered over the years, and soon Ceredig took a wife. He was deeply in love with her, and devoted in every way a man could be. He lavished her with gifts, affection, anything and everything she desired was hers. No request too large or small for his queen. But then one spring, as was the king's duty, Ceredig was called away and remained abroad for many months. Upon the completion of his task, he gathered up his men, and began the journey home. He longed to see his wife, but wishing to surprise her, he sent no word of his impending return. Upon his unannounced arrival late one night, the king was devastated to find his beloved jewel in the arms of another man. Ravaged with pain and heartbreak, he lashed out in a jealous rage and slaughtered both lovers while they were still in his bed."

"He killed the woman he loved?" I asked with horror.

"Yes, as was his right as king," she replied grimly. "But taking her life did not remove the pain. Months went by and he was unable to mend his heart. He couldn't eat, couldn't sleep. His only thoughts were of her and her betrayal. Finally, one night, overcome with heartbreak and despair, Ceredig fell to his knees and cried out to the heavens for mercy!"

Just then, in that very moment, *I* could feel Ceredig's pain. It was terrible. Terrible, and all *too* familiar. "What happened?" I asked nervously.

"Someone heard him," she replied. A cold chill swept over me. I stilled, watching and listening to what happened next. With a sudden flash of brilliant blue light, a beautiful angel descended from the sky, a woman so fair, so painfully exquisite, Ceredig could barely look upon her. Terézia's voice was full of admiration as she spoke. "The ancient scholars of my people believed her to be the goddess of Love, Aphrodite."

"What do you wish of me?" Aphrodite asked him.

Terézia sighed, holding back her urge to cry. "Ceredig threw himself at her feet and begged the loving goddess to show him the utmost mercy. No longer able to withstand the unbearable pain within his chest, he pleaded with her to remove his heart. The kind goddess took pity on him, knowing herself what it is to love so deeply. She stroked his cheek lovingly, then leaned in and kissed him with tender passion only a goddess could posses. When she withdrew, Ceredig was so moved he began to cry. Aphrodite reached out and caught the first tear as it fell from his cheek. Then, opening her hand, she extended it to him. There, in her palm was a tiny crystal. The Crystal of Anobaith—the Crystal of Despair."

Instantly, I knew what she spoke of. "The marble! That's the tiny crystal inside the marble, isn't it?"

She nodded. "Yes. It was the key to our beginning. Aphrodite produced a jewel encrusted silver dagger from her robes, and then gave it and the crystal to Ceredig. She told him that in order to remove the pain from his heart, he must pluck it out. Meaning, he had to pierce his heart with the dagger and place the crystal inside before the last beat. The power of the crystal would fill his heart with great energy, pushing out the heartbreaking pain and giving him new life—life with the ability to sense all emotion in everything. He would be able to *feel* whether a woman's feelings for him were true. He would never suffer the pain of deceit again. Without a moment's hesitation, Ceredig did as the goddess instructed him, thrusting the sharp silver blade into his chest. He collapsed to the ground almost instantly, and then with a final, agonizing cry, pushed the crystal deep into the walls of his heart."

I sat straight up, eyes open wide with revelation. "He was the first emovamp," I exclaimed with hushed excitement.

"The first Pulire," she corrected sweetly.

"Sorry, Pulire," I apologized, closing my eyes again.

She continued warmly. "When he awoke, he was strong, powerful, possessing every gift known to us and able to discern all emotion in anyone and everything. Aphrodite kissed his cheek, and then gave him a new name: Caradoc, which means 'love'. She explained that, should he find a mate who truly loved him, and whom he loved in return, he could make her *like* him. But then she warned. If the mate he chose did not love him, no matter how much he loved her, if he tried to turn her and it was not *true love* she possessed—she would die. It was the one stipulation that would ensure he would never be deceived again."

"That's why you have to possess true love to be turned."

"Yes."

I chewed my bottom lip, taking in all of this new information; ancient information, kept hidden, and Heaven only knows for how many centuries. Information even Miles and Robert didn't know. I felt privileged and overwhelmed by her willingness to share such a secret with me. Then my stomach sank. She was telling me all of this for a reason. She wasn't sharing it with me because she was fond of me, she was about to reveal something that would change everything.

"Daniela, the crystal of despair was formed out of heartbreak, its power created from the pain and anguish Caradoc felt. Once he used it, its power was gone. The crystal remained in his heart for the next fifteen-hundred years, until his death. His children took great care in removing it from his body, and though it was no longer active, they knew there was a possibility its power could someday return, and would be highly prized by any of their kind. So they hid it away, kept it safe among them for many hundreds of years. Eventually it fell into the hands of a great Japanese emperor, who entrusted its care to his daughter, a beautiful and talented lamp-work artist. She delicately spun the marble around it as a means to hide it, and then passed it on to the man she secretly loved."

"Miles," I gasped.

"Yes," she replied. "And now that it belongs to you, it has been awakened."

"But how? Why after all this time?" I asked.

"You were wearing the necklace the moment your heart was broken. Your pain, all of your grief from losing Robert was so terrible that in the moment your soul was torn, the crystal surged to life once again."

I sat back and opened my eyes, a look of terror. "What does that mean?"

She opened her eyes, gazing deeply into mine. "It means that the crystal lives, and is capable of many things, not all of them good." Her face was kind, but there was suddenly a longing in the depths of her eyes, a forbidden desire. Then blinking it away, she asked cautiously, "I trust you did not bring it with you?"

"No. Somehow I knew not to."

"You did right. This would be the worst place for it. Now that the crystal has reawakened, it must never fall into the hands of a Pulire. To do so could be disastrous for all."

"Why?" I asked.

"It would give them unimaginable power. Power so vast, anyone who possessed it would be invincible. No one would stand a chance against them. *No one*," she stressed. "Not even an army of Pulire. It must be hidden away, somewhere safe. If word of its awakening ever gets out, there are many who will stop at nothing to possess it."

"What good is hiding it? You can all feel its energy."

"That's why I had you bind it. The elements around it will mask its energy. It will still wield the same power; it just won't be detectable by any of my kind. The handkerchief was Robert's, the man who broke your heart. Your hair is a semblance of you. And the ruby petals of the anemone are the flowers of Aphrodite, formed from the blood of her dying lover. All of those components combined have formed a barrier around the energy. So long as it is not opened, it will remain shielded.

My voice quivered as I struggled to maintain my composure. "Then take it, lock it away so that no one can find it," I begged.

"Oh, sweet Daniela, I wish that were possible, but I dare not even look upon it."

"But why? I know you would never misuse it," I argued.

She looked on me with deep compassion. "I wish I could say that was true, but in reality, I don't know what I would do with it. I want to believe I would only use it for good, but an object so powerful will lead even the strongest of people to make bad decisions. Power can be good, but more often than not, it is a terrible curse and one that leads to destruction," she said with great sadness.

"Then tell me what to do with it, tell me where to hide it."

She patted my hand gently. "I cannot. I can have no knowledge of where it is. No one can. Only you can know its whereabouts, Daniela. As a human, there is no danger for you to have it. You possessing it *is,* in fact, the safest place for it."

"Of course it is," I grumbled with irritation, "It's not like I'm going to become an emovamp anytime soon—sorry, Pulire," I corrected dryly.

"Daughter, there's something you should know about the crystal, something that could change your life forever."

Instantly, my chest tightened and I breathed the words I already knew were true, "Oh God—it can change me."

Terézia nodded solemnly. "Just as Caradoc used it, so too could you."

Suddenly, my mind was a whirlwind of thought. A possibility now existed which only moments before appeared out of my reach forever. My breathing quickened, body trembled, and my heart raced with excitement!

I looked to Terézia. "I would have to…" I couldn't even finish the question.

"Yes, dear child. You would have to pluck out the pain," she said poignantly.

"How do I do it? I mean, what do I need? Does another Pulire have to be there?"

"No. You will need only a silver dagger and courage. But I warn you daughter, think long while making this decision. The crystal can be used many ways, but only once. It can give you that which you most desire, to become one of us, but it is also capable of powerful healing, even saving a life—*one life*. Once it has been used, it will become dormant again. How you choose to use it is up to you. Remember though, you alone must live with that choice *forever*."

Her tone was full of caution. Though every part of me wanted to hop on the next midnight flight home, and turn myself immediately, something else had me hesitant, extremely hesitant. This was not a decision I could rush into, no matter how badly I wanted it.

"Daniela, tell me about your dreams." Terézia's request nearly knocked the wind out of me, and I sat up rigidly.

"What do you mean?" I asked defensively.

"Specifically, what are you dreaming of?"

I chewed my lip and glanced around nervously, suddenly unable to look her in the eyes, as if hiding some dark secret. "Nothing really. Mostly just of Alistair and Tobias. The usual nightmares—them chasing me, beating me, trying to kill me—your basic run-of-the-mill nightmares," I said with disdain.

"And they don't bother you anymore?"

I shook my head and answered truthfully, "No, they honestly don't. I'm not afraid to die anymore, so…"

She nodded, but didn't look entirely pleased by my reasoning. "Are they the only ones you dream of?"

I swallowed hard. "Yes," I lied.

"You're sure there's no one else?" she asked, as if awaiting another answer.

This was my chance to come clean about the other man who visited my dreams, with the golden mask and soulless eyes who called to my body in a way I didn't understand. I should have told her, relied on my instinct and entrusted her with my secret desire to see him every night. I should have, but I didn't. I couldn't. I *wanted* to see him, to touch him, to keep him to myself. No one was going to come between me and the man with ebony eyes.

I opened my mouth and replied, "No. There is no one else."

Chapter Thirty-Seven
Daniela

Miles was waiting outside at the entrance to the castle just as promised. I was never so relieved to see him, and felt like it had been days since we'd last seen each other. He wasted no time pulling me in for a hug and ushered me into the awaiting car, eager to hear every last detail about my visit with the Oracle.

He was, of course, crushed when I explained that I couldn't tell him anything, but was equally understanding in my having no choice on the matter. I felt terrible. I wanted to tell him everything; about the crystal, about the history of his kind, about the choice I now had to make. But I couldn't. This sat better with him, than me. Inside I was throwing a temper tantrum. I didn't like keeping secrets, especially this one.

At the end of the day we had retired to the hotel and were both in our PJs, lying on the bed and playing checkers. Well, he was in PJs; I was wearing a frilly nightgown that was far more revealing than I wanted. I don't know when, but at some point, Miles had taken all of my frumpy, stained clothes which I had so carefully chosen for this trip and gotten rid of them. When I opened my suitcase, I only found several new designer outfits and a nightgown. A red, sleek, satin nightie that barely covered my knees when I stood. I'd been fighting half the evening to keep it pulled down as low as possible, but it still managed to ride up thigh-high regardless.

"So, are you at least going to start letting me call you princess now?" Miles asked.

I moved my checker one space, and replied, "No. Now crown me please."

He looked down and smiled, then placed a checker on top of mine. "Would you prefer *Your Highness* then?" he asked, moving his checker one space without a moment's thought.

I rolled my eyes. "I would *prefer* you called me by my name."

"Ahhh…la mia belle," he replied. The name rolled off his tongue like honey, sweet and rich. Honestly, I loved it when he called me la mia belle, though I wasn't about to tell him that. I was trying to concentrate on my next move, but found it hard to think of anything with Miles, who was sprawled out on the hotel bed, freshly showered, smelling like a god, and wearing only a thin pair of pajama pants.

I tugged at the hem of my nightgown again and glanced at his face, which was amused by my irritation. I glared at him momentarily then tried to look back at the game. *Accidentally* my eyes were distracted and wandered slowly over his glorious chest and tummy delightedly. Without fail, he let me know with an ornery grin that he was well aware of my silent approval.

I smiled shyly, and moved another checker. "Crown me," I demanded playfully.

Miles placed another checker on mine, and then again, without thought, moved one of his pieces (letting me win no doubt).

"Miles?"

"Yes, la mia belle."

I gave a half eye roll and sighed. "Do you remember the conversation we had at the sandwich shop, the day after I returned from England?"

"Which conversation was that?" he asked casually.

I chewed at my lower lip, contemplating the question I was about to ask, then moved my checker another space. I was headed into dangerous water. I knew what this particular topic could lead to, knew what it *had* led to in my previous fantasy at the café, but I had to know. It was a question that gnawed at me since the day we first spoke of it.

"The question about you feeding on me."

265

Instantly, Miles became stilled, his hand held motionless on the checker piece he was about to move. He looked up, his eyes focused. "Yes, I remember."

"And?" I asked.

"And what?"

I let out another frustrated breath. "And—you never answered my question that day."

Miles sat up and gazed at me mischievously. "And what question would that be?"

"You know what question."

"Oh—yes, I know what question. I remember now," he replied.

I awaited his answer, but it didn't come. He looked back down at the board, stroking his chin as if seriously concentrating on his next move. At last I could take no more. I sat up and blurted, "Well—what if I gave you permission to feed on me?"

He stopped, looking at me with all seriousness. "Why do you want this?" he asked.

"I don't know," I sighed. "I just do."

He eyed me for several long, tense seconds, then leaned in and lowered his voice. "La mia belle…as I have told you, I am your humble servant. Whatever you wish, it is yours—you have but to ask." His voice was low and husky, filled with desire, his breath, sweet, warm, and minty.

I closed my eyes. I knew what I wanted, knew it with more certainty than anything. I needed this. I don't know why, curiosity maybe, or a secret need to be used. Whatever the reason, I'd made my decision, I was going to ask.

I leaned in close, "Miles?"

"Yes, la mia belle?"

I took in a deep breath then slowly whispered, "Feed on me."

He wasted no time in scooting closer, careful not to disturb the board game. Gently, he placed his hand beneath my chin, tipped my head back and breathed, "As you wish…" Slowly he ran a finger down the long length of my neck. A shudder ran through my body, my breathing quickened. He leaned in close, his lips stopping just short of touching me. I could feel his breath just below my ear as he added, "My love..." I squeezed my knees together with anticipation.

Suddenly, Miles reared back and with a loud growl, thrust his teeth against my neck and bit me!

"Miles!" I shrieked, pushing him off and swatting at him, "You ass! I was being serious!" I scolded.

"Sorry, sorry!" he apologized with a laugh, holding up his hands in a defensive motion. "I was just playing around. I couldn't help it, it was just too perfect." I folded my arms and scowled with irritation. "Okay, here, I'll really feed on you this time," he said, trying to take hold of me.

"I swatted his hand away. "No, forget it now. You had your chance and you blew it."

"Come on, Dani, I was just teasing. Give me another chance, please," he begged with sad puppy eyes.

"No."

"Pretty please? I promise I will behave and do it right this time." I eyed him speculatively. "I promise, really," he assured.

At last I lowered my shoulders and uncrossed my arms, "Fine."

Slowly he scooted in again, and leaned his forehead against mine. "I really am sorry." He caught my eyes with his and held them. "Truce?"

I narrowed my eyes, then let out a submissive sigh and smiled. "Alright—truce."

"You ready?"

I took a deep breath, closed my eyes and replied, "Yes."

Miles leaned my head to the side once more, and this time, slowly lowered his mouth to my neck. Instantly heat surged into my skin, and I felt the unmistakable pulling of him feeding. The pleasure pulsed through my body as he laid several sensual kisses on my skin, warmth spreading quickly from my head to my feet. I relaxed and enjoyed the ecstasy of this dangerous game. Of course

Miles could take my life if he wanted, but that's not what scared me. More frightening was—he could take my heart.

The feeding was intense, passionate, just as I had experienced with Robert, but like a kiss, it felt a little different with him. I slid my hands up over his broad shoulders, gripping, digging my nails in, unable to control my desire. Fire breached the walls of my chest, and a small moan escaped my lips. Miles's arm tightened around me as his mouth kissed and moved around the front of my neck and then to my other ear. My mind was going berserk, the crazy woman in my head climbing to the highest peak and jumping, plunging to her death!

Then, there was a change in the tide, and where there had been a pulling of energy, now it was being returned, he was projecting back to me. It all felt so good, I honestly wanted this exchange to continue all night. But, all too soon, he pulled away. Immediately I placed my hand over my heart. It was pounding, pounding, pounding!

We stared at each other for several long, intense seconds, both breathing heavily. Miles smiled wide, then looked back down at the game board, and made his final move. In one fluid motion, he moved his crowned checker forward and back, to the right, to the left, diagonal, jumping over every one of my pieces until all had been conquered. Miles had allowed me to think that *I* was winning this entire time. When, in fact, he had been playing a masterful game from the beginning. Plotting, strategizing, and waiting patiently to make his move.

Upon completion of his last jump, he looked up, victory in his eyes. Then, with the cocky attitude Miles was so very well known for, he announced, "I win."

Suddenly, and with no warning, I lunged at him, throwing my arms around his neck and kissing him without restraint. He was surprised by my attack, but didn't fight it. Checkers went flying in every direction as he grabbed the end of the board game and flung it off the bed, pulling me into his arms. His embrace was so firm, so tight, I could barely breath. Our tongues collided, hands roamed freely. We let loose, kissed, stroked, bit and pulled at one another! We had no reason to slow down, no reason to stop. No reason we couldn't be *together* at last! No reason at all.

...or did we?

To be continued...

Epilogue

Her eyes captivated him, her laugh infectious. With soft pink lips which curved up into a smile just for him, she made his heart dance with happiness.

A tranquil breeze picked up several strands of her long, blond hair and fluttered them gently around her face. He moved to tuck them behind her ear, but found he was unable to move his arms. He struggled against whatever had him bound, unable to break free.

He looked to Daniela, but her eyes were no longer on him. She now looked away distantly, her arms hugging her shoulders. She was dressed in a long, dark silver dress adorned with wings and standing near the edge of an enormous cliff of fire. The flames overflowed the trench and danced against a pitch black sky quietly, illuminating her skin with breathtaking shades of warm amber. Slowly, she began to walk forward.

Robert cried out, but his voice was mute, his effort in vain. He fought against whatever had restrained him, still unable to move. Daniela continued toward the raging fire, reaching her hands out, encouraging the inferno to consume her. Robert screamed her name again, at last the pain of his love for her piercing the stillness of the night air! She turned back and gazed at him with tear filled eyes. "Daniela, stop! Don't go into the fire!"

"I have to," she said eerily.

"No, no you don't sweetie, you'll burn up!"

Daniela tilted her head to the side with a look of understanding, her tone eerily unemotional. "I know, but I still have to."

"Why?" he shouted.

She smiled warmly, and then in a very calm and sure manner replied, "Because…I *yearn* for it."

Robert shook his head, fighting back tears of anguish. "But you'll die," he choked.

Daniela nodded, "Indeed, I will, my love." With that she turned back to the raging fire and once again walked forward.

"Daniela!" he shouted, "Don't do this, please!" His words had no effect and her pace never slowed. "Daniela, stop! Come back to me, come back to me! Honey, please…I love you," he sobbed.

Her feet stopped mere inches from the edge of the deep cavern. She turned around, her toes brushing the edge, sending a few loose pebbles tumbling over the side. She smiled again, then with a gentle voice said, "And *I* loved *you*…but it wasn't enough." She extended her arms wide, closed her eyes and slowly fell back, her body instantly consumed by the blazing pit.

Continue the Journey with Daniela in:

Yearning

~Deadly Desire~
A Thief of Life Novel

Just when it seems things are looking up for Daniela Moretti, her life takes another unexpected turn. She is now royalty and possesses the ability to become an emovamp. Yet, for all her power, and for all her resources, that option has never been more out of reach. Daniela is restless, tired, while others are happier than ever, and all she can do is watch as they get everything she's ever wanted and more.

Driven to hasty decisions and desperate actions, Daniela makes a mess of things and soon seeks refuge in the arms of Ryan. But just as she is breathing a sigh of relief, she is informed of a new threat, one that is hunting her. And when Emily makes a tempting offer, Daniela must consider it or face certain annihilation. Terrified and confused, she must make a decision that will forever alter her life and possibly the world. Will she choose a death sentence or continue Yearning for that which she covets most, knowing it is only a Deadly Desire?

BONUS RECIPE!

Daniela's Mile-High Coconut Pie

½ cup Sugar
¼ cup corn starch
¼ tsp salt
4 egg yolks
2 cups Whole milk
2 tbsp cold butter (cut up)
1 tsp vanilla

With mixer, blend: sugar, cornstarch, salt & yolks until creamy. In a medium sauce pan, bring the milk almost to a simmer. Using a measuring cup (any) remove about a ½ cup of warm milk, and whisk into the egg mixture (tempering). Once the egg mixture is tempered, stir it into the remaining milk on the stove. Stir continuously for 6 minutes. Remove from heat; add butter, vanilla & 1 cup flaked coconut. Stir well, then pour into prepared pie shell of your choice (I prefer a pre-baked, traditional pie crust). Chill for several hours and top with whipped cream and toasted coconut!

Mile High Whipped Cream

In a large, chilled bowl combine:
2 ½ cups heavy whipping cream (chilled)
3 ½ tbsp white sugar
2 tsp vanilla

Whip with electric mixer about 3-5 minutes until stiff peaks form. Mixture should not jiggle.